When s
light, Sonya wished for the co...
of someone to talk to....

But without a telephone, she was unable to call anyone. No, she was on her own now—either to succeed or to fail. *But I'm not on my own,* and the thought brought her upright in bed. She turned on the light and rushed over to the luggage piled in the corner where she found the white Bible.

"God," she whispered, "I feel awful neglecting You all these years, and then turning to You when I'm in trouble. But truly, God, I have no place else to turn. Was it necessary for me to be brought this low so that I'd realize how I was straying from my childhood faith? If so, help me now. Direct me to some words that will give me peace of mind and help me through this night and the difficult days ahead."

Sonya had no doubt that God heard her prayer, and she opened the Bible to the book of Psalms and read aloud, "'When I said my foot slippeth; thy mercy, O Lord, held me up.'"

IRENE BRAND

This prolific and popular author of both contemporary and historical inspirational fiction is a native of West Virginia, where she has lived all of her life. She began writing professionally in 1977, after completing a master's degree in history at Marshall University. Irene taught in secondary public schools for twenty-three years, but retired in 1989 to devote herself full-time to her writing.

After a long career of publishing magazine articles and devotional materials, in 1984 her first novel was published by Thomas Nelson. Since that time, Irene has published fourteen contemporary and historical novels and three nonfiction titles with publishers such as Zondervan, Fleming Revell and Barbour Books.

Extensive travels with her husband, Rod, to forty-nine of the United States and twenty-four foreign countries have inspired much of her writing. Through her writing, Irene believes she has been helpful to others and is grateful to the many readers who have written to say that her truly inspiring stories and compelling portrayals of characters of strong faith have made a positive impression on their lives.

Child of Her Heart
Irene Brand

Love Inspired

Published by Steeple Hill Books™

STEEPLE HILL BOOKS

Steeple
Hill™

ISBN 0-373-87019-1

CHILD OF HER HEART

Printed in U.S.A.

And we know that all things work together for the good to them that love God, to them who are the called, according to *His* purpose.

—*Romans* 8:28 (KJV)

And we know that all things work together for
good to them that love God, to them who are the
called according to His purpose.

—Romans 8:28 (KJV)

Chapter One

If you get burned, you'll have to suffer alone with the blister!

The thought flashed unbidden into Sonya Dixon's mind as she paced the floor of her third-story apartment. With her marriage crumbling around her, why would she remember a remark her father had made over two years ago? She had paid scant attention to what he had said then, and she hadn't thought of the words since, for she had loved Bryon so much it hadn't occurred to her that the future could hold any problems.

Sonya paused at the double windows, pulled the heavy draperies and watched as darkness settled over Omaha. She opened one of the windows and shivered at the hint of frost in the air. In the distance she heard a school band playing at a football game. Seemed like only yesterday she had changed the clocks to daylight saving time, looking forward to a long summer of fun, but the wonderful season had ended in a nightmare of misery and frustration.

You might as well stop dawdling and deal with that letter, Sonya's conscience prodded, but she stared out the window until the streetlights came on and the scent of exhaust fumes stung her nostrils. The room behind her was unlit, but when she turned, the white envelope lying on the floor made a little island in the darkness.

She picked up the letter, flipped on a light, kicked off her shoes and flopped down on the couch.

"It's only a joke, so why should I let it upset me?" she muttered. She crushed the letter in her hand, refusing to read it again. When the telephone rang, Sonya threw the wadded paper across the room and, with a smile, lifted the receiver.

"Okay, Bryon, it was a good joke, but I didn't appreciate it much," she said immediately.

"Sonya?" The voice on the line wasn't Bryon's. "Oh, Mother." Sonya's smile faded and disappointment drenched her spirit.

"What was that all about?" Marilyn Sizemore asked. "What joke has Bryon played on you?"

"Only a little argument between us, Mother. I'll tell you about it sometime. What's new with you?"

"What's new with us?" she gasped. "You write and tell us we're going to become grandparents again, and then ask, 'What's new?' What could be greater news than that? Are you feeling all right?"

"Sure, I'm great. I've been to a doctor, and he's says I'm right on schedule. So don't worry about me."

"How's Bryon? Is he excited?"

"He's a little slow to catch on to the idea," Sonya said dryly. "How are Dad and the rest of the family?"

"Everything is fine here." Her mother rambled on about news of the family in Ohio, and Sonya made the proper responses when her mother paused.

"Say, Mother, I'm expecting a call from Bryon, so maybe we shouldn't talk any longer."

"Is he away?"

"Yes, on a business trip."

"But you always go with him. Are you sure you're all right, or are you keeping something from me?"

With a laugh, Sonya tried to assure her mother. "You're borrowing trouble. I told you, I'm fine."

"I want to be there for the birth. You say the baby is due in March?"

"Yes, around the first of the month. Goodbye, Mother. Thanks for calling."

Sonya terminated the conversation with relief. Bryon was sure to telephone in a few minutes, and she wanted the line open.

While she waited for the phone to ring again, Sonya surveyed her surroundings. Plush brown sectional furniture rested on a beige carpet. The draperies picked up both the brown and beige tones of the other furnishings. A superscreen television stood in one corner of the room with two reclining chairs arranged around it. Bryon's golf and bowling trophies dominated the mantelpiece. Most of the wall hangings had been gifts from Bryon's parents, as were the two antique oriental vases on the end tables. Mrs. Dixon had found the vases in China when they had stopped there on their round-the-world tour last year.

"Be careful of these, Sonya," her mother-in-law cautioned. "If Tom knew what I paid for them, he would cancel my credit cards."

With trembling hands Sonya lifted a framed portrait standing beside one of the vases. *Their wedding picture!* All of her friends had been envious because she had been the one Bryon had chosen—he was considered the catch of the university campus.

It was not only the splendor of his tall, well-muscled body that made Bryon attractive, but he was handsome, as well. His eyes and hair were brown, his teeth straight and startlingly white, and he possessed a personal magnetism that had captivated Sonya at their first meeting.

Sonya's blond beauty marked a vivid contrast to Bryon, although she, too, was rather tall with a slender body. In the picture her large blue eyes gleamed soft and gentle and happy. Long blond hair hung loosely over her shoulders. Sonya fingered the short curls covering her head now and wished she had never complied with Bryon's wishes that she cut her hair.

When the phone hadn't rung by ten o'clock, Sonya prepared a vegetable salad and turkey sandwich and took them to the living room. She placed the food on a snack tray and went back for a cup of hot tea. She avoided the dining area, although she should have been accustomed to eating alone, after the past six weeks.

Sonya turned on the television to watch the news while she ate. She had no interest in what was happening outside her own walls, but she needed to hear the sound of a human voice.

While she watched the numerous commercials leading up to the newscast, Sonya couldn't forget the crushed letter lying beside the couch.

"Good evening," the anchorwoman's voice entered the room. Sonya listened as the anchorwoman reported the world's events, yet Sonya's thoughts kept returning to the crisis in her own life.

The doorbell rang, and Sonya eagerly flipped off the television. Had Bryon forgotten his key? She ran to the door and jerked it open, kicking the letter to one side as she did so.

"Bryon, what do you think—" Sonya began, but the words died in her mouth. "Oh, hello, Leta, I thought Bryon had forgotten his key again."

Sonya didn't want to be rude to her neighbor, who owned the apartment building and lived across the hall, but could she possibly listen to Leta's problems tonight?

"Are you busy, Sonya?" Leta Barton's dark eyes wore a woebegone expression, and Sonya couldn't turn her away.

"No, come on in. I'm waiting on a call from Bryon."

"I thought he was due home yesterday."

"I thought so, too, but apparently I was mistaken in the date. Do you want a sandwich or some tea? I'm having a late dinner tonight."

"I'm too mad to eat, but I'll take some tea."

Sonya brought a cup and the pot of tea and placed them on the table in front of Leta. "Help yourself." Sonya sat down opposite her friend, who had curled her petite frame into a roomy chair. Leta looked lovely as usual, Sonya noticed, with her coffee-brown skin and dark hair complemented by the rust and gold hues of her stylish autumn dress.

"That woman has been bothering me again," Leta said.

In the two years they had lived beside Leta, her neighbor had gone through a second divorce, and Sonya had been obliged to hear a blow-by-blow description of each shattering episode.

"She follows me around. Everywhere I go, she's there. If she wants my ex, she's welcome to him, but I want her to leave me alone."

Sonya had often given Leta advice on how to deal with her marital affairs, but tonight any suggestions she might offer seemed almost laughable.

"I'm sorry you're having these problems, Leta, but I don't know what you can do about it."

"I'm going to protect myself—that's what. I'll go to the police and get a court order of protection, and if she

comes near me again, she'll have a court official to deal
with. She stole my man, and now she's trying to drive me
crazy." Her black eyes sparkled, and she poured another
cup of tea.

Sonya knew Leta wasn't serious. She had listened to
her vent her frustrations before.

"Surely she must have some reason for her behavior."

"She's jealous because the judge awarded me a huge
settlement so I can live in this luxury apartment. She
thought when she got my husband, she would get all of
his money, but my lawyer took care of that. With these
apartments, I'm set for life." Leta laughed delightedly.

"Then if you're fixed for life," Sonya advised, "you
shouldn't bother about her. If you just ignore her, maybe
she'll leave you alone."

Leta took a swig of tea and stood up. "Oh, I'd never
make trouble for her. My ex-husband will bring her
enough grief, believe me. But it does help me to let off
steam talking that way. Thanks for listening." As she
started toward the door, Leta saw the crumpled letter. She
stooped to pick it up and handed it to Sonya.

"You'd better put that in the wastepaper basket. You
know how touchy Bryon is about a messy apartment."

The letter felt like a hot potato, and Sonya had the urge
to throw it from her again. She locked the door behind
Leta, and with the paper still in her hand, she paced the
floor for several minutes. The smell of tea and salad dressing was strong in the room, so she stuck the paper in her
pocket, took the dishes to the kitchen and placed them in
the dishwasher.

Maybe I was mistaken. Perhaps it didn't say what I
thought it did. She took the sheet from her pocket and
straightened it.

Dear Sonya,
I want out! Since you're so delighted with the little
cherub, you can have it all to yourself. I won't be
coming back. Pack my clothes, and I'll notify you
where to send them. It was fun while it lasted.
                                                            Bryon

Again she thought of her dad's remark about the blister.
Had he realized even then that Bryon would be an unsta-
ble husband? Her parents had objected to her marriage,
but she had thought it was because she had left college at
the end of her sophmore year to marry Bryon, who was
going to take her to Nebraska to live.

When they had voiced their concern to Bryon, he'd
said, "I'll send her to college. The Omaha branch of the
University of Nebraska is only a few miles from where
I'll be working. No problem—she'll get her education."

Bryon had soon forgotten that promise, and because he
had been determined to have her with him all of the time,
she hadn't argued about it. She couldn't complain about
his attention to her during their two years of marriage.
He'd rented this luxurious apartment, where he often entertained business associates and their wives. He needed
a hostess for those affairs, and Sonya couldn't do that and
go to college. At times Sonya had marveled at the ease
with which she'd given up her dreams of graduation and
becoming a social worker simply because Bryon had
asked her to do so. Actually, Sonya had been extremely
flattered that Bryon had loved her so much he hadn't
wanted her out of his sight, but in light of Bryon's behavior the past few weeks, she had occasionally wondered
if Bryon really loved her that intensely, or had he been
selfishly thinking of himself, always wanting her at his
beck and call. Whenever these thoughts occurred, Sonya

had felt guilty and unfaithful. Of course Bryon loved her! He was an ideal husband.

In his position as vice president of a brokerage firm, Bryon traveled frequently, and he wanted Sonya to travel with him. How could she have been so fortunate—a country girl from Ohio having an opportunity to travel to so many large cities and resort areas? They had lived a perfect honeymoon existence until that afternoon in early August when she had come home from the doctor.

She was sure of her pregnancy even before she had consulted the obstetrician, but she hadn't told Bryon about it. She suspected he might be displeased, but she hadn't anticipated the depth of his wrath.

He'd been dressing for a dinner party when she'd scurried into the apartment. In her excitement, she had forgotten about the engagement.

"I thought you weren't going to make it. You have only thirty minutes to dress. Where have you been?" He was buttoning his white shirt and poring over his tie selection on the closet door.

Sonya laid aside her purse. "I'll shower quickly and dress." It was a relief to put off telling him.

Before she entered the bathroom, Bryon repeated, "Where have you been?"

"To the doctor."

His hands stopped in the midst of fashioning his tie, and he turned quickly.

"Are you sick?"

Sonya was gladdened by the concern in his voice. Bryon had never talked much about his childhood, but once he had mentioned that when he was in elementary school, his mother had been sick, and he'd been sent away to live with his grandmother for two years. "That was the saddest time of my life," he had said. Perhaps he was afraid if she became ill, he would be abandoned again, but surely that wasn't a normal reaction for an adult.

"Are you sick?" he repeated.

Sonya couldn't control the smile that spread across her face. "No...I'm pregnant."

Abject silence followed her statement. The anger spreading across Bryon's face took away any desire to talk that Sonya might have had, and Bryon looked as if he had been struck speechless. When he found his voice, Sonya cringed with fear.

"Pregnant," he shouted, and Sonya feared Leta would hear him. "Why have you done this? I told you to take care of that sort of thing before we married. Why did you allow this to happen? You know I don't like kids."

And why didn't he? He ignored the children of their friends so much that she was often embarrassed by him.

"I've used the same type of birth control since we were married, but any doctor will tell you that no method is completely safe," Sonya said, hastening to defend herself.

"Well, you march yourself right back to that doctor in the morning and have him do something about it."

"What do you mean?" Sonya asked, and she sat down on the water bed to still her trembling legs, but the sway of the mattress made her dizzy.

"I've told you I don't want kids. Get rid of it."

"You don't mean an abortion?" Sonya cried.

"Certainly. That's no problem anymore."

Sonya's shock turned to anger. "Forget that, Bryon Dixon," she said. "You're as much responsible for this child as I am. You'll have to learn to like it." She went to Bryon and put her arms around him, speaking more tenderly. "You might not like kids now, but your own child will be different. It might be fun to have a baby."

He jerked away from her. "Babies stink. They cry.

They vomit on you. This apartment would be crowded with toys, a crib and dozens of other things. How can I entertain my friends with a baby here?''

"The Shraders have children, and they give delightful parties."

He looked at her appraisingly. "But think how you'll look. Your beauty will be ruined forever. I want a wife to keep me company, not one who sits home breeding."

Surely he didn't consider her a possession, like the trophies he so proudly displayed on the living room mantel. Sonya's pulse raced, and her head throbbed. Bryon couldn't be saying these things!

He gave his tie a final jerk and bolted out the door without waiting for her.

He hadn't come home until early morning. It was the first night they had spent apart since their marriage, but certainly not the last one as she soon found out.

Trying to rid her mind of the incident, Sonya laid aside the letter and picked up the evening newspaper. But she could barely skim the headlines because her mind continued to think about Bryon. His behavior during the past weeks had changed completely from their first two years of marriage. He had never before spent long evenings away from home or gone on business trips without her. Now, if he entertained his friends, he did so somewhere else rather than at the apartment. He never mentioned her pregnancy. How could the mere mention of a child cause a man to change so much?

Sonya had ignored his changed attitude. When he was home, she prepared his meals. She looked after his personal needs as she always had. She hadn't nagged at his long absences. When they talked, she acted as if their relations were normal, even after he started sleeping in the guest bedroom.

Sonya privately nursed her hurt, fully believing that when the baby arrived, Bryon would be happy about it. And even with his letter, she still couldn't believe that he would actually leave her. They had shared such a beautiful love. How could he change so quickly?

If it had been true love, he wouldn't have changed, her conscience needled.

Sonya didn't go to bed until after midnight as she tensely awaited a telephone call and listened for the sound of his key in the apartment door. Then she felt his arms around her, and they shared the bliss that she'd missed so much. She gave a glad cry, which awakened her, and she sobbed when she realized that he hadn't come home—she had been dreaming.

As she struggled out of bed the next morning, she shuddered when she looked in the mirror.

"No wonder he left me," she moaned.

The combined effect of morning sickness and Bryon's rejection had caused her to lose weight. As yet, she didn't outwardly show her pregnancy, but she was only a shadow of the beauty queen that Bryon had pursued. She hadn't slept well for weeks, and the black circles under her eyes made her appear old and haggard. Even her hair looked listless and drab.

While she sat on the side of the bed waiting for her nausea to lessen, she felt a slight movement in her womb, the first outward sign she'd had that a new life grew within her. She pressed her hand to her stomach. It had been so fleeting, just a fluttery feeling, really. For a moment she thought she'd only imagined it. But no, it had been real. A real baby lived and grew inside her now. The idea was almost overwhelming.

I can't do much about the weight loss, Sonya thought as she examined her image in the bathroom mirror, but

I can at least do something with my hair. I'll call the beauty salon for an appointment.

By the time Sonya returned from the beauty shop, the mail had been delivered, and she looked eagerly through the collection of bills and junk mail hoping for a letter from Bryon saying it was all a mistake. Nothing!

Sonya put the bills in the desk where Bryon would find them and trashed the other items.

Knowing she couldn't go through another night of suspense, Sonya finally dialed the brokerage firm and asked for Riley Shrader. Riley and his wife, Lola, were close friends.

"Hi, Riley," she said. "This is Sonya."

"I didn't know you were back, Sonya. How did you like San Francisco?"

"Oh, I didn't go with Bryon this time. That's the reason I telephoned. Do you know when he's returning? I looked for him day before yesterday, but I must have been wrong. Has he been delayed?"

A long silence ensued, and Sonya said, "Riley, are you still there?"

"Yes," Riley answered, and his voice sounded strained. "I was checking to see if I could find Bryon's schedule. I don't seem to have it."

"Then I won't bother you anymore. Let me know if you learn anything."

Why had Riley thought she'd gone with Bryon? Had he told his friend that? She had wondered why Lola hadn't telephoned during the past week. Had Bryon shared his dissatisfaction with the Shraders?

Sonya settled down to another evening of waiting and wondering. Surely Bryon would telephone tonight, if for no other reason than to learn her reaction to his letter.

When the bell rang at eight o'clock, Sonya moved

weakly toward the door. This had to be Bryon, but she took the precaution of checking through the peephole. Riley and Lola Shrader stood in the hallway.

"Have you heard from Bryon?" she whispered as she opened the door. "Is there something wrong?"

She swayed on her feet, and Riley led her to the couch.

"Steady, Sonya," he said. "I'm sure Bryon is all right. We stopped by to check on you."

"I appreciate it," Sonya said hoarsely. Her mouth felt dry and hot.

"You don't look so well," Lola said. "Are you sick?"

"I'm pregnant," Sonya admitted. Because of Bryon's attitude, Sonya had told no one except her parents about the baby. "I'm having the usual morning sickness, and I'm not sleeping well. I'm tired all the time. The doctor says this is normal, and that I'll feel better soon."

Riley and Lola were the parents of three children, and Sonya expected them to be happy about her condition, but instead, tears came to Lola's eyes, and Riley refused to meet Sonya's gaze.

"What do you know that I don't?" Sonya asked with bated breath.

"I suppose you have to hear it," Riley said. "Bryon asked for a transfer to the San Francisco branch, and he starts work in that office tomorrow. He's been there this week looking for lodging. None of us at the office had any idea that you weren't with him, until you telephoned today."

Sweat drenched Sonya's hands, and she clutched the arms of her chair. She stared at Riley. Was this really happening, or was she dreaming again?

"When did he ask for the transfer?"

"About a month ago. Didn't you know he was doing this?"

She shook her head, and Lola cried, "But what's happened? I didn't think there was any happier couple in Omaha than you two. What went wrong?"

Sonya rose wearily from her chair, picked up Bryon's letter and handed it to Riley. Lola moved close to him and read the message over his shoulder.

"Bryon mentioned before we were married that he didn't want any children, and I didn't care one way or another. He blames me for becoming pregnant, although I haven't done anything different than we've always done. He demanded that I get an abortion, and when I refused, he hasn't had anything else to do with me. We've been living under the same roof, but that's all."

"The brute!" Lola said.

"I've been patient, thinking that he would change his mind when he got used to the idea, but I never suspected that he would go this far. All day long, I've been asking myself if I've deluded myself into thinking he loved me, but in spite of my doubts, I can't give him up."

"Is there anything we can do?" Riley asked.

"I don't know what to do myself," Sonya admitted. "I suppose I'm still in shock. I keep thinking it's a bad dream."

"I wish it were, but he's gone," Riley said. "He cleaned out his office and took everything from his desk with him."

"Did he go alone? Has anyone else from Omaha been transferred?"

Riley stared at the toe of his shoe, but he finally said, "No one else has gone."

He stood and laid a sympathetic hand on Sonya's shoulder.

"If he doesn't telephone me, I'll get in touch with him some way," Sonya said. "Perhaps you can give me the address and telephone number of the San Francisco branch.'' Sonya put her arm around Lola. ''I do appreciate having you come by.''

''Would you like me to spend the night with you?'' Lola offered as she hugged Sonya tightly.

''No, I'll be fine.'' Sonya forced a smile, but the moment the door closed behind the Shraders, she picked up one of the oriental vases that Bryon's mother had given them. She hurled it across the room, and when it hit the opposite wall with a crash, fragments shattered all over the carpet.

''Maybe there's a little Leta in all of us,'' she muttered.

Grabbing a pair of scissors, she headed for the guest bedroom. ''I'll pack his clothes for him,'' she said, and she jerked shirts and trousers off the hangers, threw them in a heap on the floor and tramped over them. Lifting his ties from the rack, one by one, she cut them in two and tossed the pieces on top of the clothing.

When the last tie was mutilated, Sonya hurled the scissors from her and, sobbing, she collapsed on the bed where he had slept. The scent of his cologne enveloped her, and in her fancy, Bryon lay beside her, holding her in his arms, moving his lips over hers. *How can I live without him? How dare he walk off and leave me?*

For two days Sonya cried. She didn't leave the apartment, no one phoned, and the doorbell was silent. She didn't shower; she didn't eat. She didn't care much what happened to her. Each day when the mail fell through the slot, she searched it quickly—nothing but bills and junk mail, no word from Bryon.

When she awakened on the fifth day after she had received Bryon's letter, Sonya stirred with a new determination.

"Even if I don't care what happens to me, I have a life growing within me. I have a responsibility to it, so I'm going to start fighting. I have to survive." But in spite of her brave words, Sonya was scared. What if Bryon didn't come back, and she had to rear the child by herself? For a moment she hated Bryon intensely for worrying her so much, but she swiped the tears from her eyes. Of course, she didn't hate her husband; she loved him.

Chapter Two

The doorbell rang before Sonya finished her breakfast. Eager to speak to someone, she hurried to the door. Through the peephole, she saw Leta.

"Come in, neighbor. Join me for a cup of coffee."

"Bryon already gone to work? I don't want to interfere with his schedule."

Was there any reason for further secrecy? she asked herself.

"He isn't here," Sonya said, heading back to the kitchen. She poured a cup of coffee for Leta and asked, "Do you want some toast, too?"

"No, just the coffee. You look terrible. What's the matter with you?"

"Bryon has left me."

Leta strangled on a sip of coffee and stared at her. Did it take something this drastic to shock Leta into silence? Sonya wondered.

"When did that happen?" Leta finally asked.

"He went on a business trip to San Francisco ten days

ago, and I've learned it's a permanent move.'' She briefly apprised Leta of the events of the past few days.

"You mean he didn't tell you he was leaving! The dog! Another woman, I suppose?''

That thought hadn't occurred to Sonya. Surely not! Bryon often laughed about the girls at the office who flirted with him, but he'd never indicated he took any of them seriously.

"No, there's no other woman. He left because I'm pregnant, and he didn't like that.''

"My word, Sonya, you do have trouble! At least when my two men walked off, I didn't have a passel of kids to trouble me. Men often start straying when their wives are pregnant. How far along are you?''

"A bit more than three months.''

"Of course, even if it is another woman, he'll probably beg to come back after the baby's born and you regain your good looks.''

"I don't know what to do, Leta. Bryon took care of all our business affairs, and if he's gone, I won't even have an income.'' Sonya hadn't thought of this before, but now it filled her with panic. What would she do for money?

"You need to see a lawyer. Bryon needn't think he can walk off and take no responsibility for you and that child. Don't you have any idea about your finances? He always paid his rent with a check, so you have a checking account.''

"His uncle died and left him several thousand dollars a few months back. That's in a savings account. Of course, Bryon makes a big salary, but we spend lots of money, too.'' Sonya thought about their affluent tastes. Bryon wouldn't have anything but the best clothes and furniture. He loved his fancy, foreign car and eating out at the best restaurants in the city.

"I have an electrician coming to do some work, and I have to go," Leta said, "but I'd advise you to check into your affairs quickly. If he's the kind of skunk who won't assume his responsibility as a father, it's hard to tell what he'll do."

"I still think this is just temporary," Sonya insisted. "He really isn't the kind of person to act this way."

"You poor thing! You still love him, don't you?"

"Of course I love him. When you've been in love with someone for three years, you don't forget it overnight."

"More the pity for you! If a man mistreats me, I can fall out of love mighty quick. I tell you, see a lawyer. When a man starts to stray, he keeps it up. You'll be better off without him."

"I don't feel that way, Leta, although I may be stupid to still care for him," she added sadly.

When Leta left, Sonya showered, styled her hair and dressed in brown knit slacks with matching cotton blouse. After applying her makeup carefully, she peered in the mirror.

"I really don't look too bad now." No one would suspect by looking at her that she was pregnant, so surely Bryon hadn't left because of her appearance.

The long day loomed before her. What could she do? She needed milk and bread, so perhaps she should go to the grocery store. She checked her purse—less than ten dollars—that probably wouldn't be enough, but she wouldn't need many groceries if Bryon wasn't coming home.

Their checking account was joint, so she could write a check, even though she didn't often do that. Since Bryon had been an accountant before he became a stock broker, it had seemed simpler to let him take care of paying bills.

She couldn't find the checkbook, nor could she find the

file in which Bryon stored the statements of their savings account. Sonya's hands shook, but she still refused to believe the obvious. She searched the desk for an hour, but she couldn't find any of their financial records. In her purse she found one check that she carried for emergencies. She could buy groceries with that, she supposed, but what if there wasn't any money in the checking account? They overspent occasionally, causing Bryon to borrow from his father.

Frantic with worry, Sonya left the apartment hurriedly and walked three blocks to the branch bank where Bryon conducted their business. She handed her ID card to the teller.

"I'm Mrs. Bryon Dixon. I'd like to know the balance in our checking and savings accounts, please."

"Just a moment," the young woman said. She punched some information into the computer on her desk, and Sonya waited impatiently drumming her fingers on the marble ledge in front of her. The music wafting throughout the bank, intended to be soothing to the customers, rattled on her nerves like a nail drawn across a windowpane.

"There's a balance of $929.38 in your checking account, but the savings account is closed. One withdrawal closed it two weeks ago."

"Thank you very much," Sonya said through lips so stiff she could hardly move them. She stumbled out of the building and paused. *Which way do I turn to go home?* She wandered around a few minutes and finally stopped an elderly man.

"I'm looking for the Sandhill Apartments. Could you direct me to them, please?"

"Turn north, ma'am. You can see the roof of the building from here."

Strange she could remember the name of the apartment, but not the location. *Was she losing her mind?* she wondered as she trudged home.

When the elevator reached the third floor, Sonya ran down the hall to Leta's apartment. The electrician was still there, but, noting Sonya's agitation, Leta dismissed him quickly. When the door closed behind the man, Leta asked, "What has happened?"

"Bryon has taken all of the savings, and there's less than a thousand dollars in checking. I don't even have a checkbook. What am I going to do?"

"The first thing is to take the money out of that checking account before he snatches it."

"I have one check in my purse."

"That's all you need. Go to the bank and close that account. This afternoon I'm taking you to see my lawyer."

Sonya didn't think she could walk to the bank again, and when she went for the car in the garage beneath the apartment house, she noticed Bryon's empty parking place. She had supposed his car was at the airport, but no doubt he had driven to California since he didn't expect to return. When traveling by plane, they usually took their old car to leave at the airport, but she hadn't questioned his decision to drive the new car and leave the old one for her. Come to think about it, she hadn't questioned anything that Bryon did. She loved him and trusted him completely, why should she have doubted him?

Sonya filled out the check for $929.38, drove to the bank's drive-in and received the total amount in cash. Returning to the apartment, she spent the rest of the morning looking through Bryon's desk. The gas and electric bills, car payment, and credit card statements totaled more than the cash she had.

Leta rang the bell at one o'clock. "Ready?" she said.

"Why is it necessary to see a lawyer? For one thing, I don't have any money to pay attorney fees."

"Lawyers are used to waiting for their money until the divorce settlement is made."

"Divorce! I don't want a divorce."

"Even if this is just a separation, you'll have to make some arrangements for him to support you."

"I'll get a job."

"That's assuming you can find a good job right away! Besides, Bryon should pay child support." She pointed to the desk where Sonya had stacked the bills. "Someone will have to pay those, and you know you can't. If you get a job tomorrow, it will be weeks before you would receive a check."

"When is our rent due?" Sonya gasped, realizing that she hadn't considered that obligation.

"You're paid through the rest of this month, but don't worry about that."

Sonya reluctantly followed Leta out of the apartment building. As Leta drove along busy Dodge Street, she said, "The lawyer's name is Daniel Massie. He represented me in my last divorce. Before I went to him, I'd heard he was always on the woman's side, and I believe it. He surely held my ex's feet to the fire."

Leta parked in an underground garage. "Massie's office is on the fourth floor of this building. I telephoned and made an appointment, so I'll introduce you and then wait in the reception room. You'll be more at ease if you talk to him alone."

"I don't know what to say, and I'm scared."

"No need to be. He's a gracious man."

Sonya's stomach heaved, and she nearly retched during the elevator ride to the fourth floor. She pressed sweaty hands to her abdomen and leaned against the wall, thankful that no one else except Leta had witnessed her discomfort.

Daniel Massie greeted Leta warmly when they entered his office, and after the introduction, he turned to Sonya with a smile and shook hands with her.

"I'll be in the waiting room," Leta said.

Massie motioned Sonya to a chair beside his desk. Daniel Massie was a man at whom people, especially women, took a second glance. Even as he leaned back, at ease in his leather chair, he exhibited a hint of latent authority. He was not handsome in the usual sense, yet his face was made up of winsome features—brilliant gray eyes, small wrinkles at the corners of his eyes and a warm smile. Yes, it was a face meriting a second glance, but although he had the kindest eyes she'd ever seen, Sonya couldn't meet his gaze.

What kind of person must he think she was when her husband had deserted her?

"What can I do for you, Mrs. Dixon?"

"I don't know," she murmured. What a dumb remark! And she made it worse by stammering, "I didn't want to come, but Leta thought I should."

What had happened to her self-confidence? she wondered.

"How old are you?" the lawyer said.

"Twenty-three. I've been married two years."

"Not quite as old as my mother was when my father went off and left her with two children to raise. That was twenty-five years ago when I was five years old, but I still remember the problems she had."

Sonya twisted her purse straps. The telephone rang, and Massie engaged in a short conversation with another client relating to an automobile accident. Water gurgled in the aquarium in the corner, and Sonya riveted her eyes upon the black and gold fish zipping gracefully through the bubbling water. The leather furnishings of the room weren't new, but they had quality, and Sonya deduced that Daniel Massie had a thriving law practice much beyond what she could afford.

When he replaced the receiver, he said, "Mrs. Barton briefly outlined the nature of your problem, but perhaps it would be better if I hear it from you."

In halting sentences, Sonya unburdened the trauma of the past two months, leaving out nothing. It was easier to talk to a stranger than her friends. "The worst thing about it is that we had been very happy up until that point. I just can't believe that my life could change so drastically."

"On what criteria do you judge the happiness of your marriage?"

Was he suggesting that they hadn't been happy? The nerve of the man!

Almost belligerently, Sonya said, "We lived in a large apartment in the best part of town, lavishly furnished, and we vacationed at luxurious places. Bryon bought me expensive jewelry, and he insisted that I buy nothing but designer clothing. Of course we were happy."

"But it takes more than material things to make a happy marriage. You've mentioned nothing about tenderness, mutual respect and devotion."

"We had those, too," Sonya said with downcast eyes. But had they? Daniel Massie had given her something to think about.

"Do you want me to contact your husband?"

"Oh, no, I don't want to make him any angrier. And I can't have you working for me when I can't pay you. Perhaps you can just advise me."

The lawyer pondered a moment. "Do you have family to help you financially?"

"My parents live in Ohio and would probably help me if I asked, but I won't ask them. They were opposed to my marriage, and I remember my grandmother's old adage, 'If you make the bed, lie in it.' It's my problem, and I don't expect to burden them with it."

"Then it might be a good idea for you to talk with a marriage counselor. You'll need help from someone."

"I'll handle it myself. I still think Bryon will come back."

"Even so, I suggest that you send those current bills to your husband. If he's been caring for the finances, he'll have to continue to do so. Also, if you won't let me contact him, you'll have to. Find out exactly what he intends to do. And I must warn you, Mrs. Dixon, from his actions, I think he means to make this a permanent break. If he sues for divorce, you'll need an attorney."

"I don't believe in divorce."

"You may not have a choice, and if he files, you must have help." Daniel Massie smiled slightly. "You won't let me help you. You won't call upon your parents or a marriage counselor. But you must face reality. Mrs. Dixon, I've been through this with many other women. You can't handle it alone. You'll need help to get through this," he added gently.

Sonya stood to leave and found that her legs scarcely sustained her body. She held on to his desk for support. The lawyer quickly left his chair, came to her side and took her arm.

"Perhaps you should sit down for a few minutes," he said, with concern in his voice. "I'll call Mrs. Barton to assist you."

Sonya shook her head. "I'm all right now. How much do I owe you, Mr. Massie?"

"Nothing at all today, since I haven't done anything for you."

"I won't accept charity."

"It isn't charity—I never charge for a consultation of this type. If you need further help, then we can consider a fee. But there is one thing you can do for me."

She looked at him questioningly, suddenly suspicious of his motives. What kind of woman did he consider her?

"I'd like to have you talk to a friend of mine, a professional counselor as well as a minister." He picked up a notepad, wrote a name and handed it to her. "His name is Adam Benson, and he and his wife, Marie, will come to you anytime day or night when you have a special need. I've written down his home and office phone numbers."

"I don't need to talk to a minister or a counselor. I can handle this alone."

"I'm sure you believe you can. But there comes a time in each life when human resources, and our own self-determination fail us. When those times occur, people who don't have a higher power to sustain them will be overwhelmed by the pressure. I don't want that to happen to you, Mrs. Dixon. Please take this card."

This man is really concerned about me, Sonya thought, and she took the card from his hand.

"Thank you," she murmured and walked weakly from the office.

Leta took Sonya's arm and helped her to the elevator, and Sonya was thankful to have a friend to lean on.

"What did you think of Daniel?" Leta asked, as she drove out of the parking garage.

"He was all right, I suppose."

"He makes a good appearance before a judge. I think he's very handsome."

"Maybe so. I was so embarrassed to be telling my problems to a stranger that I hardly looked at the man, but I was surprised that he seemed to be really interested in my welfare. After all, he must see dozens of people with such problems in a week's time. How could he be interested in each one?"

"I don't know, but he is. He makes all of his clients believe that solving their problems is his first priority. I've heard of a few cases when he's represented abused women in getting their divorces and has charged no fee at all, simply because they couldn't have gotten a divorce otherwise."

Sonya thought about that. It was rare to find a person who helped others so selflessly. Daniel Massie was an unusual man.

The letter she'd been looking for had arrived when Sonya entered the apartment. She tore open the flap of the envelope with trembling hands:

Dear Sonya,
By this time you will have recovered from the shock of my earlier letter. As you may have gathered, I want a divorce. I hope you'll be reasonable and not cause trouble about this, for I have no notion of returning to Omaha. You can send my clothes to the address below.

Bryon

Sonya dropped the letter on the floor and stamped on it. She picked up the second oriental vase and hurled it across the room. The shattered pieces joined the fragments of the other vase she hadn't cleaned up from the carpet. If she was only a possession to Bryon, perhaps if she destroyed everything else, he would turn to her.

She went to the desk, picked up all the bills that had accumulated in Bryon's absence and stuffed them into a stamped envelope. Angrily she scratched out a note. "If you want your clothes, you can come after them." Before she lost her nerve, she sealed the envelope, ran downstairs, and dropped it in the mailbox in front of the apartment house.

The next morning Sonya went to the unemployment agency and applied for work. Even as she filled out the blanks, she realized that she was a poor candidate for a job. She had no experience at anything. Being the wife of a successful stock broker wasn't much of a recommendation for employment, and she'd taken only basic subjects her two years in college, so she had no training in any field.

What was it her father had said? "Please don't get married before you finish college, Sonya. The day will come when you'll wish you had that degree." But Sonya had ignored her father's advice and listened to Bryon instead. "But I don't want to wait, Sonya. If I leave you here and go off to work somewhere else, you might find another man you want to marry. I want you with me always. Don't I mean more to you than a college diploma?"

Sonya shook her head to rid her mind of such perplexing thoughts and continued to fill out the job application.

The clerk who interviewed her was sympathetic and kind. She suggested that Sonya should enroll in some kind of job training at a vocational school. After scrutinizing Sonya closely, apparently taking in her expensive clothing, she said, "If you need financial help, there are federal grants available."

But that wouldn't take care of her living expenses in the meantime.

"I'll give that some thought," Sonya told the woman. "Thank you."

Acting upon Leta's advice, Sonya spent the next week going from one business establishment to another filling out work applications. Each personnel officer was kind, but the answer was always, "We'll telephone you if there's an opening." Meanwhile, Sonya's small hoard of money dwindled rapidly.

Several times she looked at the telephone number that Daniel Massie had given her. Did she need counseling? She found it difficult to discuss her problems with anyone, even her mother, who had telephoned again, wondering why they hadn't heard from her, but Sonya hadn't mentioned Bryon's absence.

Finally, when she had given up hearing from him, Bryon telephoned. The joy she felt when she heard his voice made her body tremble like a breeze-wafted aspen leaf.

"Oh, Bryon, I'm so glad you called."

"I doubt you will be when you hear what I have to say. First of all, tomorrow, I'm sending a friend of mine to pick up my belongings. Be sure you send everything."

"Bryon, please, don't you intend to come back?"

"I think I made that plain to you before. I intend to divorce you."

"But you can't do that! Bryon, I still love you. I need you. Why are you treating me this way?"

She began to sob and he hung up on her. It was hours before Sonya stopped crying. She would have been better off if he hadn't called, as she'd developed a numbness about his absence, and now her heartache started again.

His clothes still lay where she had thrown them two

weeks ago, and she picked them up lovingly, chagrined at the mess they were in. She worked for hours pressing the garments to make them as neat as he liked his clothing. There wasn't anything she could do about the mutilated ties, and she questioned whether she should send them. If she didn't, he would probably demand to know where they were, so she stacked them with his other things. Sonya had hoped that this menial service for Bryon would serve as a catharsis to rid her mind of the unkind thoughts she'd been having about her husband. Instead she actually felt unclean to love so wholeheartedly a man who no longer loved her, and perhaps never had.

She telephoned Leta early the next morning. "Bryon is sending someone after his clothing today. Do you have any large cartons that I can use for packing?"

"I'll have the janitor bring some to your apartment, and I'll help you pack. You shouldn't have to do that by yourself."

When Leta saw Sonya's stricken face, she was unusually quiet, and she didn't make any caustic comments about the tears Sonya shed as they tied the boxes. Leta put comforting arms around Sonya's shoulders and said, "Cry all you want to. I know you won't believe me now, but you'll get over this. You'll be happy again."

"You're a good friend, Leta, and I've found I don't have many. Bryon has been my life for three years. The friends we had were *his* friends. The Shraders are the only ones who have shown me a bit of kindness since Bryon left. I feel like a pariah. Bryon is the one at fault—why does everyone shun me?"

"I don't know," Leta answered, patting Sonya's trembling shoulders. "Mostly it's because they don't know what to say to you. They don't intend to be unkind."

"And I'll have to lose you, too, Leta, since I can't go

on living in your apartment and not pay rent. The rent will be due next week, and as you know, I can't pay it.''

"Hush that kind of talk. I'll carry you until you get on your feet.''

"But I can't afford this apartment on what I'll be able to make. And I hate to ask you, but could you buy the furniture? I don't know that I have the right to sell it, but if you could buy it, that would give me some money to rent a smaller place. You could rent this as a furnished apartment, couldn't you?''

"I often have calls for furnished apartments, and I'll buy the furniture if you're determined to move, but don't decide now. I have plenty of money, and I have no intention of setting you out on the street.'' She kissed Sonya's cheek and released her. "This is a tough break, little lady, but you'll come through it all right. Let me know when they come for Bryon's clothing, and I'll have the janitor carry the boxes down to the lobby. You shouldn't lift them.''

All day Sonya waited, but it was after five o'clock before the doorbell rang, and she was surprised to see Gail Lantz, one of the women from Bryon's office. Gail had attended most of the parties they'd had in the apartment. She was a divorcee, but she usually came in the company of a single man from the office. Sonya and Gail met occasionally for lunch.

"Hello, Gail,'' Sonya said. "Come in. I'm glad to see you.'' What a relief to know that all of their old friends hadn't deserted her!

"I don't have time to visit. I came for Bryon's things.''

Gail was a petite brunette with a helpless look in her eyes, who prompted protective instincts from others. Until today, Sonya had never detected any arrogance in her personality.

"Oh, I didn't know who he was sending." She stepped back into the apartment. "They're boxed and in the bedroom. The janitor will carry them downstairs."

"Two of the men from the office are with me. They'll carry the boxes."

The men, both of whom had often visited their apartment, pushed a luggage carrier down the hall. Mute, Sonya motioned them to enter. They spoke, and after that, refused to meet her gaze.

Sonya followed them into the bedroom. They stacked the boxes on the carrier while Gail riffled the dresser drawers. She added Bryon's jewelry box and several books to the stack. When she picked up Sonya's jewelry box, Sonya said, "That happens to be mine. Or do you have orders to take my things, too?"

Gail fingered several of the gold chains and lifted the diamond necklace, Bryon's last-year's Christmas gift. She dropped it back into the box and closed the lid. "You'd better put those in a safer place. You won't be getting any more."

From the nightstand drawer, she took an album filled with pictures of Bryon's childhood and youth activities. She brushed by Sonya and went back into the living room, where she collected the trophies and plaques that Bryon had won at bowling and golf tournaments.

"Where are his golf clubs and bowling ball? He wants those, also."

Sonya pointed to the closet beside the hallway. She had lost the power to speak. Gail handed Bryon's sports equipment to the waiting men, and as Sonya listened to the carrier squeaking down the hall removing all evidence of Bryon from the apartment, she couldn't have been any more disconsolate if they had been wheeling Bryon out in a casket.

Before Gail left, she took a letter from her purse. "Bryon also wanted me to give you this." Her brown eyes flared maliciously.

Sonya couldn't lift her arm to take the E-mail letter, so Gail laid it on the table, exited into the hall and slammed the door.

Gail! Was she the other woman Leta had warned her about?

Sonya locked the door, as she didn't want anyone to come in. She had about reached the end of her endurance, and if she came completely unwound, she didn't want anyone to witness it.

She forced herself to pick up the message Gail had placed on the table.

Sonya,

I've paid the bills you sent, and I think it's only fair to tell you that I'll pay no more. I've arranged for the telephone to be disconnected, and the electric and gas will be shut off the last of the month. If you had been reasonable when I asked for a divorce, I wouldn't have gone to this extent. As far as I'm concerned, you can fend for yourself.

                              Your "loving" husband, Bryon.

The last of the month. So she had three more days to live in this apartment. Even if Leta permitted her to stay rent free, she couldn't live here without utilities.

The telephone rang several times before Sonya finally answered it.

"Mrs. Dixon, this is Doctor Hammer's office. When we submitted the statement for your last office call, the insurance company rejected our request stating you were no longer on that policy. I'm sure it's a mistake, but I thought you should check it out."

"Thank you for calling. I'll look into it."

"And don't forget your next appointment in two weeks."

Sonya replaced the phone. Of course, there wasn't any mistake—Bryon had removed her from the policy. What could she do? She had no job, no money, no insurance for the birth of her baby, no friends, no nothing.

Laughing wildly, Sonya charged around the room kicking the furniture. She looked out the window. What did she have to live for? Three floors down. One quick jump would end it all. It would be practically painless and easy. She unlatched the window and climbed out onto the ledge. The traffic roared below her. She looked down fearlessly. On the count of ten, she would jump.

"One."

I've always feared heights. Shouldn't I be afraid now?

"Two."

The clouds are pretty today. They remind me of the sky in Ohio when I was a child. I used to pick out all kinds of figures in the clouds—animals, continents, states. Can I do that now? Why, yes, that one looks like an angel. Is it my guardian angel? "I looked over Jordan, and what did I see? Angels coming to carry me home," she sang dreamily.

"Three."

The first time Bryon had seen her, he'd said, "Gee, you're beautiful. Where have you been all my life?" She had been so proud that Bryon had chosen *her*. Was that why she had always done what he'd wanted her to? Come to think of it, she had never refused to do anything he'd asked until he had demanded she have an abortion. Maybe Bryon wasn't as perfect as she'd thought. Was she only a possession to him? Was he kind only when he had his own way? But she refused to believe it, for to concede that Bryon's character contained many flaws would reflect on her own judgment.

"Four."

The trees above her were beginning to display colored foliage. She had always liked fall; too bad she would miss all of the beauty.

"Five."

Would Bryon feel sorry when he heard the news? Would he realize he had caused her death? Maybe she should have left him a note.

"Six."

I should have written my parents, but there's no time. If I don't do this now, I might lose my nerve.

"Seven."

The pavement looked inviting. *I must remember to fall on my head.* Sonya envisioned that her landing would have the sensation of settling into a water bed.

"Eight."

When I awaken, where will I be? That was a sobering thought, but Sonya counted on.

"Nine."

She released her hold on the brick wall and leaned forward, but she staggered back when the ringing telephone shattered the stillness.

What am I doing on this window ledge? she thought frantically. When the telephone continued to ring, she scampered back inside the living room.

Grasping the receiver as if it were a lifeline, she said breathlessly, "Hello."

A resonant voice answered her. "This is Adam Benson.

Daniel Massie gave me your name. When would it be convenient for my wife and me to call on you?"

"Could you come right now?" Sonya gasped. "I'm desperate. I'm afraid of what I'll do if I'm alone anymore. I need help. Please come right away."

Chapter Three

By the time Adam Benson rang her doorbell, Sonya shook like a woman with the palsy. Her throat was dry, and when she opened the door she seized the man's arm.

"I'm Adam Benson, and this is my wife, Marie." His brown eyes gleamed with compassion, and he murmured, "My dear, trust us."

Marie Benson put an arm around Sonya and led her to the couch.

Adam said to his wife, "Make some tea, and see if you can find something for her to eat."

"I'm not hungry," Sonya murmured between stiff lips. Marie disappeared in the direction of the kitchen, and Sonya heard her opening cabinet doors as if she were at home.

"I almost did a terrible thing," Sonya confided to Adam. "When the telephone rang, I was standing on the window ledge ready to jump to my death. How did you know I needed help at that exact moment?"

"You've been on my mind since Daniel suggested you needed some counseling. This evening when I was praying, I felt an overwhelming urge to telephone you. Daniel has also been praying for you.''

''I can't believe I'd do such a thing. It was almost as if I were in a trance. I knew what was going on, but I seemed to be standing outside my body watching the whole thing.''

''It's quite common for a person who's been driven to the depths of despair to have suicidal tendencies.''

Marie returned with a pot of tea and some sandwiches, and the aroma of the tea nauseated Sonya. She clutched her stomach.

''I can't eat anything,'' she insisted.

''But you must eat, Sonya, and especially drink the tea. Adam and I will eat with you. We didn't take time for dinner.''

''I've not eaten much for several weeks. My stomach feels as if it's been tied in knots. I hate to eat alone.''

Marie sat beside Sonya and patted her hand. ''Try to relax. You don't have to bear your burden alone anymore. We're here to help you.''

The Bensons were middle-aged. Adam was a short, slender man, who wore brown-rimmed glasses. His wife tended to plumpness, and she had dark hair sprinkled with gray. Her gray eyes glistened with warmth and friendliness; her voice was soft and cheerful.

Nibbling on sandwiches, the Bensons talked to each other, discussing ordinary happenings around Omaha—the ball games and the fall and winter concerts planned by the fine arts department at the university. Sonya occasionally added a comment to their upbeat words. They didn't refer to her problem, and to her surprise, in a short while she realized that she had eaten a whole sandwich and her tea was gone. She poured another cup of tea and settled back on the sofa feeling better than she had for a month.

When the food was gone, Adam said, "Sonya, we're here to help you, not interfere in your affairs. If you want to tell us about your situation, we're ready to listen."

"What did Mr. Massie tell you?"

"Only that you had some problems, and that you might contact me."

"My husband has left me," and, having had the courage to admit that, Sonya launched into the experiences of the past months. She talked for more than an hour, often breaking into sobs and occasionally walking around the room twisting her hands. Marie finally pulled her gently to the sofa and sat holding Sonya's hands tightly as she talked. When she faltered, Adam asked a brief question to encourage her to continue.

"What worries me," Sonya said as she finished, "is what did I do wrong? Why did this happen to *me?* I've tried to be a good wife. I've been faithful to my husband. Why did this happen to me?"

"I know this is small comfort to you," Adam said, "but there are thousands of young women in this country who have suffered a similar fate. And I don't think you have done anything wrong. Your husband is obviously a selfish man without any consideration for others."

"That isn't true!" Sonya hurried to defend him. "He's always been considerate of me until this incident. It's out of character for him to behave like this."

"Then let's just say that your husband has a problem. A man who walks out on his responsibilities should seek help himself."

"I doubt he would see it that way," Sonya said, realizing that her two statements about Bryon were inconsistent. "But I have been wondering if there is something in

Bryon's past that I don't know about, some incident that would cause him to resent my bearing a child. I can hardly believe it, for his family seems well adjusted and live a normal life-style, and they are prosperous. I feel sure that he wouldn't see any need for change in himself.''

"Then if he won't seek counseling, either jointly or alone, all we can do is work with your situation. You must believe that you're going to surmount all these difficulties and come out of this a stronger woman than you've been before.''

"I don't see how I can make it.'' Sonya shook her head. "I've looked for a job with no luck. I must move out of this apartment soon, and my money is dwindling rapidly.''

"Please believe me—you're going to make it all right. Tomorrow, we'll discuss plans for your future. Our immediate problem is to bring you safely through the night.''

"I'll stay with her,'' Marie said.

"Oh, I couldn't let you do that. I'll be all right.''

"It's quite likely you will have other despairing moments as you struggle to deny what has happened. If you won't allow Marie to stay, then I'll give you two telephone numbers. There are counselors at these phones around-the-clock ready to listen, and whenever you feel that life is more than you can handle, telephone them. They'll listen or give advice, whichever you need most.''

"But my telephone service will be discontinued tomorrow!''

"Sometimes it takes a few days for the telephone company to follow through on those orders. We'll trust that will be the case in this instance.''

Before they left, Marie handed Sonya a small book, entitled, *No Easy Way Out*.

"Please read this book,'' Adam said. "It's the story of a young woman in this town who went through a difficult marriage. She thought she was taking the easy way out, but the woman who wrote the pamphlet believes healing comes through facing one's problems.'' He took Sonya's hand. ''How is your relationship with God, Sonya? I feel I must ask that.''

''My parents started taking me to church when I was a tiny girl, and Bryon and I go to church occasionally. I do believe in God.''

''How long since you've read your Bible?''

Sonya dropped her head. ''Not since I've been married.''

''Then I would suggest that you read it. God can help you, but you need to reach out to Him.''

Desperation surged over Sonya again when the door closed behind the Bensons. She looked out the window and then checked to be sure the latch was securely closed. She pushed several chairs in front of the window to deter her if she tried to climb out again. The street lamps radiated brightness, and blurred streaks of automobile headlights pierced the darkness. Sonya shuddered when she thought of where she might be now if the Bensons and Daniel Massie hadn't been concerned.

She looked at the two numbers Benson had given her. Would there be someone to listen if she telephoned? She dialed one of them, and a pleasant voice answered, ''We Care. May I help you?''

Sonya laughed nervously. ''I only wanted to know you were there in case I do need you. Adam Benson told me to call when I have a problem.''

''Someone will be here all of the time,'' the woman assured her. ''When you feel a problem coming on, telephone. We'll listen.''

Sonya ran the sweeper, dusted the furniture and did a load of laundry. Still not sleepy, she picked up the pamphlet Marie had given her. She started reading the story of Alice Simmons.

She tried to remember where she had heard that name, but couldn't quite recall. Then she remembered, she'd heard the woman's name on the news some months ago. Alice Simmons was related to someone well known in the city—Sonya didn't remember who.

She did remember that Alice's death by her own hand had attracted a great deal of attention in the local news. Alice had married a hardened criminal without any knowledge of his illegal activities. She had suffered abuse of all kinds, and had finally left the man to live with her grandmother. Her husband had continued to harass her, and unable to get rid of him, she had finally committed suicide. Sonya could see her own situation in that of Alice, and again she longed for the release that death would bring.

But the pamphlet continued, ''There's no easy way out. Trust God with your problems. Deal with them head-on, rather than ignore them.''

These words spoke to Sonya's immediate need, for she had been feeling guilty that she had actually planned to take her life. She couldn't imagine why she would be tempted to do such a thing, but in light of Alice's experience, her action must be a normal response to what she had been through.

During Adam's counseling, he had told her to remember, ''When your burden seems the worst, a way out will be provided.'' She repeated the words over and over, and she went to bed, clutching the paper Adam had given her. She dreaded to turn out the light, but she went to sleep right away. Suddenly she awakened overwhelmed with heaviness and despair.

God can't help me. Adam Benson can't help me. Nobody can help me. I'll do what Alice Simmons did. Surely I can be as brave as she was.

Sonya slid out of bed and headed for the window, but she became conscious of the slip of paper in her hand. Her shaking fingers reached for the telephone, and she dialed the number for We Care, fearing no one would answer.

"We Care. May I help you?"

"Yes, please. I'm considering taking my own life."

The woman's voice at the other end of the line spoke soothingly, "Tell me what's bothering you, ma'am."

At the end of a half hour, Sonya terminated the conversation feeling relaxed, although the woman hadn't said much. She had simply let Sonya talk, but that had been comforting. Remembering the woman's last words from the Bible, "Weeping may endure for a night, but joy cometh in the morning," Sonya went to sleep again.

Once more during the night, she awakened, shaking violently. She dialed the number. A man answered and, speaking calmly, he discussed the good things in life, ending with, "Why don't you try remembering all the pleasant times you've enjoyed through the years. Usually they outweigh the bad days."

After considerable effort, Sonya blocked out the past two years and thought of her childhood on the farm. She envisioned fields of growing corn, ripening wheat and the scent of new-mown hay. She eventually went to sleep, to be awakened by the ringing telephone. The sun shone brightly through her windows.

She reached for the phone receiver. "Good morning, Sonya. This is Marie Benson. How do you feel?"

"Tired, but safe, thanks to you and your friends."

"Adam and I want to talk with you again. When will it be convenient for you?"

"As soon as I shower and have breakfast. Do you know, I actually feel hungry this morning?"

"Great! That's a good sign. You've started on the road to recovery."

The warm shower took away some of Sonya's weariness, but when she started to dry her hair, the dryer wouldn't work. She tried the light switch—no power. So Bryon hadn't been fooling—he'd had the power company disconnect the electricity. No doubt the telephone would go next. Fortunately the water was provided as part of their rent, so she wouldn't be completely without utilities until she could find some other place to live.

Without electricity, she had to be satisfied with a glass of milk and untoasted bread for breakfast, but though she had felt hungry, she threw most of the bread in the garbage. Her obstetrician had given specific instructions about her diet, and she knew she must be more careful, but not this morning. She made an effort to greet the Bensons with cheerfulness, but after she reviewed her tense night, Adam said, "You probably still aren't out of the woods as far as despair is concerned, but you know how to handle it now. Let's deal with your immediate problems. As I see it you have several options, and if we had more time, we could make long-range plans, but it's obvious you'll have to make a change in living arrangements right away."

"What options do you suggest?" A sense of frustration threatened to overpower her again. If it were only herself, she could live anywhere, but she had to have a place for her baby.

"You can go to your parents and stay until after the birth of your child. Surely they would take you in."

"I know they would, and they'll be furious when they find out I haven't come to them, but when I disregarded their wishes by marrying before I finished college, I don't think they should be burdened with my mistake. My dad said if I was burned, I'd have to suffer with the blister by myself.''

''I doubt he meant that,'' Adam said with a smile. ''I have three children, and I know how your parents will feel. Besides, it will be a burden to them whether or not you go home.''

''It may come to that, but not until I've exhausted every other possibility.''

''You can go on welfare. The agency will provide you with food and shelter, as well as a health card to take care of your medical expenses.''

Sonya shook her head. ''Why should the taxpayers be burdened with my mistake?''

''Then your only other option is to take legal action immediately, to force your husband to support you until after the child is born. You might feel it isn't a problem your parents or the public should share, but you can certainly realize that he has an obligation.''

''But I want him to come back to me. If I force his hand that way, he'll be angrier than ever.''

Adam smiled. ''Since you don't like any of my suggestions, what do *you* want to do, Sonya?''

''I want my husband to come home. I want him to love our child as much as I intend to.''

''I don't mean to be cruel, but the likelihood of that happening is slim. And if he should return, I doubt it will be in the immediate future. He'll run the gamut of willfulness before he'll return to you.''

''Then if that won't happen, I'll find a job to support my baby and make a home for us,'' Sonya replied firmly. ''I want to be independent.''

''If that's your desire, we'll do what we can to help

you. It's going to be difficult for you to get much of a job until after your child is delivered, but perhaps we can find something to tide you over until then.'' Lines of perplexity creased his face as he considered her problem.

It amazed Sonya that this couple—these strangers—were so genuinely concerned about her welfare. She had never seen them until yesterday, but now they were making her future their greatest priority. Was it the depth of their spiritual faith that fostered this concern? If so, it was certainly a level of spirituality she would hope to attain.

"What about the opening at our school, Adam? She wouldn't need any special training for that," Marie said.

A smile lit Adam's brown eyes. "A good idea, dear." Turning to Sonya, he said, "We operate a day school in our church building—nursery through the sixth grade. Just yesterday, one of the aides in the nursery class resigned. You would fit in nicely, but the salary is low. I'm not sure it will support you and allow you to accumulate enough for your medical bills."

With hope dawning in her heart, Sonya said, "I'd like to try it. I'll be frugal."

Adam looked around the lavishly furnished apartment and said, "Sonya, it's a trait you'll have to *learn*, since you haven't been living that way."

"I didn't live this way before I was married. My parents reared a family of four on an Ohio farm, and we didn't have many luxuries. I'll admit it will be hard, though, because I've learned to like this way of life."

"There's an apartment complex near the church, subsidized by the government to provide housing for low-income people. They base your rent on what you can afford to pay. We'll take you there to see if they have any vacant apartments."

"You could walk across the street to work, so there wouldn't be any travel expense," Marie added.

"I'll not put you to all that trouble. I have a car and can drive there. I don't know how much longer I can afford to operate the vehicle, but at least it's paid for."

The Bensons overrode her objections and took her in their car to the Washburn Complex in a newly developed area on the west side of Omaha. They pointed out their church, the Community Lighthouse, a shingled building of modern architectural design. The four-story apartment complex faced the church.

The manager of the apartments said they did have some space available in single apartments and two-bedroom units.

"It will have to be the single apartment," Sonya told her. "I can't afford anything else."

But she was hardly prepared for the small area she was shown. The living, dining, and kitchen space was about the size of her bedroom in the apartment she'd shared with Bryon. A small bathroom contained a shower, but no tub. The apartment was unfurnished, except for a refrigerator and stove.

"If you can't provide your own furniture, we can supply it for you," the manager said. "We have a sofa that can be made into a bed at night, a small table for the kitchen and a few other items available. We can fit up the room nicely."

"I'll appreciate having you do that," Sonya said, knowing that none of her massive furniture would fit into the tiny space. Some of the enthusiasm that had been generated by the Bensons' help faded, and she wondered why Bryon would sentence her to living in such a humble place.

Sonya made arrangements to move in the next day, the

last day the rent was paid at the Sandhill Apartments. There was no need for delay. Leta had already agreed to buy their furniture, and without a telephone or electricity, the place wouldn't be livable. She couldn't take advantage of Leta's friendship and live at her expense.

Before the Bensons left her at the Sandhill Apartments, Adam said, "We'll check on you tomorrow night, and you can plan to start working on Monday morning. Will you need any help moving?"

"No, I can load everything in my car and make more than one trip if necessary. I can't express my appreciation."

Sonya's throat was dry, but her eyes watered. Bitterness filled her heart, and she wanted to rail at somebody. But not the Bensons—they had done the best they could.

"Don't try—just pass along some kindness to others who need it," Marie said with a smile.

As she walked upstairs, Sonya marveled that it had been easier to take help from strangers than from her own parents. Perhaps it was because they had not stood in judgment of her and had seemed so willing to help. Could their obvious submission to following God's will account for their generous spirits?

Leta protested Sonya's sudden move. "I think it's a mistake, but do what you think you must. If I was in your place, Mr. Bryon Dixon would have been forced to pay for your lodging and expenses in this apartment for a reasonable amount of time. You see how I'm living, don't you?"

"But you were glad to get rid of your husbands! I want to keep mine, although I admit I might be foolish to feel that way."

"You won't keep him by kowtowing to him. He'll

show you more respect if you speak up for your own rights.''

In spite of Sonya's protests, Leta helped her pack and went with her on the first trip to the apartment. When she saw the small room, Leta exploded, ''This is quite a comedown. It isn't right for you to live in such a place! You can't possibly be comfortable here.''

''I can't help it, Leta. It will take half of the salary I make at the school to even pay the rent on this apartment, and how I can eat and save any money for doctor's bills, I don't know. I'll just have to make do.'' But in spite of her brave words, thoughts of the future terrified her.

The closet was too small to hold even Sonya's winter clothing, and they left her summer garments in boxes and stacked them in the corner. Sonya had made an effort to hold back her tears, but both she and Leta were crying before they finished unloading the car.

''Look on the bright side. At least I won't have to buy any clothing—I have enough to last me for years.''

''Oh, yeah,'' Leta retorted. ''Have you given any thought to how your body is going to expand? You won't be able to wear any of these clothes much longer. Please, Sonya, go to Daniel Massie and have him contact Bryon. It isn't right for him to go scot-free while you're so hard up.''

But Sonya shook her head and bit her lips to keep them from trembling. ''All I have to bring now are my kitchen supplies and a few knickknacks. Let's go.''

Sonya thought she had cried until there couldn't possibly be any more tears left, but before she left the apartment for the last time, sobbing constantly, she looked at each item, caressing them lovingly. She and Bryon had such fun picking out their furniture. She stood a long time in their bedroom, thinking of their more personal moments. Had she failed him? What was wrong with her? If she could only get past the feeling that she was at fault, she might be able to accept it. How could she have prevented his leaving?

When she locked the door, she dropped the keys through Leta's mail slot. She absolutely couldn't talk to anyone else today.

Sonya placed a few vases and pictures in the new apartment. Even with these possessions around her, the room seemed alien. She ate a light supper, and then started her hardest task. She had to notify her parents. What if they tried to telephone and learned the number was no longer in service? She had caused them enough trouble, and she couldn't let them have that worry.

Since there wasn't any desk, she sat at the small dining table to write.

> Dear Mother and Dad,
> Bryon left me about a month ago. He's living in California and has no intention of coming back to me. I moved today to the address on the envelope. I do not have a telephone here. I'm starting to work Monday as an aide at a nursery school in a nearby church. Please do not worry about me. I'll be all right.
>   Sonya.

Adam and Marie Benson came by to check on her, but they had to call at a funeral home, so Sonya had a long evening before her. She watched the small black and white television she and Bryon had used in the kitchen, but the problems of other people soon palled.

It was still too early to retire, but she decided to see if she could unfold the couch into a bed. Considering her other luck lately, Sonya was surprised that it opened so easily. The bed was comfortable enough, but she knew it would be aggravating to fold and unfold it every day.

When she finally turned off the light, well after midnight, Sonya wished for the comfort of the We Care persons, but without a telephone, she couldn't contact them. No, she was on her own now—either to succeed or fail. *But I'm not on my own,* and the thought brought her upright in bed. She pushed the light switch and rushed over to the luggage piled in the corner. When she was packing, she had unearthed her Bible. Adam Benson had said the answers were there, if only she could find them. When she found the white Bible her parents had given them for a wedding present, Sonya turned it over in her hand as if it was some foreign object.

"God," she whispered, "I feel awful, neglecting you all these years and then turning to you when I'm in trouble. But truly, God, I have no place else to turn. Was it necessary for me to be brought this low so that I'd realize how I was straying from my childhood faith? If so, help me now. Direct me to some words that will give me peace of mind and help me through this night and the difficult days ahead."

Sonya had no doubt that God heard her prayer, and she opened the Bible to the book of Psalms. After she turned several pages, Sonya read words she didn't even remember were in the Bible. "God is our refuge and strength, a very present help in trouble." And in Psalm 94, she read of David's struggle when violent men would have overcome him, and she committed to memory the words, "Unless the Lord had been my help, my soul had almost dwelt in silence. When I said, my foot slippeth, thy mercy, O Lord, held me up."

Sonya kept repeating those words in her mind when

she returned to bed, and when worries about the future
threatened to intrude into her thoughts, she gritted her
teeth and whispered, "When I said, my foot slippeth, thy
mercy, O Lord, held me up."

Chapter Four

When she awakened again, her bedside alarm showed twelve o'clock. At first, Sonya thought it must be midnight, until she realized the sun was shining in her windows. It was the first good night of sleep she'd had since her estrangement with Bryon. She left the bed and looked across the street to see that people were leaving the church, and she was sorry she had missed going.

Her stomach rebelled at the odor of fried bacon permeating the apartment, and she rushed to the bathroom. With the adequate ventilating system and soundproof walls at Sandhill Apartments, they had hardly realized they had neighbors. But the walls here must be paper thin, she thought. Children ran in the room above her, a television played in the room beside her apartment, and the wails of a crying baby filtered in from across the hall.

Weak with nausea she crept back into bed and slept for another hour. After all that sleep, she should feel rested, but she didn't. Moving slowly to the kitchen area, she toasted a slice of bread and made a pot of strong coffee. Boxes of kitchen utensils and groceries crowded the cabinet top, and she had many other things to unpack, too. She had to generate energy somehow. She must get the apartment in order before tomorrow when she started to work.

While she sipped on the coffee and nibbled the toast, Sonya wondered how she would like a full-time job. She had worked for her parents on the farm, but she'd never had a salaried position. Such inexperience would have made any job difficult, but when she felt so lousy, she doubted she could give a satisfactory day's employment to anyone.

Sonya forced herself to finish a glass of cold milk, as her doctor had instructed. During the afternoon while she unpacked boxes, her stomach crawled with hunger, but when she tried to eat, the very scent of the food caused her to gag. The work was finished by four o'clock, and she faced a long evening.

She drew on a jacket over her sweats and went down to her car. Several children played football in the parking lot. She slid into the car, ignoring the glances of three men lounging on benches. She had intended on going to see Leta or the Shraders, but she remembered that the gas gauge had shown empty yesterday. Should she use her small hoard of money to buy gas for pleasure riding?

She got out of the car when she noticed the men staring at her, and that one of them, a short man with a handsome face, had headed in her direction. "Need any help?"

"No, thank you. I've decided to walk."

"Anytime you need any help, let me know. People are neighborly here."

She rushed out of the parking lot, trying to avoid the man's attention. Walking would be better for her, anyway, but she needed companionship.

The area around the Washburn Complex had sprouted

many housing developments. The larger houses were surrounded by a brick fence, and it was obvious that spectators would not be welcomed. Sonya walked west along a street of moderate houses until she came to a corn field. A brisk breeze rattled the dry blades, and the heavy, drooping ears on the stalks awaiting the picker reminded her of the farm at home.

Sonya retraced her steps, tears in her eyes. When she passed the Community Lighthouse, cars poured into the parking lot. Families entered the first floor carrying covered trays and picnic baskets. Momentarily, Sonya was tempted to follow them, but glancing at her dirty sweats, she moved on. She hadn't even showered today—she couldn't inflict her presence on them. No doubt Adam and Marie Benson would welcome her, but she didn't want to spoil their evening when they'd been so kind to her. She wasn't fit company for anyone tonight.

When she entered the lobby of the apartment house, Sonya went to the telephone booth. She hesitated about spending the quarter, but she had to talk to someone. Not the Shraders, for they usually ate out on Sunday nights. Surely not her parents! Leta? Maybe, but in the end, she dialed the number of Bryon's parents. She had always called his parents "Mother and Father Dixon," but would that be appropriate now?

When Mrs. Dixon answered the phone, Sonya said, without any salutation, "Hello. This is Sonya. We haven't talked for several weeks. How are you?"

"Well enough, I suppose. Tom is snoozing now. He's been golfing all afternoon. Has Bryon come back from San Francisco yet?"

Mrs. Dixon's voice sounded normal, and Sonya concluded she didn't know about her son's perfidy.

"Didn't he tell you? He isn't coming back. He's left me."

Mrs. Dixon's gasp couldn't have been feigned. "I can't believe that. What has happened?"

"I really feel that Bryon should be the one to tell you, because he's the one who initiated the separation. I'm very bitter about it, so it's best if I don't say anything until you've heard his version of the situation."

"When did this happen?"

"I had a note from him a few weeks ago saying that he didn't expect to return...and he had someone come for all his possessions. In a later letter he indicated that he would no longer be responsible for my support, so I had to move. I'm living at the Washburn Complex. I have a one-room efficiency here."

"Why that's a welfare establishment!"

Sonya laughed shortly. "It's certainly not luxury living, but it's all I can afford now."

"I'm going to contact Bryon and get to the bottom of this, and I'll be in touch with you again. Is your telephone number the same?"

"I don't have a telephone. I'm calling from the lobby. I'm sorry to trouble you with this, but if Bryon hadn't told you, I thought you deserved to know."

Sonya could hear Mrs. Dixon crying softly, and she hung up the receiver gently. She had never been overly fond of her in-laws, but she did feel sorry for them. They would feel keenly the fact that their only son's marriage had failed.

Adam Benson was on hand to greet Sonya the next morning when she timorously entered the ground floor of the church building. She arrived at eight o'clock, thinking she would be early, but numerous cars had pulled up at the door and unloaded children while she had crossed the parking lot.

"I'm sorry I'm late," she said to Adam. "What time should I come to work?"

"You aren't late because we hadn't discussed your hours. About all you can do today is meet our other staff and observe. Tomorrow, you should come at seven o'clock and plan to work until two. We try to accommodate parents who go to work early. A few children are here after two o'clock, but we have sitters with them. No school after two."

"I haven't had any experience working with children."

Adam patted her on the shoulder. "Sonya, you're going to be great at this job. Stop fretting."

But when he led her into a room housing more than a dozen active three-year-olds, Sonya's courage deserted her completely. Only Adam's hand on her arm kept her from bolting out of the room. A woman held the hands of a pair of blond girls, who were evidently twins. They tugged to get free of her hold.

Behind the woman two little boys threw play dough at one another. When Adam and Sonya appeared, one black boy raced to Adam, shouting, "Here's the preacher. Catch me," he said as he jumped into Adam's arms.

The scene was pure bedlam, and Sonya thought maybe Bryon was right about having children. But the door behind them banged suddenly, a whistle blew, and the children dived toward their assigned seats at the table. In a few seconds hardly a sound could be heard.

Sonya turned to see who had wrought this miracle. A small, gray-haired woman walked toward Sonya with outstretched hand. "Is this my new helper?" she asked. The woman radiated energy and efficiency.

"Sonya, meet our dedicated nursery teacher, Eloise

Dedham. This woman could make twice the salary in a public school as she does here. We're fortunate to have her.''

''Now, Adam, you know it's a ministry for me. I'm delighted to have you, Sonya,'' Eloise said. ''The children are always hyper on Monday morning, but once we start our activities, they settle down. Don't worry about learning everything at once. You can mostly observe today, and I'll gradually fit you into the schedule.''

Sonya was amazed at the many things the toddlers could do. They sang several action songs, listened to a Bible story, exercised, finger painted, and played with educational toys. Before lunch, they watched a video on proper table manners, and Sonya supervised three children during lunch to encourage them to observe the examples they'd watched on the VCR. The children had individual blankets for nap time, and they spread out on the nursery floor and rested for half an hour. Eloise assigned the other helper to monitor the children, and she took Sonya into her office.

''Our main purpose here is to achieve security, love and discipline for the children. We have fifteen little ones enrolled. Some of them are from broken homes, and they bring their troubles with them. Others have health problems, but some are normal, well-adjusted children. We try to meet all of their needs. Just follow my lead, and in a few days you'll know the ropes.''

''I want to do a good job, and I'll do my best.''

''It's an exacting position, but you'll do fine, and it will be good for you to be dog-tired when you go home.''

''Reverend Benson has told you my situation?''

Eloise's blue eyes gleamed with compassion. ''Yes, and we hope to extend help and healing to you.''

In the hour left in the afternoon, the teacher guided the

students in word pronunciation and numerical usage. When Eloise indicated the children should prepare to go home, Sonya looked at her watch in surprise. Where had the day gone? When most of the children left, Adam and Marie came into the room.

"What are your reactions, Sonya?" Marie asked. "Do you think you'll like this work?"

"Oh, yes. I've enjoyed today, and the time passed so quickly. I'm eager to start."

"Then we'll look for you at seven tomorrow morning. In the meantime, do you need anything? Are you settled into the apartment?"

Upon receiving Sonya's assurance that she needed nothing, Adam suggested, "You might find the adult program of the church of interest to you. Besides our Sunday and Wednesday services, we have an active singles group, which would be of help to you at this point. Every Wednesday evening we provide a fellowship dinner open to the entire congregation. You should join us. You'll meet people."

Time passed quickly for Sonya. She spent each day at the school, then went back to her apartment in a state of exhaustion. She read from her Bible each evening, and that kept her from despairing, but she wasn't sleeping well, and although morning sickness was slowly fading, she had no appetite. She ate at noon with the children, but when she was alone, she wanted nothing.

On Wednesday night she dressed in one of her most becoming dresses, noting with dismay that it was too tight around the waist, and set out for the fellowship dinner. She picked up a tray with meat, two vegetables, a salad, dessert and a roll, which cost only two dollars, delighted at the chance for a good meal at so reasonable a price.

But the room was crowded with people chatting companionably, and she felt sadly out of place.

While looking around for a seat, Sonya came face to face with the lawyer, Daniel Massie. Her face flamed, and her new courage failed her. Even here, she couldn't escape her problems.

"Hello, Mrs. Dixon. How great to see you. Come and eat with my mother and me." He took her tray and carried it to a table that still had a few empty chairs.

"Mother," Daniel said to a gray-haired woman seated at one end of the long table. "Meet Sonya Dixon. This is her first time at our dinner. Let's make her welcome."

"By all means," Mrs. Massie said with a friendly smile that thawed a spot in Sonya's aching heart. "Sit down right here next to me."

Mrs. Massie had the same sparkling gray eyes as her son, and she was almost as tall as he, but she was a lanky woman, whereas Daniel was a big man, broad shouldered though slender of hip. Mrs. Massie extended a hand toward Sonya, and two large diamonds graced the long tapering fingers. Her voice exhibited the same tone of tenderness that Sonya had observed in the lawyer as Mrs. Massie introduced her to the others seated at the table, all of whom greeted her with warmth.

"I'll bring your beverage," Daniel said. "Coffee or tea?"

"Iced tea, please." Daniel soon deposited the desired beverage at her plate.

"Now may I bring you anything else?" he asked, and at Sonya's refusal, he seated himself beside her. It was a rarity for someone to wait on her and see to her needs, and Sonya enjoyed it.

Sonya had never considered herself talkative, although she could usually carry on an adequate conversation, but tonight she seemed tongue-tied. She pulled at her garments, wondering if her pregnancy was obvious, hoping that no one except Daniel Massie could tell she was pregnant.

Her companions continued a conversation started before she arrived, and Sonya was grateful when Daniel chose to chat with her. "I'm glad to see you again, Mrs. Dixon." He lowered his voice. "I haven't been able to get you out of my mind. How are you getting along?"

"Then you don't know that I did contact Adam Benson?"

"I knew that you had telephoned him, but I've had no further report. Was he able to help you?"

"More than I can tell you right now. When I was at my lowest ebb, he and Marie came to me. They gave me a job in the nursery school and helped me find a place to live in the Washburn Complex across the street. Perhaps more than anything else, they led me to renew my faith in God and to trust Him for daily inspiration and guidance. I didn't know how low I'd fallen spiritually until I started reading the Bible."

"You couldn't be in better hands," Daniel said, and a look of relief replaced the concern previously on his face. "Working with the Bensons is the perfect place for you. They will be able to help in ways that I can't. It relieves my mind considerably to know that you're overcoming your problems."

Sonya glanced at him timidly. "Do you take such an interest in all of your clients?"

"Not all of them, although Mother does tell me that I go beyond the call of duty by becoming involved in my clients' lives."

Daniel looked up when a young man stopped by the table.

"I want to thank you, Mr. Massie, for providing the money for Johnny's camp fee," he said. "He wanted to go with the other fifth-graders, but we've been pressed for extras since my spouse has been laid off."

"Sending boys to church camp is a good investment, so it was my pleasure to do it, and incidentally, if I can help otherwise, don't hesitate to call me."

As Daniel talked to the younger man, Sonya observed him closely. She felt more uplifted than she had for months. He had left no doubt that he was sincerely interested in her personal problems as he was in the plight of this man's family. She had never encountered anyone quite like him. Bryon had never shown much interest in others' problems, and although her father had been considerate and helpful to his neighbors, on the farm he hadn't had many opportunities to meet needs.

When the young man walked away, Daniel said, "We have five minutes before the service starts. Let's clear the table, and I'll show you the way to the sanctuary."

"I don't intend to go." She looked down at her garment, which looked as if she'd been poured into it, and compared it to the neat, flowered polyester dress worn by Mrs. Massie. "I'm not dressed very well, and I don't know these people."

He made light of her excuses. "You're a beautiful woman, Mrs. Dixon. I can't imagine that you'd ever need to apologize for your appearance. Besides, you know Mother and me, and the Bensons, and since you know God, you're a member of this church family." He looked at her intently. "It would mean a lot to me to have you go, and it will be helpful to you, too. Adam is a heartening speaker."

"I've always been backward about making new friends," she admitted, "but I will go with you. I've been

spending too many evenings alone the past few weeks.''
She picked up several of the used plates and cups and
deposited them in a waste receptacle, while Daniel carried
the silverware to the kitchen service window.

The sound of piano music drifted from the second floor
and Sonya walked between Daniel and Mrs. Massie in
that direction. When a man stopped Daniel on the stairway, Mrs. Massie said softly, ''We won't wait for Daniel.
He's been advising that man about a tax problem, and he
may be delayed.''

They found a seat near the front of the sanctuary, and
Mrs. Massie informed her that the large room had a seating capacity of five hundred, and more than half of the
seats were filled. The modern stain-glassed windows lent
a worshipful air to the otherwise plain interior decorated
in variegated blue tones.

The song service had been in process for about ten
minutes before Daniel came down the aisle and sat beside
her. ''Sorry,'' he whispered, ''I didn't mean to desert
you.''

''I'm doing fine. Your mother introduced me to several
people.''

What was there about this man that caused her to feel
secure and strong when he was beside her? When she had
entered the church tonight, she felt unworthy and as low
as a toadstool. Now she actually felt like singing, and
when Daniel opened a book and extended it toward her,
she sang with a fervor she hadn't known since childhood.

What a fellowship, what a joy divine
Leaning on the everlasting arms.

It was amazing that all Daniel Massie had to do was
smile in her direction and her self-respect felt suddenly
renewed. *Where did the man get the strength that he
transmitted to others?*

When Adam called upon Daniel to pray, Sonya had the answer. She had never heard anyone pray with the earnestness Daniel exhibited. First he praised God for His mighty works in the universe and the transformation He had made in his personal life. He prayed for the needs of those who were hurting in physical and emotional ways, and Sonya knew he was thinking of her, for he reached out and took her hand. Surely some of the power he received in prayer must have been passed to her, for when he said, "Amen," she felt more spiritually aware than she ever had before.

At the close of the service, dozens of people spoke to Sonya and urged her to return again.

"Mother," Daniel said, "if you'll wait here, I'll walk Mrs. Dixon to her apartment."

"Oh, that isn't necessary," Sonya said hastily. "The street is well-lighted."

"It will only take a few minutes." He touched her arm lightly and steered her toward the side of the building that faced the Washburn Complex.

She didn't want him to accompany her, but she couldn't make a scene, so she walked silently by his side as they crossed the street. Sonya absolutely refused to allow him to escort her upstairs. The apartment was so untidy she didn't want anyone to see it, and also, though she trusted Daniel, she rebelled at any sign of intimacy from a man.

In parting, he took her hand, and the warmth of his fingers was comforting. "If there is anything at all I can do for you, Mrs. Dixon, let me know. I'm not speaking as your attorney now, but as a member of your church family. Perhaps you will need someone to take you for doctor's appointments. My time is my own. I can easily help you. Will you telephone if you need me?" When she hesitated, he squeezed her hand. "Promise me."

"I hope I won't need your help, but I will call."

He left her with a cheery, "Good night," as well as a question. Even considering the depth of his Christian faith, how could Daniel have developed such an interest in her after their short acquaintance?

Saturday morning Sonya slept late. It had been a strenuous week, but she was pleased to know she'd survived. That was the important thing—she had made it. She'd proven she could make a life for herself without Bryon if she had to, and dealing with a roomful of wiggling tots kept her mind off her troubles, but she still dreaded nighttime. When she finally went to sleep, each night she dreamed that Bryon had come back to her, only to awaken sobbing to the reality of his absence. With each heartache, she prayed, "God, if he won't love me back, why can't I forget my love for him?"

Wonderingly, Sonya rubbed her abdomen where the baby moved vigorously. Hardly a day passed now that the baby didn't prod or kick her lightly, and each time, she mourned that she wasn't sharing the experience with Bryon. She was tempted to stay in bed, but she had to buy groceries. The few items she had brought from the apartment were almost gone. Dr. Hammer had been specific about the right diet for a healthy baby, and she intended to follow his advice.

She eyed the littered apartment with distaste. Bryon had always insisted on a spotless environment, and this place didn't look like her home. She had left dirty clothing lying on the chairs, dishes were unwashed in the sink, and because it was more trouble than it was worth, she hadn't folded up the bed each day.

Bryon wasn't here now to see it, so she left the room as it was, except to pick up her dirty clothes. She took them down to the basement where the manager had told her she would find washers and dryers. After she finished the laundry, she carried the basket upstairs. The bed looked inviting, so she lay down again.

The buzzer sounded, indicating that someone wanted to enter her apartment, and she went to the speaker.

"Sonya, this is your mother. Open the door, we want to come in."

"We?" Sonya said stupidly.

"Your father and I."

Sonya pushed the button to release the lock on the lobby door and looked wildly around the littered apartment. She quickly smoothed the sheets on the couch and folded it before her parents knocked on the door.

She didn't want her parents to know the depth of her unhappiness, but when they stepped into the room, she started sobbing and threw herself on her father's husky, squarely built chest. He patted her back, whispering as he had when she was a child. "Now, don't cry, baby. You'll be all right."

"This is worse than I even suspected," her mother said, sizing up the room in horror. "Why didn't you contact us before you moved in here?"

Sonya removed herself from her father's arms, closed the door and motioned them to sit on the couch. She drew a kitchen chair close to them, took a deep breath and wiped her eyes.

"I felt it was my problem—no use to involve you."

"It's our problem, too," her father said. "We've come to take you home."

"No, I'm not leaving. I have a job, and I intend to make it on my own."

"We'll see about that," her mother said. "Start at the beginning and tell us everything."

Efficient and determined Marilyn Sizemore always had

the effect of making Sonya seem like a child again, and she found it difficult to reveal the complete facts about Bryon's infidelity. By the steely look in her father's eyes, Sonya knew he had no trouble reading between the lines.

"Do you think there's any chance of reconciliation?" her mother asked when Sonya finished.

"It doesn't seem so, but I'm not giving him up without a fight. I still love him, no matter what he's done to me."

"I can't understand why you didn't come to us immediately," her father said. "We're your parents. You should have known we would take you in."

"But you told me when I married Bryon that if I got burned I'd have to suffer alone with the blister."

Her father's face colored, and he swung his arm angrily. "It's true I didn't want you to marry him, but you should have known we would help you if you had a need."

"What's done is done," her mother said. "Let's pack your things, and we'll start home in the morning. We brought the pickup, and we can take most everything you have here."

For a moment Sonya was tempted. It would be comforting to be in her old home again, to awaken to the sounds of the farm—the lowing of cattle as they came to the barn for milking, the hum of the tractor as her father went to the fields. Her parents would shoulder the expense of the birth and support her and the baby without complaint. She would be loved and cosseted as long as she wanted to stay with them. But was that fair? Her parents had sacrificed to educate their four children, and since her marriage, they had accumulated some money and free time.

After one of their sons-in-law had become a partner on the farm, the Sizemores had been able to spend part of the past two winters away from the farm in Florida. If she went home, the money they should spend on their retirement would go to take care of her, and they would miss the small luxuries they deserved. She wanted to go home, but she wouldn't.

Sonya took them both by the hand. "I love you, and I appreciate having you come to help, but I won't push my responsibility on you. I'm going to handle this myself. I'm working now, and I'll manage."

Across the hall a door banged, and a husband shouted angry insults at his wife as he bolted down the hall. Mrs. Sizemore covered her ears.

"But surely, daughter, you aren't happy living in such a small place," her father protested.

"No, I'm not happy. I'm miserable, but I can't see any other recourse now."

"If you won't come with us, at least go to that lawyer and make Bryon give you some support."

"Mother, would you want to live on money from a man who didn't want to provide it? After being rejected the way I have, I don't have much pride left, but I do have some, and I refuse to beg from him."

Marilyn Sizemore threw up her hands in defeat. "Let's clean this place. I've never known you to litter a room like this. Don't you feel like cleaning?"

"I've lost any desire to have a clean house. There was no one to see it, and I didn't care."

With both of them working, it took only a couple of hours to clean the apartment, wash the dishes and do the necessary ironing. While they cleaned, her father checked the plumbing and electrical fixtures and took a general survey of the apartment.

"We must check into a motel," he said, "and then we'll take you out for dinner. I also intend to stock up these grocery shelves for you."

"Now, Daddy, I won't have it. I can manage on my own."

"I'll not have a daughter of mine go without food. Don't you have a birthday coming up? Count it as your birthday gift, if that will make you feel better."

"Under those circumstances, I'll accept."

"And I'm going to have a telephone installed here and pay for it until you're able to do so. I'm not doing that for you, but for your mother and me. Don't you realize how we'll worry if we can't even contact you? Forget your pride and allow us that privilege."

"I don't have any choice, I suppose, but as soon as I possibly can, I'm going to assume all my expenses. And I don't want you to send me any money, either. I'll simply send it back. Besides, I have some money—I told you I've sold the furniture. I'm not destitute by a long way."

"But if you go through a divorce, you'll need plenty of money," he said.

"Remember one of Grandma's adages, 'I'll cross that bridge when I come to it.'"

"A lot of trouble can be avoided in this life if we attempt to build the bridge before we need it," her father said. "I'll remind you of this one time, and I'll never refer to it again. If you had finished college like we wanted, you wouldn't be in this mess now. In the first place Bryon would have married someone else, and even if he had waited, you would now have a profession to provide you with a good living. As it is, you're working for wages that a high school student would scorn. And frankly, I don't believe you can possibly make a living at that school job."

Sonya knew the wisdom of her father's speech, and she didn't defend herself. She alone was responsible for her present circumstances and would have to find a solution by herself.

Chapter Five

Having a telephone gave Sonya a stronger feeling of security. She kept the numbers of We Care on the table beside her bed, and a few nights she telephoned the agency. Mostly, however, she slept long fitful hours marked by horrible dreams, awakening each morning feeling as if she hadn't slept at all. She dreamed of a reconciliation with Bryon, but in the midst of their joyous reunion, Gail Lantz would appear, and Bryon would leave her arms and go with Gail. Other times she would see accusing fingers leveled at her from the darkness, and voices echoing back and forth, saying, "Forget him. You're foolish! Stupid! Imbecile!" Another time, she was sitting on a riverbank with a fishing pole in her hands. When she landed a fish, it turned out to be Bryon, and again the accusing voices called, "Throw him back. He's not worth keeping. He's been unfaithful. Why would you want to keep him? Let him go."

To avoid going to bed early, Sonya talked often on the phone with Leta. She called Bryon's parents to let them know she had a telephone, but she sensed a reserve in her mother-in-law's manner, as if she preferred not to talk to Sonya. No doubt they had been in touch with Bryon and had his version of their problem, so she didn't contact the Dixons again.

One night she telephoned the Shraders.

"Hello, Lola," Sonya said. "How are things with you?"

"I'm glad to hear from you, Sonya. Riley and I think of you often. When I couldn't reach you at the Sandhill Apartments, I didn't know what had happened to you."

"I couldn't afford to live there, so I have a much smaller apartment in west Omaha. I didn't have a telephone at first, but I do now, and I wanted to let you know how to reach me."

"That's great. How about lunch someday?"

"I would love that, but it will have to be on Saturday, as I have a job now." She explained about her work at the nursery school.

"That sounds like a good place for you—you'll receive firsthand experience to help in raising your own child. How are you feeling?"

"All right, I think. Having never been through this before, I hardly know what to expect. I seldom have morning sickness now."

"Good. Could we meet at Pierre's Saturday at twelve? Riley will be home then to care for the children. Let's make a day of it—we can shop afterward."

Sonya hesitated momentarily. Could she afford Pierre's on her salary? But she didn't want to take a chance of losing Lola's friendship, so she agreed, "I'll be there. Telephone if you can't make it."

Sonya thought about the luncheon engagement all week. She had acquired new friends at the school, but she still missed the friendships she had made through Bryon.

Thinking about seeing Lola brought back the enjoyable times spent in Bryon's company. The longer he stayed away, the more she tended to forget how he'd treated her the past four months, remembering only the love they had shared.

Saturday morning she was downstairs before seven o'clock to do her laundry, and she made short work of cleaning the apartment. She'd stopped cluttering, so it didn't take long to shape up the place. Her messiness had been intended to aggravate Bryon, but he wasn't there to see it, so why make her own life miserable?

Now that she could no longer afford a hairdresser, Sonya styled her own hair, but she wasn't pleased with the results this morning. Since Bryon's absence, she'd allowed her short hairstyle to grow out again. She had no extra money for beauty salon appointments. She knew her hair would look mighty plain compared to Lola's modish hairdo. But she chose a dress that was full enough to disguise her expanding waistline and finally approved of the image she saw in the mirror.

Already Sonya had learned the truth of Leta's words about her clothes—there was hardly anything she could wear. She had gained five pounds, which the doctor said was normal now that she was four months into her pregnancy, but she had only a few dresses that were comfortable.

The gas gauge registered empty, and she grudgingly stopped at the service station for five dollars worth of fuel. She had received a paycheck yesterday, and although it was meager, she was thankful to have even that much. She guarded tenaciously what Leta had paid for the furniture to secure her hospital confinement, though she had drawn on that account to pay a month's advance on the apartment.

Lola waited in the lobby at Pierre's, and she embraced Sonya.

"I'm pleased to see you looking so well. I know this separation has been a blow to you, and I feared that you might have a complete breakdown."

As they were shown to a table for two, Sonya admitted, "I'm having lots of rough times, but working each day has helped me retain my sanity. I try not to think about the future, nor the past."

"I want the special," Lola said to the waiter. Sonya noted that the special cost fifteen dollars, and she knew she couldn't pay that price.

"Bring me a chef's salad and hot tea," she ordered, and to Lola she said, "My appetite still isn't good, and often I throw away food. I'd rather not order more than I can eat, especially at these prices."

Lola refused to meet Sonya's gaze. "I'll be happy to buy your lunch."

Sonya flushed and stammered, "It isn't that. I have money, just not much appetite." She forced a smile. "I may have some dessert later if I'm still hungry."

Perhaps sensing Sonya's embarrassment, Lola hurriedly changed the subject to chat about her children.

"Does Riley ever mention Bryon?" Sonya interrupted to ask.

"Not much," Lola said shortly. "He knows I've lost all patience with your husband, but he did say that Gail Lantz had been transferred to San Francisco. So you know what that means. I always thought she was on the make, ready to pick up the first man she could find dangling."

That information dulled Sonya's appetite, and she pushed the salad aside.

"What could I have done to keep him?" she whispered weakly.

"I think your question should be, 'Why would I want to keep him?' He's acting despicably. If he didn't want any children, he could have done something about it and not thrown all the responsibility on you."

"I know what you say is true," Sonya agreed quietly, "but I still want him."

Softening, Lola said, "I shouldn't be so bitter, I suppose, and no doubt I would feel differently if it were Riley."

"Do you think Bryon will ever come back to me?"

"No, I don't, and I think you should make up your mind to that fact."

Lowering her head into her hands, Sonya answered, "I can't give him up yet." Although, more and more, Sonya was wondering if her relationship with Bryon had been as perfect as she had considered it, she couldn't admit that to anyone else.

Lola patted Sonya on the shoulder. "If you want him that badly, keep hoping. He won't be the first man who's strayed and then returned home." Picking up her purse, Lola continued, "But enough of this gloomy talk. Let's go shopping. We can look at baby things, and you'll probably need some maternity clothes. I would let you borrow mine, but I'm so much shorter than you, they wouldn't fit."

"Maybe just one new dress. Most of my clothing is too tight now." Sonya knew she couldn't afford any new clothes, but she didn't want to admit her poverty.

Lola led the way to the exclusive shops where they'd always made their purchases.

"You shouldn't tempt me this way, Lola. You know pretty dresses are my weakness, and I haven't bought a new one for weeks."

"High time you did then." Waving the salesperson

aside, Lola shifted the garments on the rack. "How about this pink one? You always look stunning in pink. And here's a jumper dress—just right for your coloring. Try both of them."

"I really shouldn't, Lola. I have to conserve my money now."

"But you'll need some maternity clothes! Buy one of them at least."

The dress featured a striking earth-tone print jumper over a seven-button rust-colored Henley T-shirt. Although it was a comfortable one-piece with an elastic waist and straight skirt with back vent, it looked like a two-piece outfit. When Sonya took off her tight garment and eased into the jumper dress, she felt as if she'd been let out of jail. The price was almost a hundred dollars, a bargain price at that shop.

She modeled the dresses for Lola. "The jumper dress is definitely *you*, Sonya. And the way it's made, you can wear it throughout your pregnancy."

Normally, Sonya wouldn't have thought twice about buying the dress, as Bryon always insisted that she be stylish, but she had only fifty dollars in her purse, and that had to last for the next two weeks until she was paid again. She had used most of the groceries her father had provided.

Sonya replaced the two garments on hangers and carried them from the dressing rooms. She handed them to the salesperson. "They're very nice, but I don't have enough money with me to buy them."

"You have an account here, Mrs. Dixon. I'll be glad to charge them."

"I'd forgotten about that."

"You can surely afford this one," Lola insisted as she held the jumper dress for Sonya to take another look. Not wanting her friend to know the depth of her poverty, Sonya said, "Oh, I guess I can at that. I'll take it."

Sonya drove home with a warm glow in her heart. The afternoon had been good for her—she loved to shop, she loved to buy new clothes, and it was great to have Lola treat her as she always had. Sonya hustled upstairs to her apartment and tried on the dress again. The dress would be serviceable all through her pregnancy, for the bloused waist would facilitate any weight she gained. Humming one of the songs the children sang at nursery school, Sonya made out a grocery list and went down to the car again. It was only five blocks to the shopping center, but that was farther than she wanted to carry groceries. After two blocks, the car lurched sideways.

"What happened?" Sonya wondered aloud as she braked to a halt.

She hurried around to the right rear of the car. The side had blown out of one of her tires.

"Oh, no!" she muttered. She was parked in front of a service station, and Sonya motioned to the attendant.

"Trouble, ma'am?" he said as he approached. Sonya pointed at the tire. "Guess you do have trouble. Take a new tire to fix that."

"I have a spare in the trunk." She lifted the lid, and the man punched the tire. "Tread is worn thin on the spare—it would do for a few miles in an emergency, but you'll be asking for trouble to drive far on it. Fact is, you need a whole set of new tires."

Sonya recognized the wisdom of his words when he pointed out the worn places.

"I don't have the money for a new set of tires."

"Take my advice and buy some before winter, or else leave the car parked when the streets are snow covered."

"How much will it cost to replace the damaged one? That's all I can afford today."

"I've got a good retread here that I could sell you for $40."

Which will leave me exactly ten dollars for two weeks' of groceries.

Sonya returned to the apartment as soon as the man replaced the tire. She draped the new dress over her shoulders and smoothed down the twill challis fabric. Glancing at the clock, she knew she must hurry. She reached the dress shop just a few minutes before it closed.

"I've decided to return the dress," she said to the salesperson.

"But I thought you liked it."

"I do...but I can't afford to buy it." Sonya felt her face grow warm as she forced herself to admit the truth.

"Perhaps I could lay it away for you, and you could pick it up later."

"No, thank you, and I want you to close my account. Anything I buy from now on, I'll pay cash."

Tears blinded her eyes as she stumbled out of the shop.

Sonya stopped at the grocery store and searched the shelves for inexpensive items. She passed by the produce and meat counters, although these should be part of her diet, and bought several cans of soup, some crackers, bread and milk. The total came to more than ten dollars, and, embarrassed, she asked the clerk to deduct one can of soup. The woman in front of her at the checkout counter had a cart piled high with groceries, and she paid her bill with food stamps. Would she come to that? If the choice lay between welfare and starving, she would have little choice.

Sonya warmed one of the cans of soup for her supper, wishing she had the chef's salad she hadn't finished at the restaurant. As she washed the dishes, she thought how long it had been since morning. She'd started out so happy, but the day had gotten steadily worse.

The doorbell rang, and Sonya moved toward it with lagging feet. She kept the chain on the door all the time for she didn't trust some of the neighbors in the apartment complex. So she opened the door just a crack. It was Adam and Marie Benson, who had been visiting an elderly woman on the first floor.

"Come in. May I offer you some refreshment?" Sonya asked, wondering what she would do if they said yes.

"No, nothing, thanks," Adam said. "We wanted to see how you're doing."

"We can stay for a few moments, though," Marie said as she took a seat on the couch. "The apartment looks nice now that you've brought your own possessions here."

"It's small, but about all I can take care of with my schedule at the school. And I do thank you for giving me that job. It's been a lifesaver."

"Our director is satisfied with your work. I wanted you to know that," Adam said.

Sonya flushed with pleasure. "I needed that compliment after today."

"What went wrong today?" Marie asked, peering keenly at Sonya.

"Nothing in particular," Sonya answered, loath to burden the Bensons with her problems, "just a Saturday."

"Are you still having financial problems?" Adam asked. "We don't want you to be pressured beyond your means."

"No, I'm doing fine," Sonya insisted. She couldn't let the Bensons know that she was out of money; they had done enough already. "My parents came to visit, and when I wouldn't go back to Ohio with them, Dad paid for the installation of a phone, and he'll pick up the tab until I'm doing better. They would provide more, but I won't accept it.''

''Do you know that we have a clothing and food bank at the church?'' Marie asked thoughtfully.

''No.''

''We're going to stop at the church this evening so Adam can pick up some notes for his morning sermon. If you would like to go with us, you might want to look at the clothing—we received several nice maternity garments last week, and I think they would be your size.''

Sonya shook her head stubbornly.

''Have you ever given to the United Way or other benevolent funds?''

''Yes, Bryon was always generous with charities.''

''Then you shouldn't hesitate to receive when you're in need. You can't possibly make enough at our nursery school to provide a full living. Look at it this way—you're doing us a service by working at the school for less than you could get in many other jobs. Take some of the clothing and groceries and count it as part of your pay,'' Marie persuaded.

Sonya sobbed, and Marie gathered her close as Sonya divulged the events of her shattering day.

''Pride may be your worst problem, Sonya,'' Adam said.

''But it's also hard to become humble when you've had as much as she's had,'' Marie said severely, and Adam lapsed into silence.

When she could control her voice, Sonya told them, ''I'll take the clothes and some food with thanks,'' she said. ''Again God has sent you to me when I had a great need. I'm not sure I would have been able to make it through the night."

"Come along then. Let's see what we can find."

While Adam went to his office, Marie took Sonya downstairs to the clothing room.

"Why, this is almost like a store," Sonya said in amazement when she saw the numerous items available.

"Some of the clothing is unfashionable, but there aren't many changes possible in maternity garments," Marie said. "Look at these. I thought when they came in that you should have them."

She lifted several dresses from the rack, and while none of them were as pretty as the one she'd wanted at the shop, still they were adequate and looked almost new. Sonya chose two similar long-sleeved dresses with high waists and six-button front plackets. One dress was fashioned from royal blue wool, and the other in a multicolored polyester fabric.

"I imagine these belonged to a woman who only wore them through one pregnancy. And here are some large blouses that you can wear with those maternity slacks. You may need to lower the hem in the slacks though."

"I shouldn't take all of these," Sonya objected.

"No reason not to," Marie said. "After your baby is born, you can bring them back if you like." She motioned Sonya to another part of the room and opened several metal cabinets.

"Please choose enough food items to see you through the next two weeks."

Sonya covered her face with her hands. "I feel so cheap doing this."

"Sonya, will it help you to know that when Adam was in seminary, and we had two children and another on the way, there was never a month that we didn't have to take food from the church supplies?" Sonya looked at her with wondering eyes. "You see, I know how you feel."

"I'm ashamed for being so ungrateful. Of course I'll take some food."

She chose several cans of beef stew, tuna and macaroni and cheese mixes. She took a large box of cereal and some dried milk. Adding several cans of fruit, she decided she had enough.

"I'll help you across to the apartment house with these items," Marie said.

After Marie left, Sonya put away the foodstuffs and tried on the clothes with a spirit almost as light as it had been when she'd started out this morning. Another obstacle had been surmounted.

Chapter Six

Sonya went to early worship service the next morning and, upon Marie's invitation, attended the coffee hour between worship and Sunday School. Sonya already knew several of the parents who brought their children to nursery school, but Marie introduced her to many others. She received invitations to the singles group that met each month, but she didn't feel "single" yet, so she didn't intend to go.

When she left the church, the sunshine and breezy conditions made her think of summertime. She couldn't bear the thought of spending the afternoon inside, and she watched enviously as the families gathered into cars and started home. Even Daniel Massie, who was unmarried, drove off with his mother, both of them waving in friendly fashion.

She moped upstairs to the apartment, barely acknowledging the greetings of the other apartment dwellers. She hadn't made any effort to meet any of her neighbors, and she didn't intend to do so. She telephoned Lola, but didn't receive an answer. What could she do for the afternoon that wouldn't cost any money? She checked her stock of groceries and telephoned Leta.

"Say, Leta, how about coming over for lunch? Then we can drive to Fontenelle Forest and hike this afternoon."

"Are you sure you're up to it?"

"I'm fine, and I can't stay inside on this beautiful day."

"I'll be over soon. Don't fix dessert—I'll buy a strawberry pie."

Sonya had enough celery to make a bowl of tuna salad. She made grilled cheese sandwiches, and warmed some soup. She was mixing a pitcher of iced tea when Leta rang the bell.

"I've missed seeing you, Sonya. I returned from my mother's yesterday, but I was too late to telephone you." She looked Sonya over closely. "You're picking up some weight, aren't you?"

"Five pounds."

"You seem a little happier."

"I'm making friends at the church, and I keep busy at the nursery school, so that doesn't give me much time to brood. I'm forcing myself to accept the fact that Bryon may not come back, and if he won't, I have to go on living."

"Heard anything from Bryon?"

"Nothing since I moved out of your apartment."

"He probably doesn't know where you are."

"I telephoned his mother and told her, and I imagine she's relayed my whereabouts."

Sonya enjoyed her meal much more with someone to talk to, and she listened to Leta's chatter with satisfaction. The lives of her tenants were discussed at length.

"I've not rented your apartment yet. I want to be especially particular about the tenant who lives across the hall from me, and with your expensive furniture, I want someone who's responsible.''

"If Bryon comes back to me, we might be able to move back in.''

Leta gave her a look mixed with disgust and sympathy. ''I suppose you'll take him back on his own terms if he shows up.''

"I married him for 'better or for worse.' I've had the better for two years, and I won't give him up when I experience the 'worse.' ''

Leta swallowed her last bite of pie. ''Some people like to be martyrs, though I didn't think you would be one of them. But enough of that. We need to start if we're going to do much walking. The daylight hours are getting shorter all the time. Let's take the rest of this tea in a thermos.''

Leta insisted on driving, and Sonya didn't argue much, for she didn't want to be out of town with her unreliable automobile. They headed south to Fontenelle Forest, the largest unbroken tract of forestland in Nebraska. The paths were crowded with many others who desired a last taste of summerlike weather before winter arrived. After two hours of hiking, both of them agreed they'd had enough. Leta suggested they drive north along the Missouri. By the time they started south again, darkness had descended.

"Shall we stop at a restaurant for a snack?" Leta suggested.

Sonya didn't want to admit she didn't have any money, so she said, "There's still some of that pie left. Why can't we eat that?"

"Good idea.''

Sonya left the nursery school at noon to keep a doctor's appointment. At the apartment she changed into the blue hand-me-down maternity dress. As she appraised her appearance in the mirror, she noted that her daily walks had given her skin a healthy tinge. She'd always heard that pregnant women glowed with an inner beauty, and although during the first months of unhappiness, she couldn't see anything beautiful about her body, she looked much better now. The woolen dress, obviously an expensive one, raised her self-esteem.

As she drove several blocks to the doctor's office, she peered constantly at the gas gauge. She hesitated to change doctors now, but knowing she must reduce expenses, she thought she should seek an obstetrician closer to the apartment.

Since she was midterm in her pregnancy, she was scheduled for several tests, including a sonogram and an Alpha fetoprotein test. The doctor commented favorably about her low weight gain and said her general health was excellent. He assured her that she had nothing to worry about, but when she received the statement for his services and the lab work, Sonya cringed—almost five hundred dollars!

"I don't have that much money with me," Sonya muttered to the receptionist. "I'll go to the bank, then come back and pay you." She had deliberately refrained from starting a checking account so she wouldn't be tempted to overspend.

More gasoline wasted to drive to the bank, where she withdrew five hundred dollars from her savings account. If she had any more expenses like this, she wouldn't have enough money left to pay for the delivery of her baby. She returned to the hospital and paid the bill, but when the receptionist started to schedule her next month's appointment, Sonya said, "I'm sorry, but I can't come for any more checkups. I can't afford it."

"But Mrs. Dixon, Dr. Hammer insists on seeing his obstetric patients regularly. Surely you can make arrangements to pay for that."

"I have just enough money to pay for the delivery costs, and I must save that for my confinement. If he doesn't want to deliver without seeing me regularly, I'll have to find another obstetrician," she said hotly, for the receptionist's loud voice carried throughout the crowded waiting room.

"I didn't suggest he wouldn't deliver your baby. It's just an unusual situation. I'll discuss it with Dr. Hammer." The receptionist gave her a pitying stare. "You poor thing," she said.

Sonya said nothing.

Hoping none of her acquaintances had heard the conversation, Sonya abruptly turned away and rushed out of the room. Her pride couldn't stand much more.

She hurried into her apartment, for once glad to be enclosed within its four walls. She didn't know if she would ever have the nerve to stick her head outside again. What a humiliating experience! It was bad enough to struggle to pay every bill without having it broadcast over the city.

Suddenly Sonya felt hatred toward Bryon for what he had done to her. Up to this point, she'd considered herself at fault for the situation, but now she transferred her resentment to Bryon. She jerked off the secondhand maternity dress and flung it across the room, where it fell in a heap. She unfolded the bed and collapsed on the wrinkled sheets, wondering how she could ever find comfort for her breaking heart. Her greatest agony came from her suspicion that the unconditional love she had reserved for her husband had not been mutual. Had he *ever* loved her?

She lay there until the room was completely dark, hoping she could go to sleep. She roused when a knock sounded on the door, snapped on a light and took a robe from the closet. She considered not going to the door, for it had to be someone from the apartment building. Checking to be sure the security chain was in place, she opened the door slightly. The short, handsome man who'd often tried to converse with her stood in the hall.

She started to close the door, but he stuck his foot in the opening. "I thought you might be lonesome and want some company," he said.

"When I do, I'll choose my own company. Take your foot out of the door."

He stood indecisively a few moments, and Sonya panicked, wondering what she could do if he refused to leave? But he withdrew his foot. "Sorry, ma'am," he said. "Guess I made a mistake."

Shivering, Sonya shut the door and staggered back into the room. She slumped into one of the straight chairs and leaned her head on the table. *So this is the opinion they have of me.* Her pregnancy was obvious now, and she supposed her new neighbors had deduced that she was an unwed mother. Had it come to this? That she appeared to be fair game for any lecherous man who crossed her path? She felt the child move in her body and she shuddered again. How could she possibly make a decent life for it?

The outside buzzer sounded, and Sonya eagerly went to answer. Maybe it was the Bensons! They always seemed to know when she needed help.

"Yes," she said.

"Sonya, this is Bryon. I want to talk to you."

Suddenly Sonya had trouble breathing, and she grabbed at a chair for support.

"Did you hear me, Sonya?"

"Yes. I'll release the door. I'm in apartment 405."

She looked wildly around the room. She rushed to fold

up the couch. She picked up her dress from the floor and threw it in the closet. She recoiled at her image in the mirror, but before she could do anything with her personal appearance, his knock sounded at the door. Her heart pounded wildly, and her legs trembled so much they hardly supported her as she opened the door. His virile, stimulating presence overwhelmed her, and she threw her arms around him.

Bryon pushed Sonya aside; he wasn't alone! Gail Lantz preceded him into the room—a Gail Lantz, sleek and tantalizing, in a woolen suit that probably cost more than the doctor's bill Sonya had paid today.

Sonya didn't ask them to sit down, and she waited for Bryon to speak. Her throat was too dry to utter a sound.

"Why did you move into a place like this?" Bryon demanded, as if her dwelling had insulted him.

"I didn't have any choice."

"Why didn't you go back to your parents? I thought that's what you would do—the reason I cut off your expenses. I wanted you to leave Omaha."

"I had my own reasons," Sonya said shortly. Why bother to defend herself to Bryon? Why had she allowed him to put her on the defensive? She should have attacked him first.

"What did you do with our furniture? This stuff is junk," he said as he glanced around the room.

"I sold the furniture to Leta and put the proceeds in a savings account to pay for my confinement. Maternity care is expensive."

"I wouldn't know," he said. He motioned Sonya toward the couch and drew up one of the straight chairs for himself. Gail still hadn't said a word, and the other two ignored her.

Bryon smiled, and Sonya saw him as the person she'd

loved so long. "Sonya, I want to be fair with you, but I don't want to be married to you anymore, nor do I intend to be saddled with alimony payments. Let's admit we made a mistake, agree on a onetime payment and call it quits."

"But, Bryon, don't you even intend to acknowledge that you have a child?"

"No, I don't." His smile disappeared, and his face hardened. "You're responsible for the child, since I depended on you to prevent one. I'll give you a settlement that will pay for your medical expenses and support you for six months, and after that I'm through."

Sonya caught his hand and, ignoring Gail's presence, she said, "Bryon, how can you forget so quickly the love we shared? Don't you love me at all?"

His face softened, and his gaze failed to meet hers. He hesitated and returned the pressure of her hand, but Gail laughed ironically.

"Maybe I'd better leave, and you two can take up where you left off."

Her comment broke the spell, and Bryon threw an angry glance in her direction, but he dropped Sonya's hand. "What about it, Sonya? Will you agree to a onetime settlement? I'll be generous with you. That way we can both start our lives over again."

Sonya felt tears stinging her eyelids, but she refused to cry with Gail in the room. She lifted a hand to still her trembling lips.

"You can't expect me to make this decision without giving it some thought. How long will you be in Omaha, Bryon?"

"Three days. I'm here to attend the annual board meeting of the firm."

"Telephone me in two days, and I'll give you an answer."

Bryon's manner with Gail was curt as he ushered her out of the room, and Sonya had a feeling she hadn't cemented her relationship with Bryon by the comment she had made.

Sonya sat in a state of numbed shock after they left. Her mind rioted with unanswered questions. Why had Bryon brought Gail with him? Was he afraid to be alone with her? Afraid he would succumb to their former relationship? How should she react to his suggestion of a onetime settlement? She had to talk to someone. Should she telephone her parents? Lola and Riley? The Bensons?

After more than an hour, she telephoned Leta.

"Bryon has been here."

"What! Tell me all about it."

Eager to hear the story, Leta didn't interrupt while Sonya related Bryon's visit. "And I don't know what to do next," she concluded.

"Go to see Daniel Massie. You'll have to consult a lawyer, and I don't imagine he'll think much of this onetime settlement."

"But what about his fees? I don't make enough money to pay my current expenses."

"I told you that lawyers often add their fees to the divorce settlement. He'll get his money out of Bryon. If necessary, I'll loan you the money, or give it to you for that matter. It would be worth it to help some woman escape the clutches of a man like Bryon Dixon."

"But, Leta, for a few minutes tonight, he was like the old Bryon that I love. I believe if Gail hadn't been along, he might have agreed to come back to me. I wonder if that's why he brought her."

"Possibly. But let's not stray from the point. Are you going to contact Daniel Massie?"

"I guess I'll have to."

Sonya telephoned Daniel from the church office the next morning and set up an appointment for after work at the nursery school. To save a parking fee and gasoline, she took public transportation to Daniel's office. While she waited at the bus stop, a young woman, whom she recognized as a resident of the apartment complex, arrived at the stop with three small children in tow.

Because of Bryon's visit, Sonya had forgotten about the man who had tried to come into her apartment the night before. Perhaps it was time she made her marital circumstances known to her neighbors.

"Hello," she said to the young woman. "I'm Sonya Dixon, and I live in Washburn Complex. Haven't I seen you there, too?"

"Yes," the woman said stiffly. "I've spoken to you several times, but you didn't act like you wanted to be friendly."

"I'm sorry, but I haven't been fit company for anyone, not even myself. My husband walked off and left me three months ago, and I haven't been able to deal with it very well. When I moved into the apartment, I couldn't have told you that, but I'm finally accepting the fact."

"Are you divorced?"

"No, and I'm hoping we won't be. He came to see me last night, and I'm going to a lawyer this afternoon, but I'm pregnant, you see, and I'd like to keep our home together."

"We'd kinda wondered if you had a husband. Lots of young women in the complex don't have a man. My husband tells me not to have anything to do with them, but a body's got to have some adult company. I'd climb the walls if I didn't talk to anyone but these kids, day in, day out.''

"Maybe we can meet for coffee someday. I'm sorry I haven't been friendly.''

"Sure, I understand. My sister went through the same thing.''

"Does your husband work away?''

"He's a migrant worker, so he's gone most of the time. He'll be home next week for the rest of the winter.''

"There comes my bus. Is this the one you're taking?''

"No. By the way, my name is Loretta Slinde. I live in 212.''

"My number is 405. Let's have coffee one day soon.''

Sonya was early for her appointment with Daniel, and though she wanted to shop for a few minutes, she pushed temptation aside and went on to his office. She had to wait for a half hour, but reading one of his magazines wasn't going to cost her any money; shopping might break down her self-control.

Because she'd seen Daniel quite often at the church, she wasn't ill at ease in his presence as she had been on her previous visit. She explained briefly about Bryon's proposal for a divorce settlement.

"I won't have any money to pay for your services unless he does make an allowance for me, so there won't be any hard feelings if you don't want to represent me. I wouldn't blame you at all.''

"Then your salary at the nursery school isn't adequate?''

She shook her head. "It might be if I didn't have anything except general living expenses, but last week I had to replace a tire, and my doctor's bill was five hundred dollars. I make enough for rent and food, but not for one thing extra, although I hope to manage my finances better.

I'd sell the car if I could, but Bryon's name is on the title. So I'm using it as little as I can, and I've canceled my doctor's appointments. When my baby comes, I'll just have to enter the hospital as an emergency patient and take whatever doctor is on duty.''

"Not a very wise procedure, Mrs. Dixon." When they'd met in church, Daniel had been calling her "Sonya," but here in the office, they were on a professional footing, which made it much less embarrassing for her.

"I don't seem to have any other choice."

"Oh, you have several other options, but you didn't choose any of them. Don't worry about my fee. Your husband will eventually have to pay it, or I'm not worth much to you. About the settlement, I think you're unwise to do anything until after your child is born. If the baby should have health or emotional problems, medical bills could run into thousands of dollars. There's no way those problems could be anticipated in a predivorce settlement."

"Then you think I should tell him no," Sonya said, with a lighter heart. The longer she could put off divorce, the more likely that Bryon would come back to her.

"He would only have to wait another three or four months, and he's unreasonable to refuse that."

"He won't like it, but I'll hold firm."

"Refer him to me if he becomes difficult."

Sonya dreaded Bryon's call, and it was almost a relief when he didn't contact her that night, but she fretted all the next day, knowing she couldn't put off the controversy any longer. She hoped that he would come to see her, but the phone rang soon after six o'clock.

"All right, Sonya, I need your decision," he said briskly.

"Bryon, is there no possibility that you'll change your mind? You know I don't want a divorce."

"Don't start that. I only have a short time—our meeting reconvenes soon. But since you bring it up, I don't want a divorce, either, but neither do I want a child. If you'll give the baby up for adoption as soon as it's born without even seeing it, and have an operation to prevent another pregnancy, I'll forget about the divorce and come back as soon as you're back to normal. I only want you if we live as we did before you got yourself in this mess."

In other words he wants my undivided attention, wants to put me up on a little pedestal and have me decorate his home.

"I don't believe that would work, even if I'd agree to such a horrible suggestion. I'll admit that I don't particularly want a child, either, and with all the trouble it's caused, I have trouble looking forward to it. But I'm going to overcome that, and even if I don't love the baby, I can't deny my responsibility to it. I've seen the problems of too many unwanted children at the nursery school."

"That's my only bargaining point, and apparently you're rejecting it."

"Bryon, why don't you like children?"

He was silent for a few minutes, and Sonya didn't interrupt his thinking. She had wondered about this often and hoped for an answer.

"I really don't know. Actually, I don't dislike children in general. I just didn't want any of my own. As long as I had you, I didn't need anyone else in my life."

Sonya's heart lifted. "Then you still love me?"

Her heart seemed to stop beating while he hesitated, and she waited for him to speak.

"We're straying away from my reason for telephoning. When can we meet with our lawyers to agree upon a divorce date and settlement? It's all over, Sonya, and you might as well accept it.''

Sonya was so disappointed that she replied angrily, ''It isn't all over for me and won't be for some time. I went to a lawyer yesterday, and he advised me to refuse any settlement until after the baby is born. That won't be until another three months.''

''I won't accept that. Who is your lawyer?''

She told him, adding, ''But I won't agree to a divorce, so you're wasting your time to contact him.''

''Then you needn't expect any support from me, no maternity benefits, nothing.''

''I've been getting along for three months on my own. I'll make it, Bryon. If you can live with yourself by denying your responsibilities, I can live without any support from you. You and Gail will just have to wait for a while.''

''Not that it's any of your business, but we aren't waiting.''

With a curse, Bryon slammed down the receiver, terminating the conversation and confirming Sonya's suspicions. They were already living together!

Chapter Seven

The classroom seemed unusually quiet. The children had gone for the day, but Sonya had stayed to help Eloise take down the turkey and pumpkin display on the bulletin boards and to put up the Christmas decorations. Each day she lingered beyond her scheduled hours, because she hated going home to an empty apartment. If she worked until she was exhausted, she could fall into bed at an early hour. Most of the time sleep wiped out her trauma, except for those nights when she dreamed—dreamed of Bryon still loving her, dreamed of Bryon in Gail's arms, dreamed of Bryon gone forever.

Adam and Marie stopped by the nursery room when Eloise and Sonya had almost finished. Plastic snowflakes tumbled at random on the windows, and a nativity scene, with figures as large as the children, stood in one corner of the room. On a low table a Christmas tree blinked red and green, and brightly wrapped packages dangled from the ceiling on colorful tinsel ropes. Each child would receive one of those gifts on the last day before the Christmas break.

Sonya loitered until Eloise was ready to lock the door. As they left the room, Marie put her arm around Sonya.

"Sonya, don't overdo. You don't look well. We appreciate all the work you're doing here, but you must be careful."

"I was doing fairly well until Bryon came to see me. I'm developing a bitter attitude toward him. I resent the way he's treating me. And, too, I'm not looking forward to the Christmas season."

"Are you going to your parents' for Christmas? The school will be closed for ten days—you would have ample time."

"My mother is expecting me to come and insists on sending me a plane ticket, but I haven't decided yet."

"If you don't go away, we want you to share Christmas dinner with us," Marie said. "And in the meantime, we're always as close as your phone."

"Thanks. I'm still using the We Care numbers, but not as often as I did. And I'm finding much comfort in the Bible, but I fear my faith is still very weak."

As she trudged across the street and up to her apartment, Sonya wrestled with her decision about Christmas. During the past two holiday seasons, she and Bryon had enjoyed a succession of dinners and parties that started with Thanksgiving and continued through the New Year. She had hoped that she would still be invited to some of those festivities, but she hadn't heard from anyone, not even the Shraders. Lola and Riley always had a brunch on Thanksgiving morning, but Lola hadn't called her for several weeks. Not since their lunch date. She realized that a single would be a "fifth wheel" at a couples party, like the brunch, but couldn't Lola still remain a friend, anyway?

She'd made it through Thanksgiving with Leta's help.

Leta had spent Thanksgiving Eve with Sonya. They'd attended church together, and then Leta had come back to the apartment and stayed until midnight. The next morning she'd come for Sonya, and they'd gone to a restaurant featuring a large buffet. Since the weather was good, they'd driven east on the interstate to Des Moines, and by the time they'd gotten home, Sonya was tired enough to sleep.

But Leta would visit her mother in St. Louis for Christmas, and although it was kind of the Bensons to ask her for the holiday, she had no intention of intruding. Sonya was gradually becoming more self-reliant. She had learned that when she helped one of the children at school overcome a big problem it made her own situation more bearable. *It's time I search for others who are as lonely as I am and reach out to them. I must stop expecting people to do for me. Perhaps I can find healing by helping others.*

Sonya heard the phone ringing when she reached her apartment, and she hurriedly opened the door.

"Hello, Sonya. You're late tonight."

"Yes, Mother. We decorated the room for Christmas after the children left."

"I need to know what day you're coming, so I can arrange for your plane ticket. If I don't do it soon, you may not get a reservation."

"I've decided not to come to Ohio for Christmas."

Her mother cried, "Sonya, do you realize you haven't been home for Christmas since you were married?"

"I know, and I'm sorry to hurt you, but, Mother, I'm hurting, too. I want to be at home, but my pride won't let me come back alone, proving that I've failed at marriage. Perhaps when the baby comes, and I have something to show for three years of 'wedded bliss,' I may lose my hurt, but I can't face my friends and the extended family now. Thirty or forty relatives on Christmas Day is more than I can handle. Please try to understand.''

"What are you going to do?"

"The Bensons have invited me to spend Christmas with them." Her mother needn't know that she wouldn't accept the invitation.

"What can we send you for Christmas then? What do you need?"

The ogre of the hospital bill loomed closer and closer and without thinking, Sonya said, "Why don't you send what you would spend for a plane ticket, and I can apply it to my medical expenses when the baby is born?"

"Why, Sonya, don't you have insurance? Isn't Bryon taking care of that?"

Too late Sonya realized what she had done. So far she'd carefully concealed Bryon's total parsimony from her parents. Was that pride, too? Not wanting to admit that the man she'd chosen could behave so shabbily.

"I'm finding out there are many expenses besides medical bills," she said, trying to repair the damage she'd done. "I had no idea what baby clothes cost! I wasn't begging—I'm getting along all right—but you will buy me a Christmas gift, anyway, so it might as well be what I need rather than something frivolous. Or if you would rather, you can buy some baby items. You've reared four children, so you know what I'll need better than I do."

"I might just do that—it's fun to buy for grandchildren. But you're sure you aren't in actual need?"

"Mother, I'm doing fine, and I have to salve my ego by proving to myself and Bryon that I can manage alone."

"You don't think he'll come back to you?"

"It doesn't seem likely, but I'm still hoping."

"I can't understand why you would want a man who deserted you, but it's your decision."

This thought had often filtered into Sonya's mind, but it annoyed her to have her mother express it so bluntly.

"Daddy never left you, did he?"

"Of course not!"

"Then don't judge my reactions, Mother. You can't know how I feel. I love you, but I have to work this out myself."

Physically drained after the phone conversation and the long hours at school, Sonya made short work of dinner preparations. She warmed a can of soup and washed an apple. With these and a few crackers on a tray, she sat on the couch to watch the news while she ate. The ringing phone awakened her, and she glanced at the tray. She'd eaten about half of the food before she had fallen asleep. As she answered the phone, she noted the time was nine o'clock.

"Sonya, this is Daniel Massie. Am I telephoning too late?"

"No, not at all."

"I have something to discuss with you. Could we have dinner together tomorrow night?"

"Uh," she hesitated. "Is it something about Bryon or the divorce?"

"No, I want to discuss a proposition that might solve your financial problems."

"And you can't tell me what it's about?"

"I'd rather talk to you in person."

"Then I suppose we could go to dinner."

"Fine. I'll pick you up at your apartment. Will six o'clock be all right?"

Sonya sat for a long while before she took the tray to the kitchen and dumped the cold food into the garbage.

She pulled out the couch and made up her bed, although she wasn't sleepy. What did Daniel want? Why couldn't he have told her on the phone? Although she didn't suspect Daniel of any romantic ideas, still she didn't want to be in a man's company. The more she thought about going out with any man who might approach her romantically the more upset she became. Sonya spent most of the night tossing and turning, unable to sleep. She couldn't go through with it.

But with morning, her common sense took over. Even during the years with Bryon, she had lunched occasionally with some of their mutual male friends, and she knew that Daniel Massie was interested only in her spiritual and material welfare. He was friendly toward all the women at the church—married or unmarried—so why make such an issue about a simple dinner engagement? There was something special about Daniel, Sonya had to admit to herself. She always got a good feeling being around him. He was so warm and kind. He seemed so sure of himself; confident, but not in an arrogant way like some men. No, it was his strong faith, she decided that made him seem so calm and clear-sighted. So grounded. She envied him that. And thinking about Daniel, she was amazed at how light her spirits were during the day as she looked forward to the evening.

Although she usually dawdled after school, when her duties ended for the day, she rushed out of the building, eager to get to her apartment and make preparations for the evening. She took the blue dress she had discarded, after that disastrous incident at the doctor's office, downstairs to the laundry, and after running it through the wash and dry cycles, she was pleased with its appearance.

After showering, she styled her hair in soft waves, and her blond hair flowed freely around her shoulders. With her makeup kit that she hadn't used for months, she applied colors that brought out the gold tints in her hair and, draping the blue dress over her shoulders, she saw that it emphasized her blue eyes, making them seem brighter, but just a bit on the mysterious side.

Her hands hovered indecisively over her jewelry box. Bryon had pressured her to dispose of all of the jewelry that she'd had before they were married, so all that she possessed had been gifts from him. Would it be proper for her to wear his jewelry when she was dining with another man? She thought longingly of the gold chains she'd been given by the boyfriend she'd been dating when she met Bryon. She remembered Bryon's tirade when she'd worn one of those chains on their honeymoon. Hoping to avoid future unpleasantness, she had readily agreed to give away her jewelry, and he'd bought her more expensive necklaces. Did it show a lack of character on her part that she'd gone along with all of Bryon's suggestions? Boy! She had been putty in his hands.

Recklessly Sonya reached inside the jewelry box and withdrew the diamond necklace and earrings. Adding those to her attire really made her look elegant, and when Daniel sounded the buzzer, she went to meet him with a self-confidence that she hadn't felt for months.

For the first time Sonya was aware of Daniel's masculinity that Leta was always raving about. At the office he wore dark suits, but tonight he was dressed in a casual tweed sport coat with a tan shirt opened at the collar. He complimented Sonya on her appearance, took her arm and ushered her into his car as graciously as if she were royalty.

Driving away from the apartment house, he said, "And where shall we eat? Do you like Chinese, Mexican or plain old American food?"

"Yes."

He looked at her inquiringly, and she laughed. "I mean I like all of them, so choose any restaurant you want. My grandmother used to admonish us, 'Eat what's put before you,' so we grew up with a taste for all food."

"Then let's go to a steak house. I know a good one a few blocks from here."

The restaurant he chose was one where she had gone often with Bryon, and she almost asked Daniel to drive on to another place, but if she was ever going to forget Bryon, she might as well start tonight. But her resolve suffered a setback when they encountered Lola and Riley Shrader dining with another couple from the brokerage firm.

Sonya tried to maintain her emotional equilibrium as she introduced Daniel to her former friends, but her mind rioted as she and Daniel continued to their table. This will be all over town by tomorrow, and Bryon will be sure to find out. Why did something have to happen to remind her of Bryon tonight? Even in his absence, did he monopolize her life?

Perhaps realizing the emotional jolt she had received, while they waited for their meal, Daniel asked about her childhood on the farm.

"We have a dairy farm, milking Holsteins and a few Jerseys. Dad owns two hundred acres of beautiful, fertile soil. My brother-in-law has been operating the farm since Dad retired two years ago, although he still does a lot of the work."

"Didn't you have a brother who was interested in working the farm?"

"No brother, although I have three sisters. Needless to say, being the youngest in the family, my siblings often accuse me of being spoiled, which isn't true because our parents showed no favoritism. Dad sacrificed to give all of us a college education, and then I had to disappoint him by marrying Bryon.''

''Without any brothers, did you girls have to help with the farm work?'' Daniel asked, deftly shifting the conversation away from a subject that disturbed Sonya.

''My two oldest sisters did, and they became very good with the farm machinery. Dad took me to the fields when I was sixteen, but after I plowed out two rows of his best corn, he decided that tractors weren't my forte.'' A smile flitted across Daniel's face. ''After that I helped mother in the garden some of the time, but mostly the two younger daughters were expected to help with the housework.''

''Do you miss the farm?''

''I've been home only once since I married, for Bryon didn't want me to go alone, and he was always too busy to take me. I missed the family at first, but I've grown accustomed to being separated from them.''

''I've always been interested in farming,'' he said. ''My grandparents owned a farm in central Nebraska, and I spent all of my childhood summers there. Grandpa thought that I'd become a farmer, but my life took another direction.''

''You're probably better off as an attorney. Farming is hard work.''

''Any profession is hard if you give it your best, and that's what I try to do.''

''What made you decide to become an attorney?''

''Several factors influenced my decision. I mentioned when you were in my office that my father abandoned my mother when I was a child. Of course, a five-year-old isn't very observant, but I still remember my mother crying late into the night when she thought my sister and I were asleep. My paternal grandfather helped us, or we would have gone hungry because mother had married young and didn't have any job skills, nor did she have anyone to care for us if she had worked."

"I can see why you compared my situation to hers."

He nodded. "And although I'm not proud of this, growing up without a father was difficult for me, and I started running around with the wrong friends. I refused to go to church with mother, my grades were poor, and I failed the eighth grade. That summer I was accused of breaking into a store and stealing a television set. I hadn't done it, but my reputation was bad, and when the police took me for questioning, I was terrified. If it hadn't been for a family friend who was a lawyer, I would have been punished for that crime. He believed that I was innocent and represented me without compensation. I was so happy when I was proved innocent that I made up my mind to stop my rebellion, to study law, and become the kind of attorney who would be more concerned about justice for his clients than his own aggrandizement. I especially wanted to help boys who needed guidance."

Daniel paused while the waitress replenished their beverages and took away their salad plates, and Sonya noted particularly how considerate Daniel was of this woman as he stacked dishes and handed them to her.

"I started studying, and during my high school years, I managed to be an honor student." Daniel continued. "About the time I was ready for college, my grandfather died and left his entire estate to me, so it was easy to finance my education and embark on the goal I'd set for myself."

"You have certainly fulfilled your goal. You've been such a comfort to me, and I'm extremely grateful to Leta for bringing me to you. It's obvious to me that you are a caring person.''

"I take little credit for that. I owe it to that attorney who set a good example for me, my grandfather, and to God. When, as a teenager, I was struggling to find some meaning to my life, wanting to make new friends and chart a different path, I read a promise in one of the Psalms that I claimed for my own. *I will instruct you and teach you in the way you should go; I will counsel you and watch over you.* There has seldom been a day since then that I haven't asked God to fulfill that promise in my life.''

"Perhaps I shouldn't ask, but if you're so interested in helping children, why haven't you married and had a family of your own?''

Sonya thought she saw a shadow flicker across Daniel's warm gaze, but when he spoke his voice betrayed little emotion.

"At first I was too busy getting an education, helping mother and seeing that my sister was educated, to consider marriage. Now that my sister is settled, and Mother is comfortably established, I intend to marry.''

"I thought the many broken marriages you encounter in your practice might have discouraged you from taking a wife.''

"Those experiences have taught me to be wary, but I do intend to marry, because I've observed enough happy couples, like Adam and Marie for instance, to know that it is possible to have a Christian home and family. That's the kind I expect to have.''

As Sonya listened to him, she was impressed by his eloquence and his rugged good looks. When she first met Daniel, she hadn't considered him handsome, so what had happened to change her mind? Perhaps it was his infectious smile resulting in a crinkle in his forehead that made her smile. She was happier in Daniel's presence than with anyone else, and that realization made her squirm uncomfortably in her chair, as she lifted a hand to her flushed face. She didn't want to become emotionally involved with another man, especially when she thought there was a chance to reconcile with Bryon, and although Daniel was a cut above most men she had ever known, he was a man, and once burned, she knew to stay away from the fire. If she could simply be his friend, she would like to be more closely associated with Daniel, but could she see him often without wanting more than friendship? Sonya knew that she yearned for love, but could she ever trust another man with her heart? *Why couldn't she have met a man like Daniel before she made her disastrous marriage?* There was no doubt in her mind that the woman who married Daniel would never feel unloved or unhappy.

By the time they'd finished their salads, T-bone steaks and baked potatoes, Sonya had pushed the meeting with the Shraders into the background, and while they waited for dessert, Daniel said, "I suppose you're wondering what I wanted to talk with you about."

Sonya laughed. "Actually, I've been enjoying myself so much that I'd forgotten there was a purpose to our meeting."

Daniel looked at her appraisingly. "Sonya, do you realize that tonight is the first time I've ever heard you laugh."

She sobered immediately. "I really haven't had much to laugh about the past few months. I used to be a happy, carefree person, who laughed a lot." She rubbed her cheeks. "I suppose that's the reason my face feels stretched. I haven't used my laugh muscles for a long time. I used to be pleasant company. I suppose all of my new friends think I'm a sourpuss.''

He reached out and touched her lightly on the hand. "Let me say that I prefer the laughing Sonya. Try to think about the future with a smile."

Sonya withdrew her hand, her skin burning at his touch, but Daniel didn't seem rebuffed.

"I wanted to talk to you about an idea that I've been rolling around in my head for a few weeks. You may need some time to think about the proposition I want to make, and you may not be interested in it, but at least hear me through."

Sonya nodded and relaxed in the chair.

"You've been open with me about your finances, so I know you're having quite a struggle. My suggestion might alleviate your financial worries, and at the same time you could be a help to someone else."

With a smile Sonya said, "That's strange. In the past few days I've concluded that I'd spent too much time brooding about my problems, and that it was time I started reaching out to those in need."

"I have an elderly client who needs someone to stay with her at night. She has a maid who takes care of the house cleaning and that type of thing during the daytime, but Mrs. York isn't too well and shouldn't live alone. However, she resists moving to a nursing home.

"My idea is that you could give up your apartment, move to her home, be there with her at night, and still work at the nursery school. Those arrangements would free your salary for the hospital confinement and other expenses. I can't guarantee that my client will look favorably on this suggestion, but I feel the arrangement could be beneficial to both of you."

"That might be all right temporarily, but in three

months, I'll have a child. No elderly woman will want a baby in her home, and if I give up my apartment for three months, I might not find another.''

"She might welcome having a small one in the house. Her last close relative, a granddaughter, passed away about a year ago, and the old lady is quite lonely.''

"Where does she live?''

"In a large house in the northwest section of Omaha. At one time her family owned a ranch there, but progress has encroached on her, and she now has only five acres surrounding the house. There's one bad part of my suggestion—you couldn't walk to work, and there aren't good bus connections. You'd have to drive, and that will take some expense.''

"When opportunity knocks, it seems as if I should investigate, but shouldn't you find out her reaction before we discuss it further?''

"Do you know Edith York?'' He observed her closely with questioning eyes as if to determine what the name meant to her.

"No, I don't think so.''

"I'll go to see Edith tomorrow morning, and if she's receptive to the idea, perhaps I could take you out to meet her in the afternoon. Or would you prefer to drive out by yourself?''

"It might be better for me to go with you. I don't know much about that part of Omaha.''

Sonya didn't go to bed until the early hours of the morning, for she kept thinking of their dinner conversation. For her nightly reading, she opened the Bible to the book of Romans, turning to a Scripture that often puzzled her. *And we know that in all things God works for the good of those who love him, who have been called ac-*

cording to his purpose. Her faith in God was more secure
now than it had ever been, but she had not yet figured out
how it could be good for her to suffer through Bryon's
abandonment and the heartaches it had brought, and now
when she had found a man who seemed to be all one
could want in a husband, she was so disillusioned that she
even hesitated to be Daniel's friend.

She had once read a poem, "The Weaver," that compared one's life to a weaving fashioned by the hand of
God, who alone could see the overall pattern. She couldn't
remember all of the words, but one line had read, "I in
foolish pride forget He sees the upper, and I, the under
side" of the weaving. The poet had further explained that
in a weaving dark threads were as important as the bright
colors, and that only the Weaver knew the final outcome.
Could this mean that to experience life to its fullest required dark, as well as beautiful days?

Was there a purpose after all to these months of trouble
she had endured? Although she could see only the present,
was God cognizant of the full scope of her existence? Was
life a chain of events all woven together? If she hadn't
married Bryon, she would never have come to Omaha,
and if Bryon hadn't deserted her, she would never have
met Daniel and through his loving concern become aware
that all men were not like Bryon, and most important of
all, if she was still with Bryon, her relationship with God
would have continued to deteriorate. It was difficult for
her to comprehend that God would go to such lengths to
order her life, but that must be true.

Sonya didn't know anything about weaving, but she
thought of the large jigsaw puzzles she and her sisters had
enjoyed fitting together when they were children. When
they first dumped the jumbled pieces out on the table, it
was incredible to think they could assemble them to match

the picture on the box. Piece by piece, however, the finished product took shape. Perhaps her life was like that, and she would never know the reason for disappointments and failures until the picture was completed. *But if life was a puzzle, where did Daniel fit in?*

Daniel stopped by the nursery school the next morning and spoke to Sonya briefly. "Mrs. York is quite eager to discuss my idea with you. What time do you finish here?"

"I can leave anytime after two o'clock."

"My secretary and I have an appointment with another attorney in that area. We'll stop by the school and pick you up, introduce you to Mrs. York, give you an hour for visiting, then bring you back to your apartment. Will that be satisfactory?"

"Yes, thank you."

While the children had nap time, Sonya asked Eloise for permission to go to the apartment to change her clothing. Being an elderly person, Mrs. York probably wouldn't want to see a pregnant woman in slacks, so she chose the multicolored polyester hand-me-down dress and was back in the classroom when Daniel and his secretary arrived.

Daniel endorsed her clothing change with a smile. "Mrs. York comes from an old line of aristocrats, and she has strong ideas about proper apparel. She'll approve of your appearance."

A beautiful old cast-iron gate marked the entrance to the buff-colored brick residence. Though Daniel had said a *large* house, Sonya wasn't prepared for the opulence of the estate. The driveway curved up a small hill toward a three-storied house that faced a magnificent lawn. A brick wall marked the rear of the property, and an iron fence based in buff brick surrounded the front and sides of the estate.

When Daniel stopped in front of the house, Sonya sensed the isolation of the place. Numerous trees on the property concealed the dwellings around it. Although others lived within a mile of the property, it appeared as secluded as it had been when the house was built many years ago.

Before they knocked at the door, Daniel said, "Please don't give Mrs. York an answer until I talk with you again. You need to know some facts that she probably won't tell you, but I didn't want you to know them, thinking they might sway your opinion. After you meet Mrs. York, I'm sure they'll make no difference."

Sonya nodded.

"And be candid with Mrs. York. She'll understand your situation."

Sonya doubted that an elderly woman who lived in these surroundings could possibly understand problems of divorce and rejection so common in the current generation, but she hoped Daniel was right.

In spite of the cold wind blowing across the wide porch, she felt hot and nervous. An older woman with a kind face answered Daniel's knock. She was a housekeeper or maid, Sonya assumed.

"Good afternoon, Mr. Massie. Mrs. York is in her living room."

Bug-eyed, Sonya followed Daniel down the wide hallway. She'd entered another world. An intricately carved walnut grand stairway led from the entrance hall to the second floor. On the landing a grandfather clock announced the time at three o'clock. A huge wrought-iron chandelier, holding electric candles, hung from the second-floor ceiling. Sonya would have suspected that a house this old would have suffered neglect, but judging from her quick inspection, the house was intact and orderly.

Mrs. York was tiny, fragile and gray-haired. Her hair was dressed in an upsweep that had been done at a beauty shop. She wore a fashionable blue dress that matched vivid, sparkling eyes, and a pair of diamond earrings dangled from pierced ears.

Sonya's heart sank when she saw this woman whom Daniel Massie thought might prove her benefactor. This woman needed nothing—she wouldn't welcome a pregnant nobody, nor would she want a howling infant to destroy the quiet and peace of this house. Sonya almost turned on her heel and walked out the door, but she didn't want to let Daniel down after he'd been so kind to her.

Daniel made the introductions, then said, "I'll return for you in an hour, Sonya. That should give the two of you time to become acquainted."

"Lay aside your coat and sit down, Sonya," Mrs. York said when Daniel exited. "Stelle will bring us some refreshments. Do you prefer tea or coffee?"

"Tea, please."

"That's what I always have. She'll be along soon."

While waiting for Mrs. York to speak, Sonya looked around the room. It might have been a drawing room once, but now it served as a bed-living-room combination. One side of the room had been partitioned into a bathroom. Near the bathroom door was a single bed. The section of the room where Mrs. York sat contained a small sofa, several chairs, bookshelves and a television. A telephone stood on the table beside the chair.

Sonya considered the most outstanding piece of furniture to be an ornately carved chest at the foot of the bed, although it contrasted vividly with the many antique items in the room. Nursery rhyme characters decorated the polished maple chest. Little Red Riding Hood and the Three Bears were delicately carved and painted on the light wood. This child's toy box seemed out of place in the room of an octogenarian.

"When is your baby due, Sonya?"

That was the last place Sonya expected the conversation to start.

"Around the first of March."

"Are you having any trouble physically?"

"No, and the baby is all right, too. I had a series of tests at midterm, and the doctor assures me all is well. My problem is emotional, but I suppose Mr. Massie told you about my situation."

"Just a few basic facts. He seemed to think it better if you told me what you wanted me to know."

Stelle entered the room with a tray on her shoulder. She placed it on the low table in front of Mrs. York. The maid poured a cup and handed it to Sonya, then she carefully measured a small portion of milk and some sugar into a cup, filled the cup half-full of tea and the rest water. She pushed Mrs. York's chair closer to the table.

"Help yourself to the cookies," Stelle said. "I made them this morning, special."

"Mrs. York…" Sonya began haltingly as Stelle exited.

"Call me Edith. My friends all do."

"My husband left me three months ago when he found out I was pregnant. He hasn't given me any support since, and I've been too proud to force him to do so, nor would I allow my parents to support me. I've been trying to make it on my own, and frankly I've had a struggle. Mr. Massie seemed to think we might be of some mutual help to each other, but seeing the way you live, I can't think I would be any help to you. Since I have a long way to go before I'll be over this situation, my company may not be good for you.''

''But I'm in need of healing, too, and I need a companion. If I can't have someone in the house at night, I'll have to go to a nursing home. I don't want that.''

''I can understand why you wouldn't want to leave here.''

''I was born in this house soon after the turn of the century, ten years after my father built it. We were out in the country in those days, but the city has surrounded us. My husband sold off everything except these five acres before he died.''

''Has your husband been gone long?''

''Almost twenty-five years.''

''I'd think you would be healed by this time.''

''Oh, I'm not grieving for my husband. I need healing because of the death of my granddaughter, whom I lost a year ago. She was my only close relative, and she was soon to bear a child, too.''

''Then won't my presence be an unpleasant reminder?''

''No, on the contrary, I think it would benefit me.''

''If you should invite me to stay with you, would it be temporary? I can't believe you would want a child in the house. I suppose I could take the baby to the church nursery during the day, but at night I would have it with me.''

''This is a big house, my dear. I'm pretty much confined to this room and the dining room now. I have a bad heart, as well as an arthritic condition, which won't allow much stair climbing. Indeed, I have no desire to go upstairs, anyway, but my point is, your quarters wouldn't be on this floor, and I wouldn't hear the child.''

Sonya laughed slightly. ''I know it sounds as if I'm trying to wriggle out of this arrangement, but how could

I be of any use to you with a child to care for and in another part of the house?''

"I have a buzzer system, which sounds throughout the house. I summon help that way. Actually, I'm ready to die, and wouldn't care if I just slipped away alone, but my doctor and lawyer are worrywarts, and they insist that I must have round-the-clock companionship."

"Haven't you been able to find people to help?"

Edith hesitated with downcast eyes, and her hands moved nervously in her lap as she said evasively, "I hardly need a nurse, and I don't feel inclined to pay for a companion when I don't need one, but in this case, when you need a home and I need a night sitter, it would probably work to our advantage. I wouldn't monopolize all of your time, but I would appreciate having you share dinner with me. You would need to prepare your own breakfast each morning, as I sleep late, and Stelle doesn't come until mid-morning. The food would be my expense. You would, of course, be responsible for the support of your child."

Sonya was ready to agree to the situation. She couldn't see anything except benefit to her. Edith York was personable. The living quarters were great, although something about the house did give her an eerie feeling, and she wondered how she would like being isolated up on this knoll with only an old lady for company. But by living here, she could save almost all of her salary if the daily drive back and forth to work didn't prove too costly.

"This sounds like a good deal for me, but perhaps it would be better if we think it over for a few days."

"That's fine with me, but you should see your rooms before you go. I would like you to stay in my granddaughter's apartment. She had a living room, bedroom, bath and a small kitchenette on the third floor. I'm sure you would find it comfortable." She rang the buzzer, and Stelle came in and picked up the tray.

"Will you show Mrs. Dixon to the third-floor apartment? She may be coming here to live, and she needs to see the quarters."

Stelle turned quickly, stared at her employer, and the tray tipped in her hands. The sugar bowl slid on to the floor. It didn't break, but sugar spread over the carpet.

Sonya looked at the woman in amazement. She had sized up tall, angular Stelle as a well-coordinated, capable woman. What had startled her into dropping the sugar bowl?

"Mrs. Edith!"

"Stop gaping, Stelle, and do as I asked you. It will be all right."

"Yes, Mrs. Edith. I'll sweep up the sugar soon."

Stelle set the tray on a hall table and motioned Sonya to the left. "Quickest way is up the back stairs." When they reached the stairway, she stood aside to let Sonya precede her. "Don't stop at the first door. Go to the door at the head of the stairs."

"Aren't you going?"

"No ma'am. I need to clean up the mess I made."

When Sonya came to the first landing, she opened the door and glanced about. This was the second floor and looked much like the downstairs. Doors opened into four rooms. Before she closed the door and continued upstairs, she admired the large chandelier suspended from the ceiling.

Edith obviously intended to put her in the servants' quarters, and she'd almost decided she wouldn't consider coming here, wondering how she could climb these stairs when her pregnancy became more burdensome. And how about carrying a baby up here each day? But when she opened the door into the apartment, she knew Edith had offered the best she had.

A large picture window commanded a view of farmland to the north, completely overlooking the houses surrounding the estate. It reminded Sonya of the farm at home. She would like that view every day.

Dust sheets covered the furniture, and the rooms had a neglected look. Had anyone cleaned the room since the granddaughter had died? Sonya lifted a sheet to peek at the furniture, finding it more modern than the rest of the furniture in the house. The small bedroom was as pleasant as the living room, and Sonya could tell these rooms, once servants' quarters, had been remodeled in the past few years by Edith for the grandchild she had loved and lost. The low ceilings gave her a sense of protection and comfort. After that one-room apartment, this place looked like heaven.

She went downstairs and entered Edith's room. The woman watched her with anxious blue eyes. "I forgot to tell you, we do have an elevator to the second floor, so you would only have to walk the last set of stairs. Did you like the rooms?"

"I do. Your granddaughter must have been very happy there."

Edith's shoulders shook with sobs, and as Sonya knelt to comfort her, the doorbell rang. Edith patted Sonya's hands and gently pushed her away. "That will be Daniel. He must not see me crying. You run along now and telephone me soon about your decision. I'm willing to have you move in whenever you want to."

"I'll be in touch soon."

Stelle reached the front door at the same time that Sonya left the room. Daniel stepped inside, bringing a flash of snow and cold with him. "Ready?"

"Yes." He held her coat for her and walked by her side out to his car.

"My secretary and I didn't finish. As soon as I take you home, I'll go back and join her."

"I'm sorry to bother you. I could have waited until you finished."

"No bother. I was eager to know how it turned out."

"I'm ready to move in anytime, and she said she was willing to have me. I think it would be great to live in that beautiful house."

"But beautiful houses don't always mean happiness. Edith has had her share of sorrow."

"Yes, she told me about her granddaughter."

"Did she tell you how she died?"

"No, now that you mention it, she didn't."

"I didn't think she would, and I didn't want you to know until you'd met Edith and sized up the situation." He paused again, and Sonya stared at him curiously. "She committed suicide by hanging herself from the large hall chandelier."

Chapter Eight

~⌒~

Sonya switched on the light and sat up, drenched with perspiration and trembling. Three o'clock! This same dream had occurred all night long. She would dream; awaken in fright; go back to sleep; dream again. Same dream, but the victim changed each time.

Sometimes it was a faceless person, and finally she saw herself swinging back and forth over the York mansion's large central hall. Then the scene changed, and she stood on the ledge at Sandhill Apartments ready to jump to her death. What had prompted Edith's granddaughter to take her own life?

Sonya left the bed and went into the kitchen. She heated water and made a strong cup of tea—no more sleep for her tonight. Why hadn't Daniel told her about Edith's granddaughter before she had gone there? The reason was obvious—he was pretty sure she wouldn't go. "Nor will I go now," she muttered. Could she ever walk into that house without remembering the tragedy? No wonder Edith didn't want to go upstairs anymore, and that Stelle avoided the third-floor apartment.

By daylight, Sonya decided that she wouldn't go. She'd made it this far without extra help. There had to be another way. She would ask Daniel to tell Edith that she wouldn't come.

As Sonya sipped on the tea, she kept remembering Edith's words, "I need healing, too." And she thought of her conviction that it was time to reach out to others, rather than to expect all of the benevolence to flow one way. Sonya wished it weren't Saturday, so she could be busy at school and forget the decision she had to make.

While she cleaned the apartment, laundered her clothes and showered, Sonya kept weighing the pros and cons of living with Edith York. Did the benefits outweigh the liabilities? She would have free room and board for herself and a home for her child, thus enabling her to save enough money to pay for her hospital confinement and to continue her regular appointments with Dr. Hammer. She would have a pleasant place to keep the child and nice wide lawns for his or her stroller. As she looked around the tiny apartment, she admitted how crowded it would be when she moved in the necessary items to raise a child.

And in daylight perspective, she considered her reason for refusing to go as ridiculous. How could the tragic death of Edith's granddaughter have any effect on her? She smiled when she realized that Daniel had used psychology—he knew life with Edith would be pleasant for her, and he wanted her to see that before she heard the debit side.

She telephoned Daniel at his home. When she told him her decision, he asked, "When do you want to move? I'm sure Edith will welcome you anytime."

"The December rent is due in two days, so I might as well give notice and move Monday. I'm sure Eloise will give me the day off to do that."

"Will you need a moving van?"

"I moved here in the car. Except for my clothes and kitchen items, there isn't much to move."

"I'll give you any help you need to settle in your new quarters. Count on me to help with the moving, and I'm sure Adam will help, too."

Sonya felt warmed by Daniel's concern and murmured her thanks. He seemed to go out of his way to help her at every opportunity and she felt grateful for his friendship. She went to the office and notified the manager that she would be moving and returned to start packing. She'd always felt uneasy in this apartment, and it would be a relief to leave. Before she accomplished much, the doorbell rang. At first she didn't recognize the frail, unassuming woman standing in the hall.

"I'm Loretta Slinde. We met on the bus. You told me to come for coffee sometime. Is it all right now? My husband's at home with the kids."

"Certainly. Come on in. As a matter of fact, I'm going to move Monday, so this is probably our last chance."

"You didn't stay long."

"I've been given a chance to move in with an elderly lady. I can stay with her at night for room and board and still work at the school in the daytime. I need some extra money, so this will be a help to me."

She ushered Loretta to the couch. "Let's sit here—it's cozier than the table. Do you want sugar and cream in your coffee?"

"Yeah, I do."

Sonya carried the snack items on a small tray and placed it near Loretta. She was glad she'd bought the cookies yesterday.

"Help yourself to the coffee and cookies. Sorry they aren't homemade."

"Where did you say you were moving?" Loretta asked as she popped half a cookie in her mouth.

"To the home of Edith York. She lives in a big house in north Omaha."

Loretta choked, and bits of cookie flew from her mouth. Her face flushed, and Sonya rose to help her. Loretta waved her away.

"I'm all right. You just surprised me, that's all."

"Would you like a glass of water?"

Loretta shook her head. Although she still struggled for breath, she blurted out, "You can't go there to live—that house is haunted."

Sonya laughed.

"No, I mean it. A young woman who lived there; the old lady's granddaughter I think, well, she killed herself because she was afraid of her gangster husband. That's the reason the old lady can't find anyone to stay with her."

Well, thanks a lot, Daniel Massie.

"I don't believe in that rubbish!"

"Well, I heard it's a scary place. No matter what you believe," Loretta concluded.

"I've already said I would go, and what you've told me only confirms my decision. Mrs. York needs somebody to help her, and that somebody may be me."

Sonya switched the subject, but when the woman left, Sonya telephoned Daniel again.

"What was the name of Edith's granddaughter?"

"Alice Simmons."

"And her husband was?"

"Wade Simmons, a notorious criminal. No doubt you've heard of him."

Sonya swallowed convulsively for she recognized the name as the one on the pamphlet the Bensons had loaned her. "Don't you think it's time for you to tell me *everything* about Edith York?"

"I've always heard that what you don't know won't hurt you," he said with a laugh.

"In this case, I'm not so sure," Sonya countered. "If the ghosts show up, I need to be prepared."

"So you've heard that. You surely don't believe in ghosts."

"Not yet," Sonya joked. Her faith would never permit such a superstitious belief and she was sure Daniel knew that.

He laughed again. "When Alice married Simmons, she didn't know he was a gangster. After she became pregnant, she went back to her grandmother, not wanting to rear a child around Simmons' friends. That's when Edith remodeled the third floor apartment for her. But Simmons wouldn't leave her alone. He wouldn't allow her to make a new life for herself. Alice finally notified the police, and they arrested him at Edith's house. I suppose the shame she'd brought on herself and her grandmother, as well as the fear of reprisal from Simmons if he should escape from prison, drove her to suicide."

"So it was suicide?"

"Evidently. Now, that's the whole story as I know it. I haven't telephoned Edith yet, so if you want to back out, you can. I feel that I have taken advantage of you, but on the other hand, I did it for your own good. It will be a good home for you as long as you like."

"Or as long as Edith lives."

"Yes, I'll admit it's a gamble, as her health isn't good."

"I still intend to go," she replied decidedly.

The more Sonya thought about Alice Simmons the more she felt struck by the shocking coincidence, that of all places, she had been led to the young woman's home. Alice's life was so much like her own, her burden so similar, Sonya felt God's hand in this matter and believed there was a purpose to His leading her to Edith York.

On Sunday afternoon Sonya went to the Sandhill Apartments and found Leta at home. Leta had heard vaguely of Edith York and Alice Simmons, but laughed at the tales about the place being haunted.

"Sounds like a dreary house," she said honestly. "But it might be a better place for you to live now."

As she left Leta's apartment, Sonya looked longingly at the closed doors of her honeymoon home across the hall. Now that had been a nice place to live—for a while. She shook her head, squared her shoulders and refused to dwell on the past. She couldn't control her dreams, but in daylight she refused to mourn. Bryon was gone, and she had to make a new life, and more and more she was considering that she might be better off without him.

Monday dawned sunny and warm for a December day, so Sonya felt no misgivings when she drove her heavily laden car away from the apartment complex. Daniel and Adam waited for her at the York house, and they carried her possessions to the third floor. Daniel's presence helped her feel more relaxed and settled about her decision to live there. She realized that she trusted him; he had only her best interest at heart and believed this situation would work out.

The dust covers had been removed and the apartment cleaned. Edith must have used high-powered persuasion to force Stelle into the rooms, but Sonya was pleased to have the clean apartment. Edith came up on the elevator, and Daniel helped her to the third floor. After the men left, Edith reached a hand to Sonya.

"You've made me very happy, Sonya. I hope you will

have some happy days here. I thought this would be a sanctuary for my granddaughter, but it didn't work out that way."

"We need to discuss a few details. What do you expect of me?"

"Just be here at night. And I don't mean that you should never go out. You're too young to sit with an old lady all the time—if you want to go to church or to other social activities, that's fine. My doctor insists that I shouldn't stay all night by myself, although that's a lot of piffle." Sonya was amused at some of Edith's casual vocabulary, which seemed at variance with such a sophisticated lady.

"When my baby arrives, I'll not be going out much, so that shouldn't prove any problem. If I'm away all day, then I feel I owe the baby the rest of my time. I'm old-fashioned, I suppose, because I think a mother should stay home and care for her child, but I won't be able to do it. The Bensons have recommended a baby-sitter until I can take him to their nursery facilities."

"As I told you before, you can prepare your own breakfast, but Stelle will serve our dinner at six o'clock. She also prepares a light lunch, and if you're here at noontime, as on Saturdays, you may eat with me."

"I suppose I can prepare my breakfast in the apartment's kitchenette."

"Of course, but you may have the run of the house—go where you want to."

"Do you mind if I receive telephone calls here? My parents check on me from time to time."

Sonya's parents had been skeptical of the move, but her mother considered the York house such an improvement over the apartment that she had protested very little.

"Of course. And if they should want to visit you, the whole second floor is available for visitors."

"Thank you. I have the feeling that this bargain is increasingly one-sided."

"You won't think so if I buzz you in the middle of the night for some help." Edith rose from the chair with difficulty.

"The buzzer is connected to this apartment?"

"Yes, Stelle and I checked it when she cleaned the rooms."

"She needn't clean them anymore. I'll take care of that."

Dinner was served in the large dining room, with china and silver and crystal. "I enjoy modern conveniences, but in some ways I'm still an anachronism. I don't mind having pizza for lunch, but in the evening I prefer to honor the traditions of my father," Edith explained.

Sonya was amazed that this elderly woman was so conversant with world affairs. She must definitely watch the news more often, or she would feel illiterate during their discussions. They spent more than an hour over the bountiful meal. Eating was much more pleasant when it was shared with another, and they appreciated the company since both of them had been without companionship. Edith invited Sonya into her room, but Sonya said, "I'll need to unpack my clothing tonight and become oriented in my quarters. I'll visit other evenings, though. Shall I check on you when I leave in the morning?"

"No, I'll be asleep. I'm able to help myself quite a lot. The cane is just insurance against a fall. Don't fret about me. If I need you, I'll be sure to give you a summons."

The strangeness of her surroundings kept Sonya alert, and long after she finished unpacking, she still hadn't gotten sleepy. Except for the hiss of the steam heat as it moved through the old-fashioned radiators, she could hear nothing. From the window, she could see the glow of streetlights above the tree line on the back of the property. It was good to know that civilization was near, since the house and lot were swathed in darkness. Before she went to sleep, Sonya read a few pages of her Bible. Every day seemed to bring new changes to her life, Sonya reflected. She was grateful for the strength and courage her faith brought her. At least something good had come from all her misery.

The days passed easily in Edith's company. One snowy afternoon, as Sonya came in from a walk, Edith called out to her and Sonya quickly went to Edith's room.

Sonya knelt beside her chair. "Is everything all right, Edith?"

Edith patted her hand. "I feel fine, dear. But you look chilled. Sit here with me for a while and warm up. I want to talk to you about Christmas. Are you going to your parents for the holidays?"

"No, they want me to come and will even pay my fare, but I've too much pride to go back home now when my life is in such shambles."

"Then would you share Christmas with me? Perhaps we could prepare the meal ourselves and give Stelle the day off."

"Certainly. My mother taught me to cook, and although I won't be able to turn out a banquet, I can prepare turkey with dressing and that type of meal. And why don't we plan to attend the Christmas Eve service at the church? Do you feel up to that?"

"I seldom go out at night, but I probably can go if you'll do the driving. I have an automobile, but I haven't driven for a few years. Stelle takes me shopping and to the beauty parlor. The Christmas Eve service is a good idea,'' she agreed.

With the matter of Christmas Eve and dinner taken care of, Sonya entered into the holiday activities at church and school with a lighter heart. She felt needed at Edith's and knew that she hadn't been asked just as a charitable act. Edith wanted companionship, too, so they would be helping each other.

A careful check of her bank balance proved that she had enough for her hospital stay and for regular visits to Dr. Hammer until her due date. That gave her a feeling of security she hadn't possessed since Bryon left. Since it just didn't seem right not to do some Christmas shopping, she decided to buy token gifts for the family. She also wanted to buy something for Leta, the Bensons and Edith. Christmas cards would have to suffice for others.

The next evening, before she went to Edith's, she drove to a mall and found a few shops with good prices on the items she wanted. Since her family in Ohio would gather together during the holidays, she could mail all of the presents to her parents and ask her mother to distribute them in order to save on postage.

Though she tried to drive memories of last Christmas from her mind, thoughts of Bryon often intruded. They had spent Christmas Day with his parents, and then they'd flown to Colorado for a three-day skiing trip. Several people from the office had gone with them, including Gail Lantz. Thinking back, she tried to remember if Bryon had paid any particular attention to the woman then. She was reasonably sure that he hadn't.

During her shopping, several times she saw items that she would have bought for Bryon, and she longed to buy for him again, but on her meager budget, she couldn't have purchased anything that he would accept. Later, when she prepared her Christmas cards, on a sudden impulse, she addressed a card to him. She kept it on the table in her living room for several days, but she finally mailed it. Although she had the address of his residence, she sent it to the office. Perhaps Gail wouldn't know he'd received it. Within a week she had the card back stamped "Return to Sender." It hadn't been opened. Had Gail intercepted the card, or had Bryon been the one to return it? Last year Bryon had bought her a diamond necklace. This year he wouldn't even accept her card. How could he have changed that much?

The incident ruined Sonya's Christmas plans, but she tried to put up a front. She was loud and frivolous at school, while at Edith's, she laughed at every opportunity. Then, disgusted at herself for such foolishness, she lapsed into silence and spoke only when it was absolutely necessary. All she wanted to do was to crawl into a hole somewhere and lick her wounds. She dreaded going to school each morning, but on the other hand, she didn't know what she would do for the ten days the school was closed. Why had she tried to contact Bryon? She always came off second-best in any encounter with him.

One evening, however, a week before Christmas, when she stopped by to see Edith after she arrived home from school, Edith smiled at her.

"You look as if you're on your last legs."

Easing down into a chair, Sonya said, "That's the way I feel. My thoughts are burdensome, and certainly my body is the same way." She patted her bulky stomach.

"You need a change of pace, and I believe I have the answer. We've been invited out on a date."

"Oh, you mean we're going to double-date. I can't imagine anyone who would want to date me."

"There's only one handsome gentleman, but he wants

to take both of us out on the town, and his mother as well.''

Sonya smiled. "Apparently Daniel has telephoned.''

"He has tickets to the university choir's musical tomorrow night, and he wants to take us out for dinner ahead of time. What about it?''

"It sounds like a great idea to me, but are you able to go?''

"Why not? I told him that if you agreed, we would meet him in town. I have some business at the bank tomorrow, and it's also the day for my hair appointment, so I'll have Stelle drive me into town, and after I'm finished, I'll meet you at the church. The performance is at seven o'clock, so Daniel said we should eat at five.''

"Sounds great to me. I've attended the choir's Christmas musicals before. They're always excellent.''

Feeling less burdensome than she had when she'd arrived home, Sonya heaved her body out of the chair. "I'll have to see if I have anything I can possibly wear. There may be something in my evening garments, but I haven't had them out of the boxes since I came here.''

Most of her evening dresses were formfitting, so had to be rejected, but she did have one floor-length black velvet gathered skirt with an elasticized waist. She removed the elastic, tried the skirt on, and it fit very well. With it she decided that she could wear a sequined, belted satin blouse that fit over the bulge in her abdomen, and although it was obvious that she was pregnant, she didn't look too bad. A mink waist-length jacket would complete her outfit.

Walking downstairs more jauntily than she had earlier, Sonya presented herself in Edith's room.

"How do I look?''

"Stunning," Edith said, surprised. "I didn't know you had such beautiful clothes."

"Bryon was very generous with my clothing allowance. He always wanted me to look better than any of the other women in our group. I used to think it was because he loved me so much, but as I look back on it now, perhaps my impeccable dressing was important to him because it indicated his prosperity."

Her eyes clouded, and Edith was quick to change the subject.

"Where will you dress tomorrow evening?"

"I'll take my clothing along and dress at the church after the children leave."

"Well, I'll have to make an effort to look as well put together as you do. Of course, Jane Massie will be dressed to the nines. She always is."

When Daniel called for them at the church basement the next afternoon, he handed both Edith and Sonya a corsage box. The orchid put the finishing touches on Sonya's garments, and as she took a quick look in the mirror of the church's rest room, she agreed with Edith. She did look stunning!

Mrs. Massie and Edith were old friends, and during dinner they chatted amicably. Daniel devoted most of his attention to Sonya. She enjoyed the way his gray eyes lit with laughter before the rest of his face expressed amusement. He had no difficulty introducing subjects that she found interesting. With Daniel, she was alive.

The musical performance combined portions of Handel's *Messiah,* as well as secular Christmas music and the beloved church carols. Much of the music brought tears to Sonya's eyes, but new hope dawned when the choir sang:

"And ye, beneath life's crushing load,
Whose forms are bending low,
Who toil along the climbing way
With painful steps and slow,
Look now! for glad and golden hours
Come swiftly on the wing:
O rest beside the weary road
And hear the angels sing."

Had God sent her this particular message? Sonya believed that He had, because life's load had nearly crushed her, but for the first time since Bryon's defection, she began to believe that glad and golden hours would come for her again. In the closing moments of the concert, she prayed silently, *Thank you, God, for sending me the message of Christmas—hope for a brighter tomorrow.*

When Daniel delivered them to her car at the church's parking lot, she said quietly, "I can't express how much this evening has meant for me, but it has given me new hope. I owe much of this to you, Daniel. Thank you for a lovely evening."

Edith was already in the car, leaning back with her eyes closed, and Daniel bent over Sonya. His eyes sparkled mysteriously in the dim light, and he said huskily, "Oh, Sonya, you don't know how much this evening has meant to *me*. You've captivated my thoughts, and I'm constantly inventing ways to be around you."

Sonya was amazed at his words and his ardor. He spoke like a man in love, but surely that couldn't be. He wouldn't talk romantically to a pregnant married woman, but she found it hard to breathe, and Daniel's eyes held hers captive. He lowered his face to hers. "Sonya, I..." The moment was shattered when an automobile with its radio blaring, whizzed through the parking lot. Daniel stepped back and shook his head, as if he had just emerged from a thick fog. A stiff breeze buffeted them, leaving Sonya's hair in disarray. Smiling wryly, Daniel brushed the hair from her forehead and gave her a brotherly hug. Sonya knew that he had intended to kiss her, and although she reminded herself that she was married to another man, she couldn't deny that she would have welcomed his caress.

Opening the car door, Daniel said, "We must get together before Christmas. I'll give you a call."

The last day before the nursery school closed for the holidays, when they were distributing gifts to the toddlers, Sonya was summoned to the phone. The staff didn't usually take calls during working hours, but because so many parents were present, Eloise told Sonya to answer the phone.

"Sonya, this is Mother Dixon."

Sonya eased down into the chair by the telephone.

"Oh, hello," she answered weakly.

"I tried to call your apartment and learned the phone had been disconnected."

"Yes, I moved right after Thanksgiving. I'm living at the home of Edith York. Do you know her?"

"I know who she is, but I'm not acquainted with her. Why would you live there?"

"She isn't well, and a mutual friend recommended me to her. I can continue my work at the nursery school and not have to pay apartment rent. It's working out quite well. You can telephone me there anytime you want to."

"I called to invite you to have Christmas dinner with us." Sonya's mind worked overtime. Why, after ignoring her for three months, would they ask her to dinner?

To Mrs. Dixon she said, "That's nice of you, but I've

already made plans for both Christmas Eve and Christmas Day.''

''Are you going to Ohio?''

''No.''

''We don't want you to spend the holidays alone.''

Why was she probing? Did she think Sonya had a date?

''I'm spending the time with Edith. She's lonely, and I'm lonely, so it will be beneficial to both of us. I do appreciate your thinking of me, however.''

''How's your health?''

''I feel fine physically—emotionally I'm not so well, as you might suspect. This is a difficult season for me.''

Mrs. Dixon ignored that remark. ''When is your child due?''

''The first of March,'' Sonya said shortly. Bryon had made it plain that this was her child, and she didn't appreciate Mrs. Dixon's questioning.

''If you can't come for Christmas, how about New Year's Day?''

''Will Bryon be there? I'm sure he wouldn't want to encounter me.''

Mrs. Dixon laughed lightly. ''Bryon is going to Hawaii for the holidays, so he won't be coming home. I'm not attempting to bring you back together if that's what you think. You and Bryon will have to work out your own problems, but I can't see why that should interfere with our relationship. We've always been on good terms.''

''That's true, and I see no reason I can't spend New Year's Day with you. I'll telephone after Christmas to confirm the date.''

Sonya replaced the receiver slowly. So Bryon was spending Christmas in Hawaii! That was to have been their next big vacation. He'd gone without her, and had no doubt taken Gail. Why did she continue to love a man who treated her this way? Here she was pinching pennies to save enough money to pay for the delivery of his child, living on the charity of others for her food, clothing and lodging, and he flew off to Hawaii with his paramour. Why couldn't she see that she was better off without him?

But when she thought of Bryon, she never pictured him as a wayward husband, but rather she remembered the handsome Bryon, the catch of the campus who had pursued her until he'd won her heart.

Chapter Nine

The organ was playing when Edith and Sonya entered the candlelit church sanctuary on Christmas Eve. The room was crowded already, but an usher approached them, saying, "Jane Massie told me to bring you to her pew. Come this way." Sonya welcomed this consideration since Edith was breathing heavily, and she didn't want to keep her standing while they looked for a seat.

Daniel smiled and placed Edith at his mother's side and made room for Sonya beside him. Daniel's sister and her family had come for the holidays and they sat beyond Mrs. Massie. Sonya was surprised at her personal serenity tonight. She almost believed that the Angel's message was for her alone.

Fear not: for, behold, I bring you good tidings of great joy, which shall be to all people. For unto you is born this day in the city of David, a Saviour, which is Christ the Lord.

She should be lonely spending Christmas Eve away from her family with people she hadn't known a year ago, but these three people had wrapped her in a love that couldn't be compared to familial devotion. Sonya missed a lot of the service because her thoughts had turned inward on her difficulties, recalling how the people in this church had united to help her.

At the close of the service, Daniel introduced Sonya to his sister's family, and under cover of Edith's conversation with them, he said softly, "I'm concerned about the two of you being alone on Christmas Day. Won't you and Edith spend the day with my family? Please say you'll come; it would make me very happy."

Sonya was touched by his heartfelt invitation but she had to refuse.

"Oh, we couldn't intrude, and besides, I don't believe Edith is up to it. Look at her—she's had trouble breathing all day, and I don't like her color."

"You're right," he said, obviously disappointed. "I'll give you a call sometime tomorrow."

He gently squeezed her hand and said goodbye.

Both Sonya and Edith were serene and content when they started home from the Christmas Eve service. The choir had presented a cantata, followed by communion, and Edith hadn't even seemed tired as they drove out of the church parking lot. As they approached a minimall, Edith said, "There's one thing we forgot that I always like for Christmas dinner. Let's stop here and see if we can buy a plum pudding. My mother always made them, but I have bought them since then. The deli at that grocery store may have some left."

The parking lot contained only a few automobiles, and Sonya went into the store to buy the plum pudding. A few shoppers like herself, who had come in for a few last-minute purchases, hustled up to the checkout counter.

Exiting with the plum pudding, she had almost reached the car when she noticed a woman running across the parking lot with a man in pursuit. She headed toward Sonya crying, ''Help me. Help me.''

Sonya stood like one turned to stone, and Edith rolled down the window. ''Hurry, Sonya, get in the car. We can't be involved in this.''

The distraught woman had reached Sonya by that time, and she grabbed her arm, begging, ''Take me with you. I must get away from him.'' A quick glance showed Sonya that the woman's face was distressed and her clothing in disarray. She dodged behind Sonya when the man reached them, but he shoved Sonya aside, and she lost her footing and fell on the concrete.

''My baby!'' she screamed, grabbing at her abdomen.

By the time she struggled to her feet, the man had dragged the woman across the lot and shoved her into a car. Tires squealed as he rushed down the street, and Sonya strained her eyes to see the license number.

Sonya leaned against the car, panting. Edith held on to the vehicle and maneuvered to her side. ''Sonya, are you hurt? Do you feel all right?''

''My heart is racing so fast I can hardly breathe, but I'm not hurt.''

''Such a fall could have caused a miscarriage.''

''That's what scared me, but I don't have any pain of any kind.''

''Let's hurry home, then.''

They drove for several blocks in silence. ''Poor woman,'' Edith whispered. ''We should have helped her.''

"I know. I'll never forget the look on her face. I didn't know what to do."

"You didn't have time to do anything. We're advised to stay out of domestic quarrels—even the police seldom interfere—but I feel sorry for abused women. My granddaughter was one."

"I'm still shaking. I wanted to help her, but right now all I want is to feel the safety of our own four walls."

Sonya helped a trembling Edith into the house and settled her on the couch.

"I know you think we shouldn't be involved," Sonya said, "but don't you think we should at least report the incident? I did get the license number."

Edith sighed wearily. "By all means, do what you think is best. I'd like to help that poor woman in some way, if we could."

Sonya dialed 911, and when the dispatcher answered, she said. "I want to report an incident that happened at the Farmer's Mart parking lot on West Dodge street. A woman was running away from a man who forced her into a blue Plymouth Voyager. I believe the license plate was 1-679A, and the left front fender of the van was of a different color, maybe a light brown."

"Lady," the dispatcher said, "if we investigated every fight between husbands and wives tonight, we wouldn't have time to deal with real emergencies. You've done your duty, so just forget it."

Sonya angrily replaced the phone receiver. "So that's all the thanks we get for trying to help someone."

"Go on to bed, Sonya," Edith said, "and sleep late in the morning. We won't concern ourselves with a big dinner."

"I'm going to put the turkey in the oven before I go

to bed, and I can prepare the rest of the food when I get up. We won't have to eat until mid-afternoon.''

Sonya did stay in bed later than usual, not because she was asleep, but because she didn't want to disturb Edith. The incident of the night before continued to haunt her. She couldn't forget the terror displayed by that woman. She knew Bryon's treatment of her was a form of abuse, but at least he hadn't done her any physical harm. This Christmas Day would necessarily have been bleak, without the added trauma of seeing a woman mistreated.

Stelle had prepared a cranberry salad and rolls the day before, so all Sonya had to do was cook green beans and mash the potatoes. She set the table with Edith's bone china service and sterling silver, lit the candles and was pleased with the festive table when she summoned Edith for dinner. The woman trembled with fatigue, but they both ate a hearty meal.

Sonya filled the dishwasher and joined Edith, who was looking toward the small Christmas tree in the corner that Stelle and Sonya had decorated. ''Do you realize we haven't opened our gifts? Are you too tired to look at them now?''

Edith watched with interest as Sonya unwrapped the gifts from Ohio. Several boxes contained baby clothes as she'd requested, and a large one held a lovely maternity dress. The elegant two-piece red linen dress featured a jewel neckline and quarter-length sleeves with navy trim. Navy also marked the deep patch pockets, and the sharp knife-pleated skirt was accented by a navy band at the hem. Sonya could hardly wait to model the dress, but that would have to wait until tomorrow.

Leta's package contained two ballet-length nursing nightgowns delicately edged in lace trim. Scooped necklines and ruffled cap sleeves modified the versatility of the garments, which concealed nursing vents under center pleats. Just what she needed for her hospital stay.

Most of Edith's gifts had been received a few days before—a poinsettia from her nephew in California, and several fruit baskets sent by her elderly friends in the city. But she opened with pleasure the colorful scarf Sonya had chosen for her and a pair of house slippers, a gift from Stelle. While Sonya was disposing of the wrapping paper and ribbons, the doorbell rang, and she looked questioningly at Edith.

"Were you expecting guests?"

"No," Edith replied. She looked puzzled. Then a mischievous sparkle lit her eyes. "Unless..." Her voice trailed off and she smiled at Sonya. "Better answer it, dear. I think it's a caller for you."

Sonya reached the front door when the bell sounded again.

"Who is it?" she called loudly, through the thick wooden door.

"Ho! Ho! Ho!"

"Who is it?" she repeated.

"Santa Claus. Didn't you hear the sound of his sleigh and reindeer?"

Laughing, Sonya opened the door to a gift-laden Daniel. His broad shoulders filled the doorway and his smile warmed her. She held the gifts while he took off his coat and hung it in the hall closet.

"Sorry not to be here sooner, but it took a long time to open our gifts and eat a big dinner."

"Thanks for coming," Sonya said sincerely. "Edith will be glad to see you."

Daniel took the gifts from her. "And aren't you glad to see me?"

"Of course. It's cold in this hallway; let's find the comfort of Edith's room."

Edith opened her gift first—a high-intensity reading lamp. Then Daniel handed Sonya three gifts.

"Why three gifts?"

"Read the cards."

The small box bore her name, but two of the parcels were labeled "For Baby-to-Be."

"After hearing what I'd bought for your baby, my sister, who's the mother of three, said she wouldn't want me shopping for her children, but I believe in buying practical gifts."

Sonya's hands trembled as she opened her gift—a bottle of expensive perfume. It was her favorite and she wondered how Daniel knew. Then she recalled he'd complimented her once on the scent and she'd told him the name. But that was so long ago. His thoughtfulness and efforts to please her were touching, despite her resolve to remain just friends. Then she took the ribbon from the baby's gift and finding a football, dropped her head to the box and sobbed.

Daniel was on his knees beside her immediately. "Why, Sonya, what's wrong? I didn't intend to make you unhappy!"

She reached a hand to him, and he held it securely while she continued to sob. At last she lifted her head and wiped a tearful face.

"You didn't make me unhappy. You see, I've been concerned because no one really wants this baby. His father has disowned him, his paternal grandparents have practically ignored his coming, and my own parents would have preferred that I not have a child under these circumstances. And dare I admit that most of the time I haven't wanted the baby, either? I've done all I can to ensure its health and a safe delivery, but I've looked on the birth as an ordeal that I want to put behind me.''

Daniel still held her hand. ''I imagine those are normal reactions under the circumstances.''

''But when you bought this football, you were thinking of my baby as a person. He was real to you. I thank you for the perfume, Daniel, but the greatest gift you've given me is the realization that this child is going to be an important part of my life.''

''We're all looking forward to his birth. Mother is planning to grandmother him. She doesn't want Edith to have all of the fun.''

''Well, enough of the tears,'' Edith said, ''I want to know what's in the other package.''

Smiling now, Sonya tore away the wrappings.

''A computer!'' she shouted.

Shamefacedly, Daniel said, ''I didn't think it was too soon to start the hi-tech stuff, but my sister disagreed with me, saying I didn't know anything about shopping for newborns.''

The box indicated that the toy computer was designed for ages one year and up. Daniel took it from the box, inserted the necessary batteries that he took from his pocket and demonstrated the utility of his gift.

''The man at the store showed me how to do this. There are several program disks available in the packet. This one, for instance, is designed to teach the child the alphabet. He can hit the *A* key, and a large capital *A* and cursive *A* appear on the screen. At the same time, a voice says, '*A.*' These programs will help a child learn the colors, plants, animals and all kinds of useful information.''

Daniel spent the next half hour demonstrating the versatility of the computer, still convinced of the usefulness of his gift. His running commentary kept Sonya laughing and smiling as usual.

"I don't know whether my baby will learn from it," Sonya said, "but it's certainly entertaining for adults."

When Edith went to sleep, Daniel hurriedly took his departure. Sonya went down the hallway with him.

"She seems very weary tonight," Daniel said.

"And with some reason, too." Sonya told him about the incident they'd observed the night before.

Daniel shook his head. "There are always numerous incidents of spouse and child abuse during the holidays. Unfortunately the authorities can't investigate them all. Let's hope no harm came to the woman you saw."

Sonya agreed. Then she added, "Thanks again, Daniel. Between you and Edith, you've made this a Christmas to be remembered fondly, not a dreaded one as I had expected."

She reached out her hand, and Daniel took it, but then he leaned forward, tenderly brushed her hair aside with his hand and softly kissed her cheek. It was a gentle caress, but one that kindled a flicker of emotion in the region of Sonya's heart that she had never expected to feel again.

"Merry Christmas, Sonya, and I pray that your New Year will be a happy one."

As Sonya went back down the hall, she pressed a hand to her trembling lips, realizing that this had been the most satisfying Christmas she had experienced since her marriage.

The next morning when Edith was too weak to leave her bed, Sonya insisted on telephoning the doctor.

"I don't suppose he'll make a house call, so perhaps I should take you to the hospital."

"When I die, I'm going to die in my own bed. But

he'll make a call here—his father was our doctor for years, and his son took over the practice two years ago."

Sonya didn't stay in the room when the doctor examined Edith, waiting instead in the hallway until he prepared to leave.

"Her heart doesn't seem to be any worse, but she should stay in bed. I've told her to have bed rest for a week, but if you can keep her in bed for three days, I'll be satisfied."

But Edith didn't even leave her bed in three days, for the evening's paper brought another shock. Sonya spent most of the day in the laundry room washing the linens they had used for the Christmas meal, as well as her own garments. When she went to check on Edith after Stelle left for the night, Edith sat with the paper across her legs, shielding her face with her hands.

"Look!" she said, handing the newspaper to Sonya.

"'Husband held for wife's murder,'" Sonya read the headline aloud. "Do you think it's the woman we saw?"

"There isn't any doubt. The murder occurred in the area where the grocery store is located, and that picture looks like the man. We could have saved that woman's life. I'll never forgive myself."

"You shouldn't reproach yourself, Edith. We didn't have time to do anything. He pushed me aside and grabbed the woman before I hardly knew what was going on. By the time I picked myself up from the ground, they were gone. Besides, it says here that an anonymous phone call led the police to her assailant. That had to be the call we made."

"The call *you* made," she said. "I didn't do anything but rush away from the scene, although I thought it best at the time. Well, I can't help her now, but if another opportunity like that comes along, I'm going to be ready.''

Because Edith hadn't regained her strength, Sonya considered canceling the New Year's dinner date at the Dixons. She didn't want to hurt their feelings, but she considered she had a responsibility to Edith. However, when she told Edith that she wouldn't go, the older woman said, "You'll do nothing of the kind. I can get up if I want to, but I feel better lying in bed. Besides, you'll be going back to school the day after New Year's, and I'll be by myself then until Stelle arrives."

Still, Sonya was uneasy about leaving Edith alone, so she arranged for Stelle to take off the New Year's Eve day and then come to be with Edith on New Year's Day. "That'll suit me fine," the woman agreed. "My old man likes to party on New Year's Eve, and we start out early." She laughed. "I may be pretty sleepy come the first of the year, but I'll be here, in case Mrs. Edith wants anything."

Sonya put on the new dress her mother had sent, thankful she had a really nice garment to wear to the Dixons' dinner. Her pride would have rebelled at wearing the hand-me-down clothes. She had gained about fifteen pounds, but the chic dress camouflaged her pregnancy. Her face and neck were too thin, but she added plenty of mousse when she shampooed her hair to give it body, and after she fluffed it around her face, she looked almost as pretty as she had a year ago. She put on eye shadow and lightened the dark circles under her eyes, then surveyed her image with satisfaction. As a final touch, she sprayed some of Daniel's perfume on her wrists and inhaled the pleasant fragrance.

As she approached the Dixon home, she drove more

and more slowly. Mrs. Dixon had said twelve o'clock, and she didn't want to be late, but the thought of entering the house without Bryon frightened her. She had never visited his parents alone. It was no wonder she was having trouble adjusting to Bryon's absence. Except for the times he was at work, they had seldom been separated. Bryon hadn't gone anywhere that he couldn't take her.

She pulled her old car into the driveway, and her hands trembled as she unfastened the seat belt. Like a specter, Bryon stood between her and the house. Had his parents told him they'd invited her? Mr. Dixon came down the walk to meet her, and he took her arm.

"Happy New Year, Sonya," he said.

Mother Dixon greeted her at the door with a kiss on the cheek. "We're so glad you could come, dear. This would have been a lonely day for us without you. Here, Tom, hang up her coat. Come into the living room. We won't be eating for about an hour."

Just like old times, Sonya thought ironically, but if the Dixons were willing to befriend her in spite of Bryon's action, what did she have to lose? So she pushed thoughts of Bryon into the background and made up her mind she would be pleasant. She might enjoy the day if she tried.

Tom Dixon brought Sonya a cola, and she sipped on it slowly. She asked about other members of their family, who usually shared their Christmas dinner. Almost as if she were hoping for a middle ground of discussion, Mrs. Dixon launched into a commentary on the aunts, uncles and cousins, until it was time for dinner.

Sonya helped Mrs. Dixon clear away the dinner things and fill the dishwasher as she always had, and in spite of Bryon's defection, she felt a warm glow to be with "family."

Before they settled into the living room chairs again,

Sonya pulled back the sheers on the picture window to check the weather. "Do you mind if we keep these open?" she asked. "If it starts snowing, I'll need to leave."

"You're welcome to stay here," Tom said, "if there's a storm."

"Thank you, but I need to go back to Edith. She's been ill this week, and the maid leaves at four o'clock."

"Do you like it there?" Mrs. Dixon asked.

"Very much. Edith York is a lovely person."

"You're looking well, Sonya," Mrs. Dixon said. "Have you had a sonogram to find out the sex of your child?"

Why should she resent the Dixons asking questions about the baby? she thought. Just because Bryon didn't want the child was no reason his parents wouldn't be interested.

"It's a boy."

"Are you pleased about that?"

Sonya shrugged her shoulders. "Doesn't matter much either way. Frankly, I've had trouble becoming interested in the child because of the difficulty Bryon and I've had."

"What do you intend to do with the baby?"

Sonya stared at her mother-in-law. "Keep it, of course. Bryon wanted me to abort the fetus or give it up for adoption, but I wouldn't consider such a thing. Tell me, Mother Dixon, why doesn't Bryon like children?"

"I don't know. As a matter of fact, I had no idea he didn't like children." Sonya saw her glance nervously at her husband. "We assumed that the two of you would have a family."

"There must be some reason. I feel very bitter toward him for the way he's treated me. It might make it easier if I knew the reason for his behavior."

Mrs. Dixon's face flushed, and Sonya knew she stifled an angry retort. *Of course, Bryon wasn't at fault!*

"You might as well tell her, Anna," Tom said.

"We've questioned Bryon's attitude as much as you have, and we've come to one conclusion. I suppose you know that Bryon isn't our only child?"

"Why I didn't know that!"

"We had another son born when Bryon was five years old. He was a Down's syndrome baby."

Sonya gasped and cradled her unborn child. He gave a vicious little kick as if to assure her he was alive and well.

"He lived only six years," Mrs. Dixon continued. "We were kept so busy with him that we probably neglected Bryon, although at the time we didn't realize it. Perhaps he resented those six years and grew to hate children in general," Mrs. Dixon explained.

"And don't forget your period of depression after our boy died, Anna. For two years," he explained to Sonya, "we had to send Bryon to his grandparents. She couldn't cope with an eleven-year-old in her condition."

"He did tell me that he had to live with his grandparents for a long time, but he seldom mentioned his childhood. Perhaps he felt rejected."

"It's possible that Bryon didn't want children because he feared you might have a handicapped child," Mr. Dixon continued. "What we went through with our son wouldn't be something anyone would choose voluntarily. You shouldn't have gotten pregnant, Sonya."

Sonya felt her face flushing, and she sputtered, "Don't blame me. I hadn't changed birth control methods since we were married. If he'd just leveled with me, discussed his hang-ups, there were many ways we could have prevented a pregnancy. I loved him so much, I would have chosen him over a child anyday."

"Tom wasn't being critical of you, Sonya, but since we couldn't find out much from Bryon, we thought you might enlighten us. We were very disappointed to learn you were having trouble. Is it all over between you?"

"Not as far as I'm concerned, but Bryon has asked for a divorce. My lawyer has advised me to do nothing until after the child is born. Now that I've learned about your handicapped child, perhaps that was a wise move, although I had an amniocentesis test that indicated that my baby is all right."

"How much longer do you intend to work?"

"Until they haul me off to the hospital, I suppose. I can't afford to lose my job."

"You shouldn't be working now," Anna insisted. "If you can't get along on what Bryon's providing, we'll be glad to help you."

So they didn't know that Bryon had cast her aside penniless. She wanted to shout the news at them, but they'd always idolized their son, and she wasn't mean enough to tell them about his conduct. She knew how she had felt when Bryon toppled from the pedestal where she'd placed him. The Dixons had always been good to her, so why should she repay their kindness by demeaning their son?

Sonya started talking about her work at school to avoid any further discussion of her husband, and the rest of the afternoon passed pleasantly enough. By four o'clock snow flurries danced around the windows, and Sonya took leave of her in-laws.

"We must get together again," Mr. Dixon said as he helped her down the steps and to the car. "Be careful and don't fall. This walk could be slick."

As she drove homeward, Sonya experienced a warm glow of thankfulness that she had spent some time with Bryon's family, who'd been a part of her life for two years. But her forehead creased with worry. What if she had a handicapped child? Was that the reason for Bryon's actions? And although the Dixons hadn't admitted it, Sonya could read between the lines. Bryon had apparently been neglected during the sickness of his brother and the time of grief following the child's death. Was that the reason he wanted to control her completely? Had he been determined that Sonya would be only his, afraid that a child would wean her affection away from him? But even that couldn't excuse his actions toward her, she reasoned.

With all of these things to worry her, Sonya didn't anticipate the advent of a new year.

Chapter Ten

Within a week Edith had recovered and seemed to be as well as usual, though she tired more easily. To escape the memory of her frustrating visit with the Dixons, Sonya enjoyed returning to the regimented school schedule, but the extra weight of the child slowed her down considerably.

The Christmas season had drained her emotionally, and she was pleased to have it behind her, but now, she had only two months until her child was born. The nearer the time came, Sonya, with dismay, realized that she dreaded having the baby—not the physical birth, but simply the thoughts of having a child around all the time. This distressed her because she didn't want the child to feel unwanted, and she'd read that the emotions of a mother before the baby was born could determine the personality of that unborn babe. Since Daniel's gift at Christmas, she was considering the birth of her son with some anticipation, but at times she blamed him for causing her to lose Bryon. She definitely had to get over that feeling, and she decided to have some counseling with Adam Benson, which would help her put motherhood in its proper perspective.

To offset her lack of enthusiasm for the child, she made an effort to be sure he was healthy. She walked around the York lawn several times each day and watched her diet religiously. Stelle, who had become a close friend, was as protective of Sonya as she was of Edith and prepared food suitable for a pregnant woman.

Daniel, too, continued to bolster her spirits as he had during the Christmas holidays. He often called at the house, and while Sonya saw him only in Edith's presence, he had a knack of knowing what to do to encourage her. He occasionally brought her chocolates, but more often, while Edith dozed, he encouraged her to talk about the activities at the nursery school. His ready laughter when she reported an amusing incident, or his compassion when she spoke of a needy child, not only filled the lonely hours of waiting for her baby, but gave her additional insight to the worth of this man. She actually enjoyed her work more, storing up incidents to share with Daniel.

One night when she met him at the door, she was chuckling. "Wait until I tell you what happened today."

He shook the snow from his hat and coat before he entered the house, and as they walked down the hallway to Edith's room, she continued, "We took the children on a tour of a church—a different denomination from ours. The children are well acquainted with our large baptistry and have seen people immersed in it. On the tour, the church's pastor pointed to their baptismal font.

'This is where people are baptized,' he said, and one boy went forward, peered into it, and scoffingly said, 'Baptized in that *little* old thing!'"

Both of them were laughing when they joined Edith.

"Wait until your son gets here," Daniel said. "He'll be saying the same kind of cute things."

Daniel referred to her pregnancy often, and one evening, he said, "Sonya, I want you to telephone me when you need to go to the hospital for the baby's birth. It doesn't matter what time of day or night, I'll be ready."

"That's good of you, but Leta has already volunteered. She also plans to assist me in the delivery room." Daniel appeared disappointed, but Sonya felt uncomfortable imagining a man other than her husband helping at such a time—even Daniel.

When Sonya considered that the child would be born in eight or nine weeks, she knew she had to make plans for it. She needed clothing and a bed or bassinet. And where could she stay when she came from the hospital? She wouldn't be very active for a week or so, and she couldn't ask Edith to share that burden. What could she do?

Eloise lightened her load somewhat by suggesting one day, "If you don't have all the baby things you want, a friend of mine is having a garage sale tomorrow. She has some beautiful items. Her house is located along your way into work. Why don't you stop there in the morning?"

Sonya took her advice and bought a bassinet and a boxful of clothing for only twenty-five dollars. That evening after supper she spread out her purchases for Edith to see.

"I've wanted to ask you what you needed for the child, but until Christmas, you seemed so reluctant to talk about your pregnancy that I hesitated. However, I have several things you're welcome to use."

Leaning on her cane, Edith went to the chest at the foot of her bed, and she motioned for Sonya to follow her. When she unlocked the chest, Sonya saw layers of baby clothes, some still wrapped in their plastic coverings.

"I bought these for my granddaughter before her untimely death. I haven't felt right about giving them away, but I would be happy to see your child wear them. I've become quite fond of you."

Sonya lifted a small sweater and booties and held them to her face while she tried to stifle her tears.

"I'll be proud to use these, but when the child comes, shouldn't I go someplace else? It's an imposition on you to bring a baby here."

"Why, I thought that was the plan," Edith said, dismayed. "I'm looking forward to having a baby in the house. It will remind me of the time when my own son was toddling around this room."

"Then you'll *have* a baby in the house, but if the situation becomes a burden to you, please let me know."

"A burden? Nonsense, my dear," Edith said, "I'm looking forward to the baby so much that I've come up with a plan that might keep both of you here all of the time."

Edith shuffled back to her chair, and Sonya sat on a footstool at her feet.

"I want to stay here. You know how grateful I am to you for taking me in, but I'll have to work to support myself and the baby, and I must make some provisions to have the child cared for while I work. I'm not sure my salary will take care of a baby-sitter and the extra supplies I'll need for it. If not, I'll have to find another job. I'm so worried about all of this, and that's one of the reasons I dread having the baby."

"Don't you expect your husband to pay child support?"

"I'm sure he won't if he can get out of it, and I don't intend to force him into it."

"Would you rather stay with your child than have a baby-sitter?"

"Yes, of course. That's the way I was taught."

"Then you may be interested in my plan. I've not been able to put that young woman we failed to help on Christmas Eve out of my mind, and I've prayed for some way to make restitution."

She took a newspaper clipping from the table drawer. "Did you see this?"

The article, headed, "Help for abused women and children," reported on incidents of child and wife abuse in the city of Omaha. Sonya was stunned at the astronomical number of cases, and until this point, she hadn't really considered herself an abused wife, but the article stressed that verbal and emotional abuse brought on by desertion was just as devastating as physical abuse. The article concluded with an appeal for homes to shelter abused wives, stating that grants were available for those with suitable facilities. A telephone number was given if one desired additional information.

"After I thought about it for a few days, I telephoned that number. Seems this is a crisis-intervention agency supported by several church denominations. They check out the situations to be sure that the applicants really need help, then they send them to abuse centers. The grants also provide a small salary for a director. I've been wondering why we couldn't turn this house into an abuse center where you could be the paid director. You would have a job and can stay here and look after your baby at the same time."

"That sounds like a solution to *my* problem, but it wouldn't work for you. You're used to privacy, and I don't believe you would like having your home turned into a public shelter."

"I've considered that, but I've been pretty much confined to two rooms for a long time. As you know, I seldom go upstairs. We could put a partition in the middle of the hall, lock the door, and as thick as these walls are, I would probably not know anyone was in the house. Besides, I may not live long, anyway, and I'll die happier if I know this big house is being put to some use."

"On Sunday Adam Benson said in his sermon that when God closes one door, He often opens another one, and he urged us to be aware of the open door of opportunity. It's strange, but if I hadn't gotten married, I intended to prepare for social work, but since I didn't get a degree, I doubt that I have the expertise to serve as the director. What would I have to do?"

"We must check out those details. I didn't want to proceed further until I had your opinion. I'm sure that the salary is meager, but probably as much as you receive at the school. If you're interested, I'll telephone Daniel Massie and ask him to have dinner with us tomorrow night. We'll see what he thinks."

"I think you two women have all the trouble you need" was Daniel's instant opinion. "You would have all kinds of women and children coming here."

"The agency screens the women," Edith said.

"I'm an abused wife, and you sent me to Edith," Sonya added.

"That's another matter entirely." Daniel's gaze met hers, his eyes glittering with unspoken emotion. "I will look into it for you. Our church contributes to the agency, so I know it's a reputable group."

Daniel had his findings within a week, and he came one evening to discuss them.

"You would have to request enough money to do some

remodeling on the house. Fire escapes must be added, another bathroom and probably one of the front rooms turned into a dining area, if you intend to keep the one across the hall for your own personal use.''

''What does being a director involve?'' Sonya asked.

''A crash training course to be qualified, but that shouldn't be difficult for you, since you told me that you were interested in social work. Then, too, you would need more help than Stelle. She's busy enough now with Edith, so plan another person to help with the cleaning and night monitoring. Don't say you can handle it all, because with a baby you wouldn't have the time. I'll consider those things in the grant application.''

''For how long will we be committing ourselves?'' Edith asked.

''Two years, when you would be evaluated before you could ask for more funding.''

''Would the grant proposal include food, medical attention and other special needs?'' Sonya questioned.

''Yes. There are several drugstores and hospitals in the area that cooperate with the agency. If this facility is approved, you would be covered with insurance—most of the funds come from the city and state governments.''

''I'm rather excited about it,'' Sonya admitted. ''It sounds as if it might solve my problem.''

''I don't think you should do this, partly because of Edith's health, and the fact that this project will take you away from your child quite a lot, but you may be assured that I'll be supportive in all that you do. Call upon me for any help you need.''

When Sonya walked to the door with Daniel, he said, ''Have you heard anything more from your husband?''

''No, except he returned a Christmas card I sent him,

and his parents invited me to eat New Year's dinner with them.''

"I had a rather nasty letter from him stating that we needn't think we could rob him, and insisting that I initiate divorce proceedings. I replied amicably that I would contact him sometime in March with our proposal.''

"I'm eager now to remove him from my life, and perhaps I can start over again. Right now everything is in limbo until the baby is born.''

"Yes, that's true,'' Daniel agreed. Sonya sensed that he was thinking about their relationship as well. Did Daniel hope to be more than a friend to her someday? The thought of any man's romantic interest had seemed repellent to her not so long ago, but Daniel had become such an important part of her life. Sometimes she believed God had sent Daniel into her life for a purpose, not only to watch over her and help her survive Bryon's abandonment, but to show her that, unlike Bryon, some men could be relied upon and trusted.

"How much longer are you going to work?'' he asked.

"I've requested a leave of absence for six weeks starting in mid-February.''

"And perhaps by that time, if the grant application is funded, you may not have to go back to the school at all.''

"I hope so. I like the work, but I think my own child should be my first priority. Growing up without a father will be a big enough detriment, and if his mother is gone most of the time, the child will feel neglected right from the first.''

"You will make a good mother, Sonya.'' He took her hand in his.

She flushed with pleasure. "I'm beginning to feel more like a mother now, so I hope you're right.''

"And don't forget I'm taking first dibs on being a substitute uncle. I'm great with kids. And I know I'll love yours." His smile warmed Sonya's heart. Yes, Daniel was a good man and a blessing in her life.

The day Sonya left school for her leave of absence, the staff surprised her with a baby shower. The love and good will the women displayed meant as much as the needed items. With their generous gifts and what she'd collected, and with Edith's contributions, her child was going to be well clothed. Thinking back to the time of Bryon's desertion, when the future had looked hopeless, Sonya realized that time and God had a way of changing everything. Considering how Edith, Eloise and others had cared for her, she looked forward to managing the abuse center so she could pass along to others the good will she'd received. She thought often of Jesus's parable of the sheep and the goats. "Inasmuch as ye have done it unto one of the least of these my brethren, ye have done it unto me." Was this a way she could show her gratitude for how God had supplied her needs?

Leta agreed to be Sonya's support person during the delivery, and she attended the prenatal classes with her. During these sessions, Sonya lost what little fear she had experienced and learned many exercises to strengthen her muscles and help with the delivery. As the burden of the baby increased, and she could hardly find any comfortable position to sit or lie, she longed to have the birth behind her. She had a suitcase packed with the necessities for her and the baby, since Dr. Hammer had indicated during his last examination that she might deliver sooner than he had expected.

Daniel had also volunteered to take her to the hospital when labor began, and she told him, "If I can't locate

Leta when the time comes, I may have to call on you. Besides, my mother is coming, so I won't be alone.''

"You know you can always count on me, Sonya," he assured her. "Now more than ever."

Edith had insisted that Sonya's mother should stay with them, and Sonya had readied a room on the second floor. Dr. Hammer had set the date for March 2, and Sonya's mother was scheduled to fly in the day before.

Just a few days before her due date, Daniel reported that the grant application had been approved with funds to be available for renovation within a month.

"So that means you will be able to stay here and care for your child," Edith said, "which makes me very happy. I will look forward to hearing the sounds of a child in this house."

"If the abused women bring their offspring, you may have more sounds of children than you want," Sonya said. "But I'm happy, too, Edith, and I appreciate the help you've given me. Having this good home has meant the difference between hope and despair. I'm beginning to heal. There are days now when I never think of Bryon, and I often sleep through the whole night without any bad dreams.''

"But you've helped me, too. Without you in the house, I would probably have given up and gone to a nursing home."

"Better get ready for a quick trip out of here, Sonya," Stelle said one morning near the end of February. Because of Sonya's cumbersome body, Stelle had delivered Sonya's breakfast each morning.

"What makes you think that?"

"There's a full moon tomorrow night, so you're apt to deliver anytime, and you may have to leave without much warning if we have a bad storm. We've gone all winter without a blizzard, and we're due one. My bunion says snow, the newscaster says snow, and when we both agree it's a sure thing.''

Sonya laughed. ''I don't have any insight about the weather, but I'm sure that I won't hold on until March 2. I had lots of pain all night long. Should I telephone the doctor?''

''Might be a good idea,'' Stelle agreed as she glanced over Sonya's body. ''Looks to me like you're gonna drop that child any minute.''

By noon Sonya's pains came regularly, fifteen minutes apart. She paced the floor of the apartment all morning, eyeing the lowering clouds, which promised that the predicted blizzard was a distinct possibility. When she contacted Dr. Hammer, he concluded that he should see her. So Sonya called Leta, but there was no answer. She thought of calling Daniel, as he'd offered, but then felt self-conscious about bothering him during a workday. She was preparing to drive to the hospital herself when Daniel stopped by with some papers for Edith to sign.

''Why didn't you call me, Sonya? How could you even consider driving yourself to the hospital,'' he said sternly, taking the suitcase from her hand. ''The roads are slick, and the wind gusts are strong enough to sway a car. Stelle,'' he called as he started down the steps, holding Sonya's arm, ''give those papers to Edith and tell her I'll pick them up tomorrow.''

When the pains became more severe, Sonya was thankful that Daniel had offered to chauffeur her. He's doing what Bryon should be doing, she thought. It was a miserable trip; Sonya shook convulsively when the labor pains struck periodically, and she gasped for breath.

''Does it hurt very much?'' he asked quietly. Sonya

just nodded. "Don't worry. We're more than halfway there. I'm sorry I don't know what to do for you," Daniel added, a mixture of concern and affection in his expression. "I've never driven an expectant mother to the hospital before."

Sonya gritted her teeth and stifled a scream. Daniel laid his hand on her shoulder. "Don't fight your pain. Scream if you want to. It won't scare me." He patted her back. "I'll have you there as soon as possible." Daniel insisted on waiting out in the reception area while she saw the obstetrician. After the doctor had examined her he said, "You're definitely in the early stages of labor. Although with a first baby it may take a long time, I can't risk sending you back to that house with this blizzard blowing, and no one but an old lady to look after you. I'm going to admit you."

"I'll tell Mr. Massie not to wait for me, and then I'll need to make some telephone calls."

On trembling legs, Sonya waddled back to the waiting room. Daniel helped her into a seat beside him. His face showed his concern.

"He's going to admit me." Her lips quivered. "I've managed to be nonchalant about the delivery up until this point, but now I find that I'm afraid, terribly afraid."

Daniel tenderly folded her hand in both of his. "We're always afraid of the unknown. But you'll get through this, Sonya. I know you will. And afterward you'll have a beautiful baby. I telephoned Mother to tell her where I was, and she sent you a Scripture verse for comfort. After all the years, she says she remembers that childbirth was a frightening experience. When the discomfort seemed almost unbearable, she quoted over and over, 'Weeping may endure for a night, but joy cometh in the morning.'

Those words helped her over the rough places. She wanted you to remember them.''

''I learned those words the night Adam Benson visited me when I needed him so desperately. I would have committed suicide if he hadn't telephoned me that night. So that's another thing I have to thank you for.''

She started to rise, then groaned and grabbed her stomach. Daniel instantly came to his feet and reached out to support her. With his strong arms wrapped around her, Sonya pressed her cheek to his chest. She felt a featherlight touch of his hand on her hair. ''Dear Sonya,'' he whispered. ''Don't be afraid.'' She felt his embrace tighten ever so slightly for a moment, then he stepped back and lifted her chin with his fingertips. Gazing down into her eyes he said, ''Sonya, at this moment you feel very alone, but let me assure you that God will be with you through this experience. I'll be praying all night for your physical needs, as well as your spiritual assurance, and when this is over, you'll realize that never for a moment were you separated from His everlasting arms.''

She nodded and walked away from him, but before she turned the corner into Dr. Hammer's office, she looked back. She waved her hand to Daniel, who stood where she had left him. She yearned to know the meaning behind the pensive expression on his face.

Sonya made her first call to Stelle, and the woman said, ''Don't you worry about things here. I'll stay with Mrs. Edith. We'll be praying for you and your little one.''

When Sonya telephoned her parents, her mother said, ''I'll get a plane tonight. I can be there in the morning.''

''There's a blizzard here. You may have trouble landing.''

"The airport in Columbus should know whether or not I can land. Don't worry. I'll be there."

She made a call to the Bensons, who promised to be in constant prayer for her, and to Leta. To Leta she said, "Dr. Hammer says it won't be for several hours, so if you're here early in the morning, it will be soon enough."

But around midnight Sonya was brought awake by sharp pains, and she rang for a nurse. The intense pain, which built to a peak and then receded long enough for Sonya to catch her breath, kept her from counting her contractions, but the nurse monitored her every fifteen minutes. After a couple of hours, she said, "Mrs. Dixon, your contractions are about four minutes apart, and you're going to deliver soon. I'll put in an alert to Dr. Hammer, and then we'll take you to the delivery room and prepare you."

Sonya gripped the side of the bed until another wave of pain receded and said hoarsely, "Should I ring my friend Leta? She's supposed to be my support person."

The nurse pulled back a curtain and peered into the night. Snow swirled against the windows, and Sonya couldn't see the streetlights. Shrieking wind along the side of the building signaled that a full-fledged blizzard was pelting the city. She couldn't ask Leta to come—she would take it alone.

Because of the trying situation with Bryon, and the fact that at times she'd dreaded having a child, Sonya hadn't dwelt much on the pain of childbirth. She had often heard women talk about their difficulty during the long hours of labor. Throughout the months when she had carried the child, it seldom seemed real to her, almost as if someone else was bearing it, but now she was scared, and tears slipped from her eyes. Over and over, she kept repeating the words she had first heard from We Care: "Weeping

may endure for a night, but joy cometh in the morning.''
She sensed the prayers of Daniel and the Bensons, and
their loving concern and petitions blanketed Sonya with
the assurance of God's love.

When they took her to the delivery room and prepared
her for the birth, she was aware of what was going on,
but it was almost as if she witnessed what was happening
to someone else. But the pain was real enough, and though
the nurses made her as comfortable as possible and
coached her with breathing and relaxation techniques during contractions, loneliness overwhelmed her.

"Oh, Bryon, come and help me," she screamed once,
and then clamped her jaws tightly to prevent another out-
burst. Bryon wouldn't come, her mother and Leta
couldn't, only God could help her tonight, and she
reached out a hand to Him.

During the struggle to force the child into the world,
two strong emotions manifested themselves and fought for
control of her heart. As the pain intensified the child became real to her. He was hers, and she loved him, and
strange as it might seem, as her love for the child surfaced,
the indifference she'd felt for the baby was transferred to
Bryon. The hold Bryon had held on her emotions disappeared, and she no longer cared about him. It was such a
strange feeling—for two years Bryon had been the center
of her universe, and tears stung her eyelids when she realized that now she felt nothing for him. She hoped she
would simply remain indifferent to him, for she didn't
want to hate him, although he had given her ample reason
to do so.

"Oh, thank you," she breathed when the nurse finally
gave her a shot to ease her labor pains and drowsiness
calmed her, but she endured until she experienced an ex-

cruciating pain and heard Dr. Hammer say, "That's it—we've got a fine boy."

She awakened in the recovery room when Doctor Hammer came in with a nurse carrying a blue-wrapped bundle.

"You have an eight-pound boy, Mrs. Dixon, and he's healthy and alert. How do you feel?"

"Tired."

"You've a right to be," he said with a laugh, "and you probably won't believe this, but you had a much easier time than most women do. Physically, you're well built for bearing children."

"Rather wasted on me, isn't it, when I'm married to a man who doesn't want a family?" Sonya said bitterly. "And, Doctor, I will have to give my husband an answer now about the divorce, so I hope you'll examine the baby carefully to be sure he's physically fit."

"That's part of our routine here. We're required by law to test newborns for certain rare, inherited diseases. You can be assured that your baby will be screened before he leaves the hospital."

Sonya cuddled the baby and scrutinized his features. His little face was red, his eyes squeezed shut, and a bit of brown fuzz covered his small head. She'd seen baby calves on the farm with more beauty than that, but she smiled at the mite she held and whispered, "Doesn't matter if you're not a great beauty now, you'll change soon." She wasn't worried about the child's appearance, since both she and Bryon had more than their share of good looks. Up until this moment she hadn't decided on a name for her boy. If conditions had been normal, she would have named him after Bryon, but knowing he wouldn't want that, Sonya said, "Would you like to be called Paul?"

The baby didn't make any response, but at least he

hadn't cried over the prospect, so Sonya kissed him and said, "Paul. I like the name, and I love you."

At daylight, her mother telephoned. "Sonya, we've finally arrived at the airport, but it will be a while before land transportation can bring me into town. How are you doing?"

"Fine, Mother, and you have an eight-pound grandson."

"You mean I'm too late," she said, and Sonya sensed the disappointment in her voice.

"The baby was born three hours ago. I was in labor about twelve hours. All is well."

"I'll still come to the hospital as soon as I can make it."

When the phone rang again, Daniel was on the line. "I checked at the front desk and learned that you had already delivered. How are you, Sonya?"

"Tired, but I understand that's a normal reaction. And, Daniel, I want you to know that my faith in God's providence remained strong."

"You're a courageous person, Sonya. I never once thought that you wouldn't come through it all with flying colors. And how's your son?"

"The most perfect baby ever born."

He laughed. "They always are."

They spoke about the baby for a few more minutes and Daniel told her he'd be coming in a few hours to see this perfect baby for himself.

Right after she hung up the phone, a nurse came in with a large bouquet of roses. "How beautiful!" Sonya exclaimed. She eagerly tore open the card, expecting to see Edith's or even Leta's name. But the flowers were from Daniel with a simple but touching note: "Wishing you and your new baby great joy this morning and every morning—Daniel.''

Glowing with Daniel's good wishes and confidence in her, Sonya telephoned Leta and the Bensons, then she settled down to rest and contemplated the night's experience, destined to be a turning point for her. Becoming a mother had put her life into a new perspective. She savored a closeness to her own mother that she'd never known before and formed a deeper appreciation for what her parents had done for her. She experienced a peace that she hadn't known since Bryon had left her, but this was an incident they should have shared, and she sorrowed that Bryon had missed forever the wonder and beauty of the birth of his first child.

Mostly Sonya rejoiced in the miracle that she wanted the child, for her greatest fear had been that once the baby was born, she wouldn't feel any emotion toward him. Her apprehension that rearing the child would be a duty rather than a labor of love had disappeared forever when she first held and touched Paul. He was simply amazing to her. She had a son and she loved him! Perhaps that was the greatest miracle of all.

Chapter Eleven

With her mother on hand to help with the baby and to look out for Edith, too, Sonya didn't mind going back to the York home for her convalescent period. Her mother intended to stay for two weeks, and after that Sonya would be able to continue as Edith's companion. Edith gave Paul a heartwarming reception.

"I've longed for the sound of a baby's cry in this house, and I hope you won't think he's bothering me. Bring him to see me every day. I'll even watch him for you when your mother goes away, because you're going to be busy. Daniel telephoned yesterday that the inspectors will arrive in a few days to look over the house and see what changes have to be made to turn it into a refuge for battered women."

Sonya had telephoned Lola Shrader the news about the child, and while she was still in the hospital, Lola came to visit her bringing several sleeper outfits. Sonya had been resentful toward the Shraders that they'd ignored her during the Christmas holidays, but it was probably better that way for all of them. A single, pregnant woman didn't fit into the company Riley and Lola entertained.

Apparently Riley had reported about the child at the office, and Bryon must have heard. When Paul was ten days old, he telephoned.

"Are you ready to proceed with the divorce now?" he inquired bluntly, with no question about the baby, no comment upon Sonya's health. Wouldn't one think he would want to know his child's name, or if it were a boy or a girl? Perhaps his informant had supplied the information. Whatever the situation, his attitude annoyed Sonya, and she said angrily, "Yes, I'm ready for a divorce. I want you out of my life as quickly as possible, Bryon. I'll have my lawyer contact you."

She slammed down the phone without giving him an opportunity to answer. She punched in the digits of Daniel office.

"Daniel, my husband just telephoned about the divorce, and I'm ready to have you continue with it. When will it be convenient for me to see you?"

"I'll stop by the house this afternoon. I have to be in north Omaha, and that will save you a trip downtown."

Sonya had hesitated to contact Bryon's parents about the birth of her son, but since Bryon already knew, they probably had heard, too. The last time she'd phoned them they'd been preparing to go to California for several weeks, so she doubted that they had returned. For some reason when they didn't answer their phone, she was relieved, but she didn't feel it was right to restrain them from seeing Paul, especially since his face mirrored the distinctive features of their son. Even Sonya's mother, against her will, admitted that she could see nothing of her daughter in the child. "But let's hope he'll have your personality," she muttered.

A few months ago this fact would have frustrated Sonya, but now she could look at this little image of Bryon with unconcern. She loved Paul, but his visage didn't give her any longing for Bryon. She tried to convey something of her feelings to Daniel when he arrived for the appointment.

"I don't want Bryon anymore, so you take what measures are necessary."

Today, Daniel was her attorney instead of her friend, and he approached the matter of her divorce in an unemotional manner, but never again in his presence would Sonya be able to blot out the comfort he'd given her on the day that Paul was born. She now looked upon their relationship from a new perspective.

"What kind of divorce settlement shall we ask for? It isn't out of line to demand that he pay all of your hospital expenses, as well as child support, and even some alimony for you until you marry again."

Sonya laughed shortly. "This experience has soured me on marriage. I don't want anything from Bryon except complete custody of the child and that he sign away all of his rights."

Daniel frowned. "As your attorney, Sonya, I must tell you that is very foolish. He should pay for the care of this child. You don't realize how much it will cost to raise a child."

"I made it through the past six months on my own. I had enough to pay for the hospital bill and even a bit of money left over. I figure if I could manage that, I'll make it alone."

"I'm advising against it."

"If Bryon is sending child support each month, I'll not have a chance to forget him. I want to put the past behind me, Daniel, and I think this is the only way to do it. I do want you to make him pay your fees and any court cost involved. I don't want him to give *me* anything, but I want you amply compensated, and I know I can't afford to pay you what you're entitled to have. Bryon is the one who wants a divorce, so he should at least pay for that. Perhaps I am being foolish, and I certainly am not suggesting this as a precedent for other women to follow, but my pride prevents me from taking anything from Bryon.''

"Sonya, I have mixed feelings about this. As an attorney, I oppose your action. Your husband should pay to support your child, especially since you don't have an adequate income. Many of my divorced clients can't make a decent living for their family when they have a good job *and* receive child support. On the other hand, I look forward to having Bryon Dixon out of your life forever.''

Daniel had helped Sonya and Edith choose a well-known contractor to do the renovation, and on Monday morning three workers arrived. They first blocked off Edith's quarters by building a wall with a locking door in it.

It saddened Sonya to see the changing appearance inside the old house. She loved it because the walls had reached out and sheltered her when she needed a sanctuary, and she thought the renovations desecrated it. She figured Edith had similar feelings, because the elderly woman spent most of that day lying on the bed, but by evening the partition was in.

By the end of the week all the necessary changes in the house had been made and Sonya looked forward to starting her training classes.

Paul was a month old when Bryon's mother telephoned and asked if they could see the child.

"We returned from California yesterday," Mrs. Dixon said. "We could come by whenever it's convenient for you."

"Edith is doing quite a lot of renovation right now, and the house is rather untidy. Why don't I drive out with him tomorrow afternoon?"

"That will be fine."

The Dixons were obviously delighted with their grandchild, and Mrs. Dixon compared him to some of Bryon's baby pictures, confirming how much Paul looked like his father.

"It's almost as if we have Bryon again," she said.

Sonya stayed a couple of hours, and Mrs. Dixon held the baby all the time she was there. She seemed quite reluctant to give him up when Sonya prepared to leave.

"You said that Mrs. York is renovating her house. Seems a strange thing for her to do at her age," Tom Dixon said.

"She's turning the house into a crisis center for abused wives and children. I'm attending classes so that I'll be qualified to be the director. Since I wanted to care for Paul myself and avoid a baby-sitter, this arrangement seemed like a good idea. After my own experience, I think I have some knowledge to help other women, so I'm looking forward to the work."

"That doesn't appear to be a desirable environment to rear a child," Mrs. Dixon said.

"Oh, we have a delightful apartment for Paul and me. There will be an attendant to supervise the clients at night, so I'll be looking out for him then."

"But you don't know what kind of people will be living there," her mother-in-law insisted.

"They'll be screened carefully, and I don't have any worries about it. Actually, I have a lot of sympathy for

the women who'll need to come to our center. From what
I've learned in my training, I'll be dealing with women
caught in troubled circumstances who are finally taking
the first steps to make their lives and their children's lives
better. No doubt by the time Paul is older, I will use this
experience to find another job probably in social work as
well. But I don't want to leave him when he's a baby.''

"Would you consider coming here to live?" Mr. Dixon
asked.

Sonya stared at him, dumbfounded. "Wouldn't that be
an awkward arrangement? If I lived here, I couldn't possibly avoid seeing Bryon, and it would be too painful for
me if he should bring home another wife. In spite of how
he has treated me, I can't forget that he once loved me.
Besides, I don't believe Bryon would come home if I
lived in your house.''

"But if your divorce goes through and you have custody of the baby, we might never see him," Anna said.

"A few months ago, I was so mad at Bryon that I didn't
care whether I saw any of you Dixons again, but before
I could become the sort of Christian I want to be, I had
to learn to forgive. I've forgiven Bryon for what he has
done, and I certainly won't be mean enough to prevent
you seeing your only grandchild, but I believe Bryon will
not want you to have a relationship with Paul. If he broke
up our marriage because he didn't want a child, he won't
want to share you with our son, especially when I'm the
boy's guardian. You may have to make a choice—either
your son or your grandson.''

"I'm sure he will change his mind now that the child
is born," Anna said confidently, with a significant look
at her husband.

Sonya was glad to leave the Dixon house, and she
doubted if she'd ever go there again. She had never loved

the Dixons, but she had respected them. Maybe the break with Bryon would have to include his parents, too.

Paul was three months old, the house was almost ready for patrons, and still no word from Bryon about the divorce. Although Daniel had contacted Bryon's attorney and filed the necessary papers, he had received no response.

When Daniel telephoned that he needed to see her, Sonya wasn't surprised. "Do you want me to come into the office?"

"No, I need to see Edith on business, too, so I'll come there this morning."

Daniel's face was unusually grave when Sonya opened the door to admit him.

"Shall we sit in Edith's room? I've just brought Paul down for his visit with her. She enjoys having him for an hour or so each day. I think she pretends that he's her own great-grandchild."

"She's become quite fond of you, Sonya."

Daniel lifted Paul from his carrier when they entered the room. "How's my boy?" he greeted the baby and kissed his cheek. Paul was a happy child, and he gurgled at Daniel in reply. "He's a cute one, Sonya. And he's getting bigger every day. Pretty soon, I'll have to teach him how to toss that little football I gave him," Daniel said, testing Paul's grip on his finger as he cradled the child to his chest.

Sonya laughed. "I think we have a way to go before he's playing football, Daniel." She reached for the baby and Daniel unwillingly handed him back.

"Whatever you say. You're his mom. Maybe we'll start with the zoo, first," he added hopefully.

"Sounds like a good idea," Sonya agreed.

Daniel sat down, and he looked at Sonya with compassion. "Sonya, you have to deal with a rather difficult situation."

"Bryon?"

"No, I haven't heard from his lawyer, but now I think I know why. I had a visit from Bryon's parents yesterday. They want to adopt Paul."

"Why, the nerve!" Sonya said when she finally found her tongue.

"Apparently they believe that Bryon will not have another child, and they want an heir. If you retain sole custody of Paul, they would have no legal right to him at all."

"But what legal grounds could they have?"

"They're contending that a crisis center isn't a suitable environment for a baby, and that financially they're able to care for him, and you're not."

Sonya reached for Paul and clutched him tightly. "Can they take my baby away from me?"

"I don't think so, but they have a lot of money, and they're determined."

"And I don't have any money," Sonya said bitterly.

"I'll do everything I can for you, without charge," Daniel assured her. "That should go without saying by now."

"And you're welcome to use my money, Daniel," Edith said, and her lips trembled. "It's inconceivable that anyone would say *my* home isn't a fit place for a child."

"I don't believe there's a judge who will give them custody of Paul when he knows the true facts. We can have plenty of character witnesses, perhaps your friend Leta, Edith, Adam and Marie Benson, and the people you've worked with at the nursery school. I thought I knew your answer before I came, but I had to inquire. Your answer is no?"

"Of course."

"They said they will give you one hundred thousand dollars if you agree to their plan without a court fight."

Sonya hadn't felt such a surge of anger since she'd learned that Bryon had deserted her. She remembered distinctly the mutilation of the two Chinese vases, so she hurriedly placed Paul back in his playpen. She didn't want him in her arms if she had an urge to throw something. She paced the room while Edith and Daniel watched her.

"I'm trying so hard to come through this divorce without hatred, but it grows worse every day. Just when I think I can live at peace with everyone, the Dixons take this awful action. Do they have such a low opinion of me that they think I would sell my child? That's what it amounts to."

"If that's what they think, I'll soon take them your negative answer and then let them proceed. Though I was sure of your answer, I couldn't speak for you."

"Thank you, Daniel," Sonya murmured.

He favored her with an inquiring glance.

"For believing that I wouldn't give up my child for money."

He flashed a warm smile. "Sonya, it makes me laugh to even hear you say such a thing. There was never any question in my mind about your answer had they offered you a million dollars. What puzzles me is why they didn't work through Bryon to gain custody of the child," Daniel added. "That would be the logical way—for Bryon to fight for him."

"Bryon doesn't always do what his parents want him to, so he may have refused."

Daniel stood and looked down at Paul, who had gone

to sleep, unconcerned about the battle that was brewing over his small form. He reached down and gently touched the baby's hair with his fingertips.

"I can't understand why a man wouldn't want a baby as sweet as this one, but unfortunately, in my line of work, I see this form of rejection every day."

After Daniel left, Edith and Sonya sat in companionable silence. Sonya's thoughts were so troubled that she didn't want to talk, and Edith must have understood this for she waited until Sonya stirred and said, "I must get ready to go to my class. I'll never be able to concentrate on my studies after this jolt. Do you want me to leave Paul here, or should I take him to Stelle so you can rest?"

"Since he's happy here, leave him, and tell Stelle to look in on both of us occasionally."

Sonya knelt beside Paul and laid her hand tenderly on his face. "I can't believe they would try to take my child. For one thing, they're both in their sixties and certainly that is no age to start rearing a baby."

"I'm sure you have nothing to worry about, Sonya. Since you have such a good record, I can't see any judge taking the child from you. If Bryon fights for him, that's a different story."

"This could drag on for years, couldn't it?"

"I don't know, but there is something I do know. Do you realize that Daniel Massie is in love with you?"

Sonya turned startled eyes on the older woman.

"I was sure you didn't suspect that," Edith said gently.

"He's given no indication. I've been very grateful for his supportive friendship as well as some spiritual guidance, but love…no, surely you're mistaken."

"As an attorney, he knows you have to preserve your integrity until after a divorce is finalized, so he wouldn't ask you to do anything that would jeopardize your standing in the court. But you need to face the possibility that when your divorce is finalized, he may speak.''

''I certainly hope you're wrong, Edith. I owe so much to him that I'd hate to hurt him, but right now I feel as if I will never marry again.''

''Perhaps I shouldn't have said anything, but if he does approach you, I didn't want it to be a surprise.''

But Edith's words had disturbed her mind, and she thought of the many times Daniel had helped her during these months, and she was convinced he didn't take that much interest in all of his clients. She thought of the many quiet talks they'd had together. They'd grown even closer after Paul's birth. She thought of Daniel's warm looks, his kind words and encouragement and his tireless efforts to be there when she needed him. Was that love? She didn't know the answer. But whatever Daniel's feelings for her, she felt honored that a man with so much to offer any woman wanted to be such a large part of her life and Paul's.

And if he is in love with you, what do you think about it? Sonya could find no answer to that question.

It was over a week before Daniel contacted Sonya again, and when he telephoned, he said, ''The Dixons are going through with their demand, so I've arranged a meeting before a judge on Monday. You're to appear and bring Paul with you. Wear something sedate and conservative, but dress up. We want to make a good impression.''

''I'll wear one of the expensive outfits I used to buy. I'm almost back to my original size. They may not be fashionable now, but perhaps the judge won't know the difference. Or is it a woman judge?''

''No, we've been assigned a male judge—he's in his

late fifties and a solid family man. We have a good chance with him. Shall I pick you up?''

Sonya would have liked his comforting presence rather than to arrive at the courthouse by herself, but she remembered Edith's comments about Daniel's interest in her. If they were true, she couldn't place herself under any more obligation to Daniel than an attorney-client relationship warranted.

''No, thanks. That would be out of your way, and my old car is still running well enough. If I need transportation, I'll let you know.''

''As you wish. The hearing is at ten o'clock.''

Three days to wait! Sonya tried desperately to fill in the hours. She studied for her final exams in the social work course, willing her mind to concentrate on the book before her. The exams were on Wednesday, and if the decision didn't go in her favor, she wondered if she might fail the course.

The night before the hearing, Sonya went to her room soon after dinner. Clutching Paul in her arms and wondering if this time tomorrow night she would no longer have him was an intolerable burden to bear. She knew Paul should be resting in his crib, for she didn't want him to be fussy tomorrow, but she was reluctant to put him down. Only once before could she remember a more trying time—the night she would have taken her life except for the timely arrival of Adam and Marie. She had thought losing Bryon was the worst thing that could ever happen to her, but his desertion was nothing compared to the possible loss of her son.

Although she was worried, she didn't have the feeling of desperation she had experienced that other terrible night, for she had a hope now that she didn't have before. Sitting on the couch with Paul in her left arm, she opened the Bible to Romans 8:28. That verse didn't baffle her as much as it had once. *And we know that in all things God works for the good of those who love him, who have been called according to his purpose.*

She couldn't see why it would be right for the Dixons to take Paul, but she had experienced sufficient evidence of God working in her life to believe that, in some way, He would make tomorrow's hearing turn out for the best. She did love God, she believed He had a purpose for her life, and she had no choice except to leave tomorrow, and all other tomorrows, in His hands.

Sonya kissed Paul, laid him tenderly in the crib, and changed into her nightgown. "Weeping may endure for the night, but joy cometh in the morning," she whispered and turned out the light.

Surveying herself in the mirror on Monday morning, Sonya was pleased with her appearance. She'd found a classically styled navy wool suit, with a shaped blazer and slim skirt that seemed perfect for court. Small gold earrings and a pearl necklace completed her outfit. Most of the weight she'd gained during her pregnancy was gone, and her figure looked slim and attractive once more. The honey-toned hair flowing over her shoulders was shiny and alive. Only in her large blue eyes could one detect the unhappiness that had been her constant companion for so many months.

She dressed Paul in a new set of clothes her mother had recently sent. He looked like a miniature farmer with his red plaid, flannel shirt and blue chambray overalls. Edith was still in bed eating the breakfast Stelle had brought when Sonya walked down the back stairs and paused in the doorway.

"How do we look?" she asked, holding Paul aloft for inspection.

"Adorable! Come for a kiss. Remember, right is going to win, and it's right for you to keep this boy."

After Sonya buckled Paul into the used car seat she had found at a yard sale, she reached into her purse for a tissue to wipe the perspiration from her hands and dropped her head on the steering wheel to ask for God's help. After a few minutes she turned the ignition key with shaky fingers and drove slowly down the street. She had ample time, so she needn't hurry.

Daniel waited for her on the steps of the courthouse flanked by the Bensons, Leta, Eloise Dedham and the manager of the Washburn Complex. "Doesn't hurt to have plenty of backup troops when we go into battle," he said with a smile. "We probably won't need them, but I'm ready."

Leta took Paul from Sonya and hugged him. "Doesn't he look cute in this outfit? The Dixons will get this child over my dead body," she said dramatically.

Leta carried Paul until they reached the courtroom. "Sonya should carry him now, Leta. When we enter the room, the five of you can sit on the seat behind us. My defense will depend on what the Dixons' lawyer proposes, so I don't know when, or if, I'll call you to testify."

Daniel led Sonya to a table close to the judge's bench, and her spirits soared when she sensed her friends seating themselves behind her. She deflated again when the elder Dixons entered the room with their lawyer, completely ignoring her presence. She hated to think that their friendliness toward her since Christmas had been nothing more than a ruse to snatch her baby.

Paul began to fuss, and Sonya whispered, "Please, baby, be good today." She reached into the diaper bag and brought out a bear he liked, which silenced him for the moment. She'd brought a battery of things to entertain him and to feed him. Turning to Leta, she whispered, "If he needs to be changed, will you take care of him?"

Fortunately the judge came in at that moment, and the clerk asked everyone to rise. Sonya hoped they would have the proceedings finished before Paul became too fussy. The clerk called the courtroom to order and the judge sat behind his large desk. As Sonya reseated herself, she felt Daniel briefly squeeze her hand. "Don't worry, Sonya," he whispered. "With God's help, we'll win this. He knows we have to."

The judge scanned the papers before him and turned to the Dixons' attorney. "It's my understanding that Tom and Anna Dixon are suing for the custody and adoption of their grandson, Paul Dixon. I have in the record here that the mother of the child, Sonya Dixon, is opposed to that adoption. What is the position of the father? I assume he's still living."

"Yes, and he has no objection to this adoption. He doesn't want the child himself," the plaintiffs' lawyer said.

"The court will listen now to the arguments advanced by the grandparents as to why they want to adopt the boy."

The lawyer approached the bench. "I have here a financial statement of my clients. It's their contention that they can provide much more for the child than his mother can. She's the director of a crisis center for abused women, where she makes less than the minimum wage. She lives in that center, and my clients believe that isn't a proper environment for the rearing of a child."

"I assume that the father is paying some support for the boy. Is that considered in an estimate of her income?"

"No, Your Honor. A divorce is in process, but it hasn't

become finalized, necessarily delayed for the outcome of this hearing.''

The judge glanced momentarily toward Paul, who chortled gleefully in Sonya's arms.

"Am I to understand, then, that you bring no charges against the character of the mother?''

"No, Your Honor, we haven't investigated her lifestyle. We simply believe this adoption would be in the best interests of the child.''

The judge nodded for the attorney to take his seat, and he turned to Daniel.

"Mr. Massie, we're ready to hear your case.''

"Your Honor, I want my client, Sonya Dixon, to tell you the events of her life the past year.'' Sonya turned startled eyes upon him, and he smiled slightly. "As you can see, this comes as a surprise to Mrs. Dixon. I hadn't warned her ahead of time, since I wanted the narrative to be completely unrehearsed.'' He smiled encouragingly at Sonya. "I believe her story is the only defense we need.''

"Will you stand, Mrs. Dixon?'' the judge said.

Sonya handed Paul to Leta, and he left her arms reluctantly, howling immediately. Leta snatched up the diaper bag and hurried down the aisle with the unhappy boy.

"I was happily married to Bryon Dixon for two years, but when I became pregnant, he turned into a different man. When I refused to abort the fetus, he abandoned me.''

She swallowed and resumed with difficulty. For over an hour she talked, occasionally sipping from the glass of water that Daniel had placed on the table. She told of Bryon's surprise move to San Francisco, Gail's entry into the apartment to take away his clothes, how he had closed the savings account, leaving her with scant money, how he'd had the utilities turned off. When her voice faltered,

and she felt unable to go on, she glanced at Daniel and
drew strength and comfort from his calm, steady gaze.
Tears streamed from her face as she recalled the move
from the Sandhill Apartments to the tiny quarters, how
she was compelled to wear used clothing, depend upon
the church for food. Gaining control of her emotions, she
wiped her face with some tissues the court clerk handed
her. When she mentioned her move to Edith's home, the
judge took on a new look of interest.

"There were times when I hated my unborn child because of all the trouble he has caused, but during the night
I labored to bring his small form into the world, I fell in
love with him. I want only what's best for him, and if
Your Honor believes his interests can best be served with
his grandparents, then I won't contest the decision of the
court."

Daniel stood up and interrupted, "Your Honor, the client hasn't discussed such a statement with me. Please
don't hold her to that decision."

"Be seated, Mr. Massie. You gave your client the privilege of speaking without coaching. You'll have to take
the consequences. Continue, Mrs. Dixon."

Daniel eased back into his seat, and, taking a deep
breath, Sonya said, "But, Your Honor, I want my baby.
I love him with all my heart and would do anything in
my power to keep him safe and happy. I've provided for
myself for over a year. I changed my life-style to scrimp
and save to pay my hospital bills. If I could do that when
I was pregnant and with a newborn child, surely I can
take care of him now without doing him any harm. You
can tell that he's a happy baby and that he won't come
to any harm through me."

"Do you mean that you haven't had any support from
your husband?"

"No, Your Honor, not from him, his parents, nor mine. Since December, I've been a companion to Edith York for free room and board, and until a few weeks before Paul was born, I worked at a nursery school and saved enough to pay my hospital confinement. I'll admit that compared to the Dixons, my financial statement is meager. I own a six-year-old car and have less than two hundred dollars in the bank. Those are my total assets, except for some expensive jewelry, compliments of my husband."

"May I ask about the divorce proceedings and terms?"

Daniel rose. "May I speak to that, Your Honor."

The judge nodded and said, "Be seated, Mrs. Dixon."

"My client's husband asked for a divorce almost immediately after he deserted her, and he wanted to give her a onetime settlement to pay for the hospital confinement and her expenses until she could get a job. I advised that she refuse the divorce until the birth of the child. When he was born without any health problems, I contacted Mr. Dixon's attorney and gave him our terms. That has been over three months ago without response from them."

"May I ask what your terms are?"

"Again, Your Honor, Mrs. Dixon refused my counsel. She wants nothing from her husband except his renouncement of all claim to the child and that she be given complete custody. She wants to assume full responsibility. I think it unwise, but she is adamant."

"Mrs. Dixon, you may remain seated, but I want to ask why you're taking a stand that might not be in the best interests of your child?"

"Perhaps it's stubbornness, Your Honor." A light smile played around the judge's stern features. "Bryon has never inquired about the child, never asked his sex or his name, although I assume he knows this from his parents or from our mutual acquaintances. I feel it's degrading to Paul to demand support from a parent who won't even claim him.''

"Mrs. Dixon, I'm going to ask you a question which may be difficult for you to answer, but I want the truth. Does your husband have any reason to believe that this child is not his?''

"Your Honor!" Sonya gasped.

Bryon's father cleared his throat. "Your Honor, may I speak?'' And when the judge nodded assent, Mr. Dixon said, "We have no reason to believe the child is not legitimate, else we wouldn't have asked to adopt him. To compare Bryon's baby picture with her child, one would find them as identical as twins.''

Sonya ventured a look at her in-laws. Mr. Dixon's face was red, and he breathed with difficulty. Mrs. Dixon sat with her face buried in her hands. Had they had any idea before just how shabbily Bryon had treated her? Sonya's face seemed drawn and tight. Tears threatened to overflow again. She glanced at Daniel and the sympathy and affection in his expression soothed her.

"I apologize for asking that, Mrs. Dixon, but I had to be sure before I made any decision.''

"Your Honor," Daniel said, "if there is any question about my client's character, I have with me several witnesses to assert that Mrs. Dixon has lived an exemplary life both before and after her husband's desertion.''

"That isn't necessary at this point. Normally I would deliberate several days before making a decision of this sort, but surely even the plaintiffs and their lawyer can see that justice can only be served by refusing this request for adoption.'' Sonya dropped her head on the table and sobbed. She heard sniffing all around her, and the judge halted momentarily. Even his voice seemed strained with emotion when he continued, "Mrs. Dixon, I believe the attitude that weighed most heavily in your favor was when you agreed to relinquish your son if this court decided his interests would best be served with his grandparents.

"I remembered when a judge, much wiser than I, was faced with a similar decision. You will remember that two women came to King Solomon contesting the motherhood of a child. When the real mother agreed to give up her child to save his life, King Solomon ruled in her favor. Can I do any less than he? It may be that the grandparents will appeal my opinion, but it's my decision that their request for adoption be denied."

Mr. Dixon leaned forward and spoke to his attorney. "Your Honor," the attorney said, "the plaintiffs will not appeal."

The judge turned again to Sonya, who lifted her tear-streaked face.

"You understand, Mrs. Dixon, that my only ruling is with the case in hand. This is not to indicate that your husband may not demand custody of the child. And although it isn't my place to advise you, I would strongly suggest that you rethink the terms of the divorce. Even if you receive custody of the child, your husband has some obligation for your welfare and that of his son."

"Thank you, Your Honor."

The judge left the courtroom, and Marie Benson snatched Sonya into comforting arms. Over Marie's shoulder, she watched Bryon's parents make their way slowly down the aisle. She'd never before thought of them being old, but they walked with the tread of the aged. Bryon had ruined their lives as well as hers.

Chapter Twelve

Sonya fretted because the elder Dixons might still acquire Paul through Bryon. Even if he didn't want Paul, Bryon could demand full or equal custody and turn the child over to his parents. This specter haunted her, but she finished her social work course, passed it and waited for the first client at Blessed Hope, the name they'd given to the crisis center.

Since many people still gossiped about the tragedy that had occurred at the York house, Sonya had difficulty finding a helper, and it was imperative that they hire an extra night worker as she couldn't leave Paul by himself all night. When she couldn't hire a part-time person through the unemployment agencies, she went back to the Washburn Complex to talk to Loretta Slinde.

Although Loretta was still skeptical, she agreed to work. "My man ain't working right now, and we need some extra money."

"It will be part-time work. We can't pay you if we don't have a patron. I'll probably call you frequently in the middle of the night."

* * *

Representatives of the organization assembled at the house for a ribbon-cutting ceremony, and a newspaper reporter from the *Herald* spread the story prominently in the next Sunday's issue. They still hadn't received a client when Edith had a telephone call from her indignant nephew, the first time she'd heard from him since Christmas. Sonya sat nursing Paul in Edith's living room, and since the man spoke loudly, she heard most of the conversation.

"Aunt Edith," Albert York said, "I can hardly believe what I've just read in the *Herald*. Why would you turn your house into such a place? And who is this Sonya Dixon you've taken under your wing? What kind of influence is she exerting upon you?"

Edith's lips trembled as she slipped a nitroglycerin tablet under her tongue. "I believe the newspaper explained it all, Albert. It was *my* idea to convert the house into a shelter."

"Well, I don't like it. It's degrading to the York name for one thing. The scandal connected with Alice's death was bad enough, and people are just beginning to forget that, and you have to start a crisis center. I don't wonder that Uncle will turn over in his grave."

Still with an attempt at calmness, Edith said, "Your uncle lived with me for several years, and I doubt he would be much surprised at anything I do."

"Since you know my objections, I trust you'll close down the place immediately."

"That's out of the question. I've signed a contract with the organization for two years. And I might remind you, Albert, you don't own this property." She eased the receiver back in place.

"Albert is worried about his inheritance," she said angrily.

"I could hear. It's too bad he doesn't understand."

"Albert has a dollar sign where his heart should be. He resents it that I've lived so long to use money that he thinks should be his. He's my husband's nephew and believes he's the heir to the York fortune, but he hasn't seen that in writing."

The first call for help came at three o'clock that night. A new telephone hot line had been installed in Sonya's apartment to avoid disturbing Edith.

"Mrs. Dixon, we have a patron for you. The police will bring her by shortly. She may be suicidal, so you should watch her carefully."

Sonya put in a call to Loretta Slinde and dressed hurriedly. Paul slept peacefully, but she left the door open so she could hear if he cried.

Walking down the broad stairway to wait by the front door, Sonya shuddered at the sight of the big chandelier. She had grown accustomed to the house, and it had been a long time since she'd thought of Alice Simmons and her tragic death on that spot.

The woman who staggered into the house ahead of the policemen reeked of alcohol, and Sonya turned inquiring eyes upon the officers.

"Both husband and wife are heavy drinkers, but tonight he became abusive, beat up the woman and kicked her out of the house. We've got him in jail. Try to sober her up."

Sonya led the woman upstairs and into the bathroom, where she promptly vomited on the floor. Seating the woman on the side of the tub, Sonya bathed her face and applied bandages over the worst places. She tried to talk to the woman, who gave her name as Tracey, but couldn't carry on much of a conversation after that. Sonya tried her best to simply calm her and make her comfortable.

By the time she had the woman ready for bed, Loretta arrived, and she cleaned the bathroom. Sonya returned to bed, but she didn't sleep, wondering if she'd done all she could for Tracey.

After she fed Paul the next morning, Sonya checked with Loretta, who sat in the upstairs lounge watching the shoppers' club program. She had the volume turned low, and Sonya whispered, "How did things go?"

"Haven't heard a word out of her. I've checked in the bedroom often. She's sleeping it off."

"I'll report to the agency and see what we do next."

Sonya didn't like the monitor's report. "Her husband has paid his fine, the police have released him, and he's coming to get his wife."

Indignantly Sonya repeated the message to Loretta. "We'll have to awaken her and let him take her, I suppose. Seems futile to me."

Loretta flipped off the television, stretched and stood up. "Doesn't surprise me. I've seen abuse often at the apartment. Man and woman go on a binge, get mad at each other and call the police. When they sober up, they're lovey-dovey until they liquor up again."

"Do you think she'll want to go back with him?"

"Where else can she go? She can't stay here forever."

Loretta was right, and when a burly, unshaven man appeared at the doorway demanding, "Where is she?" Tracey meekly followed him out to his car.

After they left, Sonya telephoned the agency. "Wasn't there anything else I could have done for her? I feel as if I'm wasting my time if women like Tracey are just going to go back to the same situations. I thought we were here to help them."

"We see all kinds of cases," the director said soothingly. "When a woman doesn't want to return to her husband, you can keep her until we find a place for her to live. Each case is different. Sometimes we find foster homes for children until the mother can determine some means of support. You're going to deal with many different situations."

The woman was right, for throughout the rest of spring and into summer, hardly a night passed that Sonya didn't have one or more patrons. A few women spent a week or more at the house and actually proved a help with other clients, who came in sick or hurt. Sonya was always moved and humbled when she witnessed women who were suffering themselves reaching out to those even less fortunate.

After four months of dealing with the problems of abused women, Sonya was ready to believe that Bryon had treated her decently. He'd never hit her, never publicly humiliated her, nor had he forced sexual relations upon her. She knew she hadn't deserved the treatment he'd given her, but at least she had come to the place where she could think of it with some detachment. Both she and Daniel had thought there would be an immediate response from Bryon's attorney after the adoption ploy had failed, but the months passed without any contact.

After Paul's birth Daniel became a frequent visitor at the York mansion. Sometimes he had business with Edith, but more often, he simply dropped by for an hour or so just to visit. Sonya would have been flattered to think he came solely to see her, but she had to admit that he gave most of his attention to Paul. He fussed over the boy like a mother hen with a chick. He absolutely insisted on going with her when she took the child to the pediatrician for regular exams, and he rejoiced as much as she did when the doctor praised the baby's growth. If he visited at feeding time, he heated the formula, tested it carefully and held the bottle for Paul to eat. A few times when Sonya was busy with the shelter's clients, he even changed Paul's diaper. Since Sonya had no previous experience with children, they were learning child care together.

Sonya did appreciate Daniel's interest in Paul, for she had read articles by psychologists saying that a child's personality formed at an early age, and she thought it was important for Paul to have a male influence. Daniel was being the father that Bryon should have been, and she was grateful to Daniel for filling that void. Sonya's maternal affection, and the love he received from the Massies, as well as Stelle, Leta and Edith had molded Paul into a happy, well-adjusted child, who cried very little and smiled at everyone.

Jane Massie, too, insisted on helping with Paul, and when Sonya needed to take Edith to the doctor or attend workshops to keep updated on state regulations for the Blessed Hope shelter, she often took Paul to the Massies'. If Daniel could rearrange his work schedule, he was always there to help.

When Paul was six months old, weighing in at fifteen pounds, and displaying his first tooth, Daniel telephoned. "This calls for a celebration. Mother and I are coming to visit tonight, bringing cake and ice cream."

A warm glow spread throughout Sonya's body, and a smile crinkled her face. "You can bring refreshments, but no presents."

But when Daniel and Jane arrived, they brought several brightly-wrapped packages, which Paul liked more than the cake.

"Are you determined to spoil the child?" Sonya said in mock severity. "Daniel, it's time you married and had children of your own. Then, you can spoil them.'' Although Sonya laughed when she reprimanded him, she realized that the idea of Daniel being married was not amusing.

The house was quiet tonight with only one patron, and Sonya relaxed, for a change. This job was more taxing than she'd expected, and she seldom had a chance to sit down and think. She felt like a prisoner—she wasn't married, she wasn't divorced. She didn't know whether she could have Paul all the time, or if Bryon would contest that. If he wouldn't contact them, she intended to do something. Daniel might not approve, but she decided to write to Bryon.

Dear Bryon,

Why haven't you contacted my attorney? Although at first I opposed the divorce, I now believe it's the only way we can go. Too many things have happened between us to ever have them resolved. It's been almost a year of indecision, and I want to leave the past behind me and begin to plan a new life. Although you've never asked my forgiveness, indeed you may think you've done nothing to warrant it, I want you to know that I have forgiven both you and Gail, and I wish you the happiness that we had during our two years of marriage. And you should be happy, because if you agree to the divorce terms that I want, you won't have any extra financial burden. You give up custody of our child, and that's all I want from you. And may God forgive you as I have.

Sonya

A few days later, Mrs. Massie telephoned and talked to Edith, inviting her and Sonya and Paul for dinner. Edith didn't give her an answer until she talked with Sonya.

"Are you sure you feel up to it?" Sonya asked, for Edith seldom went out anymore. Her hairdresser came to the house, and she relied on Sonya and Stelle to do the shopping. When Sonya questioned her about her health, she always said, "I'm fine, dear, only wearing out. Remember I'm an old woman."

When Sonya finally succeeded in taking her to the doctor, he had told Edith, "You're living on borrowed time. I've told you that for years, but you always make a liar out of me. Just take it easy and do what you feel like doing."

"Sonya takes care of me. She won't let me do anything."

"And rightly so," the doctor agreed.

But Edith seemed to want to go to the Massies. "Jane Massie is one of my best friends, and I was a friend of her mother. I prefer to go for Sunday dinner, rather than some evening, if that's convenient for you."

"I can't be gone at night unless I have someone here to man the phones, so Sunday noon sounds good to me."

Edith didn't go to church, but she was ready when Sonya and Paul returned, and they drove to the Massies' in Edith's old Lincoln. Sonya looked forward to the visit as a break from her routine and as something to take her mind off the pending divorce. Although she'd agreed to the divorce, her mind wasn't completely at ease about it. She kept remembering her vow "Until death do us part."

"This house was built at the turn of the century," Edith commented as they drove up the circular driveway, "by Daniel's grandfather. The Massies have always known how to make money and to keep it. I suppose Daniel could live in ease without working a day of his life, but the Massies are workers, too.''

Daniel rushed down the steps to greet them and to help Edith into the house. ''Leave the car here in front,'' he said to Sonya. ''We don't expect anyone else. If you need help with Paul, I'll come back soon.''

''No help needed,'' Sonya said. ''By the time you have Edith settled, we'll be up the steps.''

Daniel met her at the door and took Paul from her arms. ''He's getting to be an armful. Aren't you, little guy?'' he asked Paul. The baby grabbed Daniel's hair and Daniel laughed out loud.

Daniel was so good with Paul. Sonya felt a warm glow, watching their rapport. She knew Daniel would make a wonderful father if he ever had children of his own.

Upon entering the Massies' home, Sonya's thoughts quickly turned to Edith. Sonya noted the blue shade on Edith's face, and she watched anxiously as Edith slid a small tablet under her tongue. How much longer could Edith live, and then what would happen to Blessed Hope and Sonya herself? She tried not to think of such things, but moments like these made her realize how shaky her future was.

Edith rallied and seemed in better spirits than she'd been in for days. After dinner, Mrs. Massie took Edith into a small sitting room to look at some old family portraits. Sonya could hear their voices through the open door as she and Daniel went into the large room overlooking the garden. The watering system arced in a rainbow as it tossed water on the flowers. Paul had slept through dinner and still seemed content in his carrier.

''It's nice for us to meet occasionally on something other than an attorney-client basis,'' Daniel said.

"We do that each Sunday at church. We're all members of the same family there."

"Sonya, I want to be more than that to you. And as your attorney, I know I shouldn't speak until your divorce is final, but do you realize that I love you?"

"I hadn't even thought of such a thing, until Edith suggested that you had a personal interest in me."

Daniel took Sonya's hand and pulled her into his arms. Her heartbeat quickened when she saw the yearning and desire in his eyes.

"I've tried to conceal my feelings from you, for I know you aren't ready for another relationship. I thought that love at first sight was a foolish notion, but from the first day you came to my office, I've known you were the only woman I could ever love. I tried to argue myself out of it, especially when you were still declaring your love for Bryon, but I couldn't do it." His voice was husky, taut with emotion, and when she glanced upward, she saw that his face was white and tense.

"Should we be talking about this now, Daniel? I'm still married," she protested with her lips, but her heart was hammering in her chest, and as closely as he held her, she wondered if he could feel her rapid heartbeat.

"Don't think I'm not aware of that," he groaned in dismay. "I tell myself dozens of times every day, 'She's married,' but my love is so overwhelming that I can't keep it to myself any longer. I wanted you to be free before I spoke, but I have no will power where you're concerned."

Daniel lowered his lips to hers in a brief, soft kiss that tenderly expressed his depth of emotion. Surprised at first, Sonya didn't respond, but she trembled in his embrace. Could she be excused for accepting this moment? She still didn't know the depth of her feeling for Daniel, but she did know that no embrace of Bryon's had given her the pleasure and joy she experienced in Daniel's arms.

With a sigh, Daniel lifted his head, and with a gentle hand, placed her head on his shoulder and his hand caressed her hair. "I love you for your beauty, both physical and spiritual. I respect you as one of the finest women I've ever known. You've triumphed over a situation that has devastated many women. And even if I didn't love you so deeply, I would still want to marry you. You're the woman I want to rear *my* children. I want to marry you, Sonya."

Her words were muffled on his shoulder, but she whispered, "You deserve someone far better than me—a woman embittered by a former marriage and mother of another man's child."

"I don't agree. I believe you're the one God intended for me, although He had to take the long way around to bring us together. I've often wondered why He hadn't led me to the right person when I've prayed for a Christian mate. I knew why the first day I saw you. I've been waiting for you all of my life."

While they stood in close embrace, and he waited for her answer, Sonya thought of how she had felt when Bryon proposed to her. That day she felt giddy, excited and triumphant because she had won the man so many other girls wanted. Today, her feelings were different. Being asked to share Daniel's life had restored all the self-esteem she had lost when Bryon rejected her. She felt secure, wanted, cherished. She had learned long ago that Daniel's handsome features mirrored the beauty of his soul. She would be safe with Daniel Massie; she would be loved; she would be respected. What more could a woman want?

Realizing that the silence had lengthened, she reluc-

tantly pulled away from his arms and picked up Paul who
had awakened. "I wasn't ready for your declaration, Daniel, and I can't give you an answer yet. There's a part of
me that wants to accept you now. I'm tired of carrying
the load alone, and it would be a relief to dump all my
problems on someone else. The fact that you want me has
restored my self-respect. I haven't really felt like a
'woman,' since Bryon rejected me, but when you took me
into your arms, I was all woman. You made me feel whole
again."

He smiled winningly. "Can't you give me a little
hope?"

"I'm afraid to. You see, even after my divorce is finalized, I might still feel married to Bryon. He's treated
me shabbily, but he still hasn't given me enough reason
to justify putting him out of my life if he should change
his mind."

"I knew it was too soon to ask you, and I know we'll
need time together—a real, old-fashioned courtship if you
like, for as long as you want. I want the chance to take
care of you, Sonya, you and Paul. I want to make you
happy. I know I can."

"I can't answer you now, Daniel," she said honestly.
"But whatever happens, I'll always treasure your friendship."

"I'll treasure yours as well."

Sonya heard Mrs. Massie and Edith returning, so she
said quickly, "Thank you."

On their return home, Edith smiled. "So he asked
you?"

Sonya laughed and threw a puzzled glance in her direction. "How did you know?"

"It was written all over both of you—looked as guilty

as two kids caught in some mischief. What did you tell him?''

''Nothing. If there's one thing I've learned from this past year, it's not to make hasty decisions. I've been burned once. I don't want to repeat the experience.''

''Living singly isn't any pleasure, and I'm sure rearing a child alone is difficult.''

''I realize that, but I've learned from the clients we receive at Blessed Hope that there are worse things than being a single parent. And besides, at this point, I still have a husband.''

''You've not heard anything from him?''

''Nothing, and it makes me suspicious.''

Chapter Thirteen

When the telephone rang, Sonya thought it was another case for Blessed Hope, as she was expecting no other calls.

"Sonya, this is Bryon. How are you getting along?"

His voice no longer contained the harsh, cold quality, and he sounded like the Bryon she'd once loved. She eased down on the couch and gasped to catch her breath.

"All right," she said, relieved that her voice sounded natural, but how could it when she found it difficult to breathe?

"When can I talk to you?"

"If it's about the divorce, you'll need to telephone my lawyer."

"But that's the point—I've changed my mind. I don't want a divorce; I want to come back to you."

Sonya started laughing, and she couldn't control her voice when she tried to talk. The phone jiggled in her shaky hand, and she blurted out, "I can't believe this— that you'd actually suggest walking back into my life as quickly as you walked out, especially now that I've agreed to the divorce."

"I'm in Omaha for a few days, and I must talk to you, Sonya."

"If you had suggested a reconciliation a few months ago, you would have made me very happy, but it may be too late now. I question that we could possibly have a happy marriage with all the bitterness that has passed between us."

"Certainly we could. I still want you, Sonya."

"Will you go with me to a Christian family counselor where we can discuss our differences? If you accept Christ into your life as I have, we can make a success of our marriage."

He didn't answer. "Bryon, did you hear what I said?"

His laugh was scornful. "Yes, I heard what you said, I'm not deaf, but you did send me into shock. What's happened to you? You don't sound like the girl I loved and married."

"If you feel that way, I won't talk to you anymore unless my lawyer is present. I'll telephone Mr. Massie, and if he's available, we can meet at his office at eleven o'clock in the morning."

"What I have to say can't be said before a third party."

"It has to be that way. Do you think I can trust you now? Is this something you and your parents have hatched up to take control of Paul?"

"No, it is not. My parents don't even know I'm in town. I'm at the Holiday Inn. If you can't get an appointment with Massie, telephone me here."

Sonya's hands shook until she could barely punch the digits of Daniel's number, and he listened in silence as Sonya hurriedly related the strange conversation with Bryon.

"You did the right thing," he said immediately. "As a matter of fact, your husband should bring his attorney, but he probably wouldn't take kindly to the idea if you suggested it."

"Then you can meet us."

"Yes. I may have to reschedule some appointments, but I consider this an emergency. Remember, Sonya, I have a personal interest in the outcome of this meeting."

Sonya telephoned Leta next—who better than Leta to deal with the perfidy of men?

"Doesn't surprise me at all," Leta said promptly. "Men want their little spurts of freedom until their freedom turns into a prison."

"Do you think I should take him back?"

"Mercy, no!" Leta exploded. "You have him right where you want him. Let him understand how it feels to be rejected."

"That isn't a Christian attitude, Leta."

"Ha! If I'd taken a Christian attitude in my divorces, I'd be sitting out on the street."

"Maybe I shouldn't even talk to him."

"I don't know how you can avoid it. He can keep calling you on the phone. You may as well talk it out."

"I'm afraid this is another attempt by the Dixons to get Paul. If I take Bryon back, he's liable to turn the child over to them."

"You may be right, but I'm telling you, don't take him back. Hold his feet to the fire and get your divorce. You don't owe Bryon Dixon a thing. He's on the begging end now. And, another thing, take Paul with you in the morning. If he sees the way you've bloomed out now, looking like you did when you were a bride, he's going to be determined to have you. Seeing you as a matron with a child in your arms might cool his ardor. And good luck. Be sure and telephone me as soon as you can."

Edith was still in bed when Sonya went down the next morning, and after Sonya explained where she was going, she said, "But I'm not sure I should leave you." Holding Edith's hand, she noted her pulse was faltering and weak. "Perhaps I should call the doctor."

"No," Edith said weakly. "Your situation is more important than my health. I'm going to stay in bed. Just ask Stelle to bring me some tea and toast. I'll be all right."

Sonya wasn't convinced. She had never seen Edith so low before. Cautioning Stelle to keep a close eye on her mistress and to call the doctor if her condition worsened, Sonya put Edith's problems behind her. She had enough of her own this morning.

"Paul, we have a very important appointment this morning," she said, when she left the car in the garage and caught the elevator to Daniel's fourth-floor office. "You're going to meet your father."

Bryon was already in the waiting room when Sonya entered, and she halted her steps suddenly. She had expected to be here first and to compose herself before he entered.

Bryon rose at once and came to her, and in spite of herself, Sonya forgot all of the mean things he'd done in the past fourteen months. He was the old Bryon—the man with the charm and good looks who had won and married her.

Dear God, don't let my better judgment be swayed again!

He stooped to kiss her, but Sonya backed out of his way just as Daniel opened the door of his office.

"I'm ready to see you now, Mrs. Dixon," he said as impersonally as if she were a stranger.

"Have you met Bryon?"

"Only over the phone." Daniel shook hands with Bryon and motioned them into his office.

When they were seated, Paul reached out his arms to Daniel. The attorney took him and threw him into the air a few times. Paul chortled and laughed, puckering up when Daniel handed him back to Sonya. Bryon watched the episode with a speculative gleam in his eyes.

Bryon looked closely at his son. "I'd heard he looked like me. I can't see the resemblance, but he does favor my baby pictures." He reached out a hand and patted Paul's head. "Don't you recognize your daddy?" But Paul nestled closer into Sonya's arms and eyed Bryon with suspicion.

Perhaps sensing Sonya's discomfort, Daniel interrupted the scene by saying, "Mrs. Dixon tells me that you've changed your mind about a divorce. It's always wise to discuss any legal changes with an attorney present. I'd expected you to bring your own counsel."

Bryon waved his hand impatiently. "My lawyer doesn't own me. I can make my own decisions. And what I wanted to say to Sonya is for her ears alone. It was her idea to meet here, not mine. We can work this out between the two of us, I'm sure."

"Mrs. Dixon," Daniel said, "the choice is yours—do you want me to leave the room?"

Always overawed by Bryon's dominant personality, Sonya found it hard to deny him anything, but she now had reason to fear both Bryon and his parents. Could she trust him? Her arms tightened around Paul.

"No," she said decisively. "Go ahead, Bryon. Mr. Massie knows all about our problems. After all, he's been representing me for months."

"Yes, and I'm beginning to suspect his interest is biased."

Ignoring this remark, Daniel said, "Mr. Dixon, I'll be taping the conversation, in the event we should need it for future legal proceedings."

Bryon stood up angrily. "I'm not used to being treated like this. Sonya, what's this guy done to you?"

"Why should I trust you after the way you've acted the past year? Sit down and say what you want to."

Surprisingly, Bryon did as she commanded. He turned his chair so that his back was to Daniel, and he took Sonya's hand.

"I've rehearsed over and over what to say to you, but in simple words—I've been a fool, Sonya. I knew that soon after I left you, but I became involved with Gail, and once she had her clutches into me, she wasn't about to let go. I reached the place where I hated her, but hated myself more. I was on the verge of suicide, but I don't suppose you'd understand that."

With a grimace Sonya answered, "I understand it all too well."

"My work suffered, and my supervisor suggested I needed some help, so he recommended a counseling service. I've been going for weekly therapy the past few months, and they've suggested changes in my life as well as our relationship. My therapist insisted that I delay the divorce until I was sure of what I wanted. I'm not back to normal yet, but near enough to realize I don't want to lose you."

Sonya glanced down at Paul, sprawled out on her lap, sleeping peacefully.

"Bryon, all I'm hearing is that you want to come back to *me*. You must remember that there would be three of us now, and Paul was the cause of the problem in the first place."

Bryon nodded. "I can't help it if I don't like kids. I hated my brother from the day he was born until he died. Because of his illness, my parents necessarily had to give him a great deal of time and attention. I suppose I really wasn't neglected, but I had a fixation on that idea. Until he was born I'd had all of my parents' love and devotion—when he came along, he got more than his share, or so I thought. My inner self told me the same thing would happen when you became pregnant. Does that make sense to you?"

"Yes, I believe that's the key to your problem, but now that you're at the root of the situation, how is it going to affect your behavior?"

"Don't expect me to become an affectionate father if that's what you mean. I had thought I might change my mind when I saw the boy, but I feel absolutely nothing. Why don't you give him up for adoption?"

"Why, Bryon! I wouldn't give my child away to save my life."

Daniel growled and shoved back his chair. "I can't stay and listen to this, Mrs. Dixon. I'm going into my law library."

He closed the door behind him, but Sonya was comforted to know he was nearby if she needed him.

"I have trouble believing this isn't a plot with your parents—I come back to you, and they'll take Paul."

"I haven't talked with my parents since they telephoned that they had been denied the right to adopt him, but that might not be a bad idea. He can live with them."

"No."

"Then he can live with us as long as you keep him out of my way. Hire a nanny to look after him when I'm at home. You can spend your time with him while I'm at work, but at night you're mine.''

"That won't be satisfactory. I want our son to be brought up in the security of a Christian home.''

"What goes with you and this Christianity business? Is this something new you've gotten mixed up in?''

"You know I'd always gone to church before we were married, but you discouraged it by keeping me busy doing something else on weekends. Since you've been gone, I've rediscovered the security of a Christian faith that I'd been floundering without for years.''

"What do you mean by that?''

Perhaps he was feeling the tension in the room, for Paul started fidgeting in her arms and when he began to cry, Sonya carried him into the law library. Daniel was pacing the floor, his hands knotted into fists, his face white with anger.

"Take care of Paul for me,'' she pleaded.

"Get rid of the man, Sonya, before I throw him out of my office.''

"Give me another minute. He's asked a very important question, and I want to answer it.''

She sat down beside Bryon and took his hand, looking deep into his eyes, trying to find there an image of the man she had married. She chose her words carefully for she knew that their whole future as a family depended upon his understanding.

"You asked me to explain my faith in God. He sent his Son to die and redeem mankind from sin, and to live in a right relationship with God, we have to accept His free gift of salvation. I've done that. You've heard the Gospel before—you've gone with me to church on Easter.''

"Everybody goes to church on Easter. And certainly

I've heard crap like that, but I didn't suppose anybody believed it except down and outers. I wouldn't have expected anyone of your intelligence to fall for such rot.''

Believing there was a chance that she might penetrate the shell around Bryon's heart, Sonya didn't want to antagonize him, so she concealed how abhorrent his words were to her.

"I may as well tell you that when you left me, I was so low that I very nearly committed suicide. If it hadn't been for God's providential care and my renewed faith in Christ, I couldn't have made it through the past year. I won't abandon that faith to stay with you, and I expect to bring Paul up to believe the same thing.''

Bryon laughed, and the contempt in his laughter seared Sonya's heart. "Something has happened to you—there's no doubt of that, but once we're back together, you'll forget all of this foolishness.''

"I wouldn't even listen to you if it weren't for Paul. He needs a father.''

"If it will satisfy you, give him any kind of religious instruction you want, but don't expect any help from me. I've made myself clear on that. This is just between you and me, sweetheart—neither Paul nor God are involved.''

After this conversation, Sonya couldn't see any way to redeem their marriage, but if it was God's will that she reconcile with Bryon, He could make them into a strong and loving family.

Daniel reentered the room, more calm than he had been, and handed the sleeping baby into Sonya's arms.

"I'll have to think about it. How long will you be in Omaha?''

"Two days. I'll be at the hotel in the evening and at the office during the day.''

"I'll have Mr. Massie telephone you my decision, which I need to discuss with him now."

Before he left the room, Bryon leaned over Sonya and brushed his lips over hers. Seated as she was and holding Paul, she couldn't evade his gesture, and her face flamed. "While you're considering, don't forget I love you."

Without a word to Daniel, he walked out of the office with his old buoyancy, already sure of her decision.

Daniel and Sonya looked at each other for a long time. "As I've told you before, every time it seems I have my life on an even keel, the Dixons disrupt it. What am I going to do now?"

"Go on with the divorce. You can't trust him."

"It's such a difficult decision for me, because as I told you when I first came to this office, I don't believe in divorce. As long as Bryon was pressing the action, I had no choice, so my conscience didn't bother me. Now, he's pitched the ball to my court—it's going to be my decision, and I don't like being put in that position."

"Of course, my interest goes beyond that of a client-attorney relationship, but even if I didn't have a personal feeling for you, I'd say the same thing. It's a long chance that you can ever mend your relationship."

"But there is a chance?"

"I suppose so, but not one I'd want to gamble on."

"And there's Paul. In these few months I've learned how difficult it is to be a single parent. I can give him love, but not much more. Is it fair to deny him the support of his father? I'm so confused. How I wish I'd never laid eyes on Bryon Dixon!"

"But you have, so you'll have to deal with him. However, I wouldn't do it now. You have two days, and you could take more time if you wanted to." Daniel paused; his expression grew serious. "And if it's a decision about raising Paul without a father, you know I'm more than willing to act as a father to him. If we were ever to marry, as I hope, you know I'll adopt him. I love the boy already."

The phone rang, and Sonya detected Stelle's shrill, excited voice when Daniel answered.

"We'll be there right away," he said and slammed down the phone.

"It's Edith." He reached for his coat and hat on the rack. "She had a 'sinking spell,' according to Stelle, and Stelle telephoned the emergency squad. They're taking her to the hospital."

"You go ahead. I'll take Paul to Leta and join you as soon as possible."

Sonya telephoned Leta to see if she could keep Paul, and Leta said, "Sure, I'll meet you down in the lobby to save time. Just park in front of the building."

When she delivered Paul, Sonya took time to tell Leta about the conference with Bryon. Although she was in a hurry, she thought she owed Leta a quick explanation.

"Think hard and long about it. Don't let the scoundrel rush you into a decision. You don't owe Bryon Dixon a thing. And don't let Paul's future sway you—he's better off alone with you."

When she rushed into the hospital, Edith was in ICU, and Sonya and Daniel could do nothing but sit in the waiting room. After several hours, Daniel finally contacted Edith's doctor.

"She's on the verge of a massive heart attack, and I don't see how we can prevent it, but she's rallied somewhat, so perhaps she'll surprise me. You and Mrs. Dixon might as well go home. I'll leave word to telephone if her condition worsens."

"I don't like having you up there alone," Daniel said as they left the hospital.

"I may not be alone. Remember, I'm employed as a social worker, and there may be a client for us tonight. I need to be there. As soon as I go for Paul, I'll head that way."

But she didn't protest when Leta insisted on spending the night with her and Paul.

When she arrived at the mansion with Leta, Sonya put Paul to bed, then shared a cup of tea with her friend. Leta was always good company and Sonya found herself confiding her deepest fears about Edith's condition. Edith had come to mean so much to her in such a short time. Would she lose Edith now, so suddenly? How would she cope with such a blow?

Leta offered her comforting words, but Sonya knew that Edith's condition might not improve and tomorrow could bring unhappy news. Before she fell asleep Sonya prayed long and hard for Edith's recovery.

Chapter Fourteen

Sonya awoke to the sound of the telephone. She picked up the receiver, her heart clutched with cold fear. She heard Daniel's familiar voice.

"Sonya—did I wake you?"

"Have you heard from Edith?" Sonya quickly replied.

"Yes, I telephoned at seven o'clock. The nurses said she's responded to treatment and may be moved into a regular room today."

Sonya sighed with relief. "Thank goodness. I'll visit her this morning."

"I'm sure you'll give her spirits a lift," Daniel replied. "I'll probably go see her tonight." He paused. "Sonya, don't forget that you must give Bryon an answer tomorrow?"

"I remember," she assured him, though she didn't confide what her answer would be.

She chatted with Daniel for a few more minutes, then telephoned Adam Benson. "May I see you sometime today? I have an important decision to make, and I need some advice."

"Will ten o'clock be convenient?"

"Fine, I'll be there."

When Sonya telephoned the hospital, she learned that Edith had just been transferred to a room. She was eager to see her and quickly got dressed and took Paul downstairs to Stelle.

"Stelle, I have an appointment this morning, and, also, I should like to see Edith. Will you mind looking after Paul? I'll try to return by noon."

"No bother, Sonya. Me and Paul—we're friends."

"He's everybody's friend," Sonya said with a laugh. "I don't know where he gets it—from neither of his parents, I'm sure."

"He's God's special little child, that's what he is," Stelle said and picked the boy up to give him a big hug.

Sonya put her arms around Stelle. "You're pretty special yourself. I don't know what I'd have done without you and a few of my other good friends during the past year. You've made my life bearable again."

Sonya never worried about Paul when either Stelle or Leta kept him, but she tried not to impose on her friends. She could have taken him with her to Adam's office, but not into the hospital, and she went to see Edith first.

Edith sat in her bed, nibbling on something from her breakfast tray. She gave Sonya a cheery smile.

"All of this fuss for nothing! I want to go home."

Sonya kissed her cheek. "What does the doctor say about it?"

As if on cue, the doctor entered the room and said, "The doctor says she can go home tomorrow. But it wasn't fuss for nothing—if Stelle hadn't gotten you here to hospital, you could have had a major attack. You have to remember you're not a girl anymore, and you must take it easy."

"I've outlived my quota of time, anyway, Doctor," Edith said pertly.

When the aides came to give Edith a bath, Sonya left, and when she passed the nurses' station, Edith's doctor called to her.

"I probably shouldn't release her, since her heart is mighty weak. I've considered a pacemaker, but at her age I'm not sure it's advisable. She'll be happier at home. Just protect her as much as possible."

Knowing that Edith would be returning home gave Sonya a lighter spirit to face the appointment with Adam. She told him about Edith, and he said, "I'll go to visit her this afternoon. But you didn't come to talk about Edith. What's troubling you, Sonya?"

She settled back in the roomy chair and breathed deeply. "My husband wants to come back to me. He's decided he doesn't want a divorce, and I need to give him an answer tomorrow."

"Does that make you happy or sad?"

"Do I look happy or sound elated?"

He smiled. "Not that I can notice."

"A year ago this would have made me happy, but so much has happened since then. I've built my life without him. I've found that I can get along on my own."

"Then why are you having trouble with a decision?"

"I was brought up to believe that divorce is unacceptable. You marry someone, you stay married. As long as Bryon was pushing for divorce, I felt it wasn't my decision to wreck our marriage. Now it is."

"But is the marriage already wrecked? Can the breaches be repaired?" Adam's soft brown eyes clouded with concern.

"That's what bothers me. If I thought we could return to the good marriage we had for two years, I'd be willing to try for Paul's sake. Is it fair for me to deny him a father-son relationship? I've read about the problems of single parenting. Am I ready for that? What should I do?''

"I'll be the first to admit that I don't have any hard-and-fast rule to hand out to those whom I counsel. Basically I oppose divorces because they are tearing down the foundations of family relationships in our country. Strong homes are the backbone of our society. But on the other hand, I don't approve of spouse abuse, either. If some woman comes to me, bruised and beaten, such as the cases you receive at Blessed Hope, I can't tell that woman she should live with the man until death parts them. If he continues to abuse her, it won't be long until they're parted by her death.''

"Of course, Bryon never laid a hand on me.''

"But you were abused emotionally and mentally. Changes come in a marriage that are hard to cope with sometimes.'' Adam removed his brown-rimmed glasses and rubbed his forehead. Sonya glanced out the window at the Washburn building, thinking of the miserable nights she'd spent there. *I've come a long way since then!*

Adam startled her when he spoke. "As customs have changed through the ages, so have people's ideas about divorce. What had once been unacceptable, might be per-fectly agreeable to today's society.''

"But taking a vow of staying together for better or worse wouldn't change.''

Adam laughed, and Sonya was glad someone could find humor in her situation; she couldn't. "This is a strange counseling session. It sounds as though I, the counselor, am giving you reasons for divorce and you're trying to prove I'm wrong.''

Sonya flushed. "Does that mean I want to go back to Bryon?''

"Not necessarily, and I want you to know that whatever you decide, Marie and I will stand by you. But it must be your decision."

Adam discussed several Scripture passages relating to divorce among the Hebrews and in the early church, and he said, "I'm not always sure when the New Testament is discussing the practice of divorce or talking about the ideal marriage. There are passages that seem to be emphasizing monogamy in marriage rather than dealing with the subject of divorce. The practice of plural marriages was not uncommon in Hebrew history, but slowly the trend was toward one man for one woman. The gospel writers indicated that one shouldn't search for ways to squirm out of the marriage contract, but rather stressed how two people becoming one can have a beautiful relationship that precludes any possibility of divorce."

"Do you know of any such ideal marriages?"

With a smile, Adam assured her, "Many of them. Marie and I have that kind of marriage."

"Come to think of it, so do my parents. Then it is possible in this day and age?"

"Most assuredly."

"If one divorces, then what about remarriage?"

Adam leaned back in his chair and scrutinized her closely. "Are you considering remarriage?"

"Not very much, although Daniel has asked me."

"Yes, he told me. I've had a counseling session with him. He wants to marry you, but he, too, is concerned about what is morally right."

"It would be much easier if there were only a few spiritual and moral rules to follow, allowing us to pinpoint the right or wrong."

"Unfortunately, it isn't that easy. We have to make our own difficult decisions. If you do go back to your husband, it will be necessary to forgive him and forget the past, and I doubt you can do that unless he has changed his habits. Both of you would have to change."

"Bryon has made it plain that he won't change spiritually. In fact he was very sarcastic about my Christian faith. Perhaps my biggest concern is whether I can be married to him and still live a committed Christian life."

"It can be done, but it won't be easy."

"Bryon has made no effort to change and I question that I can trust him. You can't have a good marriage without trust. Should I ask him to give me more time about this decision? It took me completely by surprise."

"I wouldn't dally long with it for you're going to be in a state of emotional suspense until the matter is resolved. And, Sonya, although I won't give you a definite answer about divorce, I am going to advise you about remarriage. At this point, you are definitely not ready for another relationship. You're not completely healed emotionally, and I do hope you'll take my advice about that."

"But sometimes I'm so tired of all this trauma that I'd like to drop it on another's shoulders."

"The very worst reason for a marriage. Occasionally marriages of convenience are successful, but my advice is to never marry again unless you meet someone you can't live without."

Sonya picked up her purse from the floor. "I have to go. Stelle is baby-sitting, and I told her I'd return before noon, but I do thank you for talking with me. You and Marie have been so helpful through all of this."

"But have I helped you with your immediate decision?"

She smiled slightly. "I don't know. I need to think about what you've said. Right now, my mind is muddled."

In spite of her need to relieve Stelle of Paul's care, Sonya parked her car along Happy Hollow Boulevard and entered the wooded area bordering the University of Omaha. She walked with downcast eyes, paying no attention to the people she met. She left the path and wandered into the deeper woods and sat under a maple tree near a small creek. She leaned against the large trunk and looked up into the foliage that was beginning to show a tinge of yellow. She watched as two squirrels hauled nuts to their winter storage. More than a year had passed since Bryon had left her. A year that had brought some heartbreaking moments, but also a year that had proven she could manage without him. She had matured spiritually and emotionally, and she had also gained friends, the kind of friends who helped without question. And she had a son! Sonya smiled when she thought of Paul, his small hands, his bubbling personality.

Yes, there was no doubt that she could live without Bryon now, but should she? She had suffered and survived. She felt sorry that she no longer wanted him. How could she have changed so much in a year's time? Should she keep the vows she'd made, "Till death do us part"? But the vows had already been broken, and she hadn't been the one to do it. She had blundered once by choosing Bryon—should she repeat the mistake?

Sonya walked back to the path and wended her way toward the car, no nearer a decision than before, until she noticed a decrepit vine growing in the graveled path. The vine had obviously tried to grow strong, only to be trampled underneath the feet of those who passed by. The vine was hardy and would continue to grow and put forth an occasional bloom, but its beauty and purpose in life would always be stunted. The vine had taken root in an unsuitable place—if it could only send its tendrils elsewhere, it would have a chance of normal growth.

That's the way it is with me, Sonya contemplated as she slowly drove away from the park. She would always be stunted as Bryon's wife. Actually, what had she accomplished in the years of their marriage? Endless parties, vacations, ski trips, collecting a big wardrobe and piles of jewelry but she had never really made her mark in the world. She had been content to dwell in Bryon's shadow. She didn't want to do that anymore. Bryon probably had changed very little, but Sonya knew that she had grown beyond him. If they could go back to what life had been three years ago, would she really want to?

The answer, of course, was no. She had found out what living meant—loving her child, caring for those who were down-and-out, denying herself for others. She would be selfish to go back to the old, narrow way of living.

Sonya had put off the most important issue until the last. She had to face reality. If she continued as Bryon's wife, her faith would suffer. Bryon's dominant personality would assert itself, he wouldn't let her rear Paul as she wanted to, and she would begin to doubt the hope of eternal life that she had now. The words of Jesus reminded her that anyone who started to follow Him and looked back wasn't fit for the kingdom of God; she couldn't forsake Him again. Considering these aspects of her relationship to Bryon, there was only one choice to make.

When she reached the York mansion, she parked the car and walked into the house with a light step and new determination as she picked up Paul from his playpen in the kitchen. She felt as if she had taken a new lease on life. She'd been fighting a war, and she had won it— maybe not all the battles, but enough of them to claim victory.

"God's in His heaven—all's right with the world," she quoted from *Pippa Passes* as she headed upstairs with Paul.

When Daniel answered the phone, she said, "I've come to a decision. I want to continue with the divorce as soon as possible."

"You sound happy about it."

"Not really happy about the divorce, but happy I've made a decision. I feel as if I'm a newborn calf frolicking around the pasture. I've been weighed down with bitterness and unhappiness for over a year. It's a relief to be free of it."

"Then I'll telephone your husband's attorney and say we want to proceed with the divorce on the terms outlined in our previous offer. I can't say much now, Sonya, but you know how happy your decision makes me."

Sonya hoped she wouldn't have to talk with Bryon again, but later that night, when the telephone rang, Bryon was on the line.

"I'm hurt by your decision, Sonya. I thought you didn't want a divorce."

"A year ago I didn't, but I've too many scars on my emotions to start over again."

"But you said you had forgiven me."

"That's true, but I can't trust you again. There's a difference."

"Are you in love with someone else? Is that why you don't want me now?"

Sonya wondered if this was the only reason Bryon wanted her. Did he still look upon her as his possession, and he couldn't bear to let someone else have her?

Daniel's smiling face and lovable personality flitted through her mind, and she wondered if she could give Bryon an honest answer to his question. Her high regard for Daniel complicated her decision about the divorce. She loved Daniel as a friend and had no doubt that romance would blossom if she gave it the opportunity. She couldn't fool herself that wanting to be in Daniel's presence was only because he was good to her and Paul. Why did her pulse accelerate when she heard his voice? Why did her heart sing when she caught his glance across a crowded room? Why did she think of him when she awakened in the morning and when she closed her eyes at night?

"You didn't give me an answer," Bryon prompted.

"When you abandoned me, you lost the right to ask that question, but I can tell you that I don't want an intimate relationship with anyone right now, including you. Except for my responsibility to Paul, I'm free, and I like it. Please, Bryon, if you have any consideration for me, go on with the divorce. If you don't, I'll sue for it myself."

"Then it's goodbye?"

"Yes," Sonya whispered, "and I'm sorry it turned out this way."

"So am I," Bryon said, and he hung up the receiver.

Although Sonya had been happy with her decision, she sat with her hand on the phone for a long time. Was there still time to salvage their marriage? She didn't even undress and go to bed for she knew it was useless. Apparently Bryon would cause her many more sleepless nights. If a spouse died, it was final because there was a corpse to bury, but how does one bury a divorce?

Two months had passed since Edith's hospital release, and she still hadn't regained her strength. It took quite a lot of Sonya's time to care for her, but the doctor had found a nurse who consented to work at night, which was a great help to Sonya.

"With this work of Blessed Hope, you have about all you can do, and you're not getting much rest sleeping on the couch in her room. As far as that's concerned, Edith isn't resting well, either, fretting for you," he had said.

"It's a vicious circle, isn't it?" Sonya said with a smile.

"Yes, and we can stop it with some extra help. Mrs. York can afford it."

Sonya was glad for the relief, since Paul demanded quite a lot of attention, too, and hardly a night passed that they didn't have at least one client on the second floor. Loretta could usually come to help, but Sonya still needed to supervise.

One morning during Thanksgiving week, Daniel telephoned, and he said excitedly, "May I come out for a minute? I have some good news for you."

"Have you straightened up all the details of the divorce?"

"No—that will be another week or so. Bryon's lawyer hasn't been very cooperative."

Daniel's excitement had piqued Sonya's curiosity, and she met him at the door. His face beamed as he thrust an envelope into her hands.

"Congratulations!"

Daniel took Paul from her arms as she pulled a check from the envelope in the amount of $10,000, payable to Sonya Dixon.

"Is this real? What does it mean?"

"Mr. Dixon visited me this morning and asked me to give you this check. They feel badly that Bryon hasn't supported you, and the check is also an apology for their attempt to take Paul. He asked my advice about giving it to you, and I told him you would accept it. That's the least they can do, so I hope you will take it. I feel sorry for Bryon's parents.''

Sonya kissed the check. "Of course, I'll take it. I want to make amends with them. It would be wrong to shun their generosity.''

"Let's go tell Edith. She'll be delighted," Daniel said.

Edith was sitting in a wheelchair looking out the window, and her features broke into a beautiful smile when she saw the check. "My word, what are you going to do with so much money?"

"I don't know. Right now, I feel like going on a spending spree and blowing every dime of it. I haven't bought any new clothes for almost two years, so, Daniel, you keep it for a few days until I calm down."

After Daniel left, Sonya pulled Paul's playpen into Edith's room and sat down to visit with her. Paul was too heavy and active for Edith to hold anymore, but she liked to watch the boy as he played. Sonya brought a basket of clothing that needed mending. The quiet scene caused Edith to doze occasionally, but once she asked, "Surely you have some idea of what you'd like to do with your money?"

"My mind has been working overtime since Daniel brought the check, and I've thought of dozens of things. I suppose the wise thing is to save it for an emergency—so I'll have Daniel invest it for me. There is one thing I'd like to do, but I may have to wait until Paul is a little older. I want to go back to school and major in subjects to train me more adequately for the kind of work I'm doing. If I'd finished college as my parents begged me to, then I wouldn't have fouled up by marrying too young. I'm sure Bryon wouldn't have waited three years for me."

"Don't let the mistakes of the past burden you any

longer. Everyone is entitled to a few of them, but it's how you deal with mistakes that determine your destiny. The idea of going back to school is an excellent one. We have good universities close by, and I'm sure you can manage financially."

"Yes, I will manage somehow," Sonya agreed. "It's what I really want to do, and I guess I've learned that I can accomplish more than I'd ever dreamed possible if I'm determined enough, and pray for God's help."

The next morning Edith's room seemed empty when Sonya walked in, and she looked around quickly. Had Stelle taken Edith out? But a glance showed that Edith was in her bed. Somehow she didn't look right, and Sonya rushed to her. One touch told her that the room was empty. Edith had died.

She rushed into the kitchen. "Stelle, come quickly." Stelle stalked into the room behind her as Sonya rushed back to Edith's side. Noting Sonya's tears, Stelle said softly, "She's gone, is she? I've been expecting it most every day."

"But I thought she was better."

"Better in some ways, but getting weaker and weaker. What do we do now?"

"I suppose we'd better telephone Daniel. He handles her affairs. I don't even know what funeral director to call. She never discussed her death with me."

Sonya could hardly control her sobs when she telephoned Daniel, for she'd grown as fond of Edith as if she were family. While she waited for Daniel to come, Sonya went to her apartment to check on Paul and to telephone the agency. She told the dispatcher about Edith's death and asked if they could be relieved of clients for a week.

"Certainly. You telephone us when you're available again."

"I don't know what will happen now. There's a possibility we'll have to close the home."

Even though Edith had signed a contract for two years, her death might cancel that. She deeply grieved Edith's death, for she was fond of her, but underlying that was concern for her own future. Maybe this was her answer about going back to college, since it would have been hard to manage Blessed Hope, look after Edith and Paul and carry a full load of courses.

Edith had left specific instructions with Daniel about her funeral. Her body lay in state in the large parlor where her parents' funerals had been. Because Edith had outlived most of her generation, there were few mourners of her own age, but many of the members at Community Lighthouse came to pay their respects, and Adam's simple funeral message would have pleased Edith.

Daniel had notified Edith's nephew, and he came to the funeral, but he hadn't chosen to stay at the house, although Stelle and Sonya had made preparations for him. He approached Daniel after the closing ceremony at the mausoleum.

"I have to catch an early-morning flight. Could we take care of the legal matters tonight? I assume Aunt Edith had a will."

"Yes. I'll meet you at the house at eight o'clock."

"Could we meet at your office? I'm uncomfortable there, never knowing when some of those women might wander in."

"There won't be anyone tonight. The dispatcher knows about Mrs. York's death, and no one will be sent."

"Very well. I'll be there promptly."

Daniel drove Sonya and Stelle back to the house, and she asked, "I'm wondering what I should do about Blessed Hope. Even if Edith's nephew doesn't like it, we have a contract with the agency that goes on for more than a year. Can he make us close the shelter?"

"I'll take care of Mr. York this evening."

Several of the church people had sent in trays of food, so Stelle and Sonya ate their evening meal from that supply. Sonya helped Stelle put away the food, and she said, "You can let Daniel and Mr. York in, if you will, please. I'll take Paul upstairs. He's about asleep now. You can tell that Leta let him play all afternoon without a nap."

After Paul was bathed and put in bed, Sonya sat down and tried to contemplate what the future held for her. Her musings were interrupted when the house phone rang. Daniel was calling from downstairs. "Could you come down to Edith's room for a few minutes?"

"I've just gotten Paul to sleep, but I'll leave all the doors open, and I can hear if he awakens. Will I be needed long?"

"Probably not."

Mr. York, robust and florid, sat pompously in Edith's chair. Stelle stood by the door.

"Come in, both of you, and sit down. As you're mentioned in the will, it's necessary for you to be present."

He didn't have to tell Sonya to sit down as her legs wouldn't hold her. She listened in stunned silence as Daniel read. At first it was a lot of legal jargon about the payments of bills and being of sound mind, but ten minutes later, Sonya pretty much understood the gist of Edith's intention. Ten percent of her estate was to be given to Stelle, ten percent to the nephew and the balance of her holdings to Sonya.

"But that's preposterous," Mr. York shouted. "This woman is little more than a servant in the house. She's moved in here, ingratiated herself with my aunt. Who knows what she's done to persuade Aunt Edith to leave her all the money!''

"Be calm, Mr. York. Your aunt was certain you would feel this way, so she gave an explanation." And Daniel read an addendum to the will, written in Edith's own hand:

> "I'm sure that my nephew will be unhappy about this decision, but I want to remind him that the estate is mine, and I personally think I'm being lenient toward him to give him ten percent. My husband paid for Albert's college expenses, and he gave him a generous sum to make the down payment on his home. In return for that he did very little to show affection toward us.
>
> "Sonya has never asked me for anything, and except for giving her and the child a home, I've done nothing for her. On the other hand, she has given me love and companionship, which I needed desperately, and she allowed me the delight of having a child in my home. She's proven that she can triumph over difficulty.''

Daniel carefully folded the document and placed it in his briefcase, and the nephew shouted, "I'll break the will. It's my uncle's money, and she has no right to give it away."

"I have a copy of the will for you," Daniel said. "Any reliable attorney will tell you that there's no way you can break this document."

"When did she make this will?"

"Two months ago. But you didn't receive any more in her previous will. Mrs. York considered you had gotten your share."

"I suppose you brought undue influence upon her. What are you getting out of it?"

"I had no idea what she had in mind, until she summoned me to this room in October," Daniel answered calmly. "And I didn't get anything out of it. In fact, I've lost a good friend and a client."

"Crooks and thieves, all of you. You'll be hearing from my attorney," Albert shouted.

He started down the hallway, and Stelle followed to lock the door behind him. Daniel smiled at Sonya. "How does it feel to be rich?".

"I still don't believe I'll receive this. Mr. York is very angry."

"I told him he wasn't entitled to any more in the first will than he was in this one, and I intend to send his attorney a copy to prove it. Before you came here, she had willed most of her estate to charities. Don't worry, Sonya, the will is airtight," he assured her.

"How much is the estate worth?"

"Maybe $100,000, plus this house. It's hard to tell what you could get out of it on the market. Sometimes people pay well for the old houses. It's not so much, not a large estate."

"Not much! Maybe not for you, but for someone who has lived as I have for more than a year, wearing used clothes from the church clothing bank, subsisting on groceries from the food kitchen, I feel as if I'm a millionaire. I only wish I could properly thank Edith for what she's done for me."

"She evidently considered that she was in your debt." He reached into his briefcase. "She also left this letter for you."

With trembling hands Sonya opened the sealed envelope.

Dear Sonya,

When you read this I will be with my Lord, so please don't grieve for me. I've lived a long, happy and rewarding life, and I'm not sorry to be gone. Believe that and dry any tears you might have for me. Your presence in my home for almost a year, and the advent of Paul, have made the declining months of my life very happy. I took courage when I saw how you battled and won against your own disillusionment and unhappiness.

When I saw the depth of your character as you accepted the directorship of Blessed Hope, I decided that you would make better use of my estate than the charitable organizations I had previously chosen to receive it. It's yours with no strings attached. If you want to continue Blessed Hope—fine. If you want to sell the house, that's all right, too, because I realize it is too great an expense for a residence. Above all, I want you to have my estate to ensure that you can control your future. In time you may want to marry again, but you won't have to for financial security if you invest my estate well. You can trust Daniel to advise you. I have found him knowledgeable and trustworthy.

Your devoted friend, Edith York

In spite of Edith's admonition, tears stained the page before Sonya finished reading it.

"Have you read this?" she asked Daniel.

When he shook his head, she handed him the letter. He cleared his throat noisily when he finished, for he, too, had been influenced by Edith's life.

"It's strange, but all of these months when I've had no money, I constantly thought of things I'd like to have for

Paul and myself. But now that I'm in funds, I can't think of anything I need, except that I want to do something for those who have helped me. I want to take you and your mother, the Bensons, Eloise, Leta and Stelle out to dinner. I'll check with Adam and see when he's free, and arrange the dinner soon. Without the seven of you, I wouldn't have made it. I want to show my appreciation."

"That's a great idea."

The dinner was arranged for the following Sunday after worship service, and it was a time of rejoicing for all of them, but an incident marred the day for Sonya. While they waited for their food to be served, Sonya saw Bryon's parents leaving the restaurant. If they had seen her party, they had ignored them. Both of the Dixons looked older, and they walked dejectedly. For some reason Sonya felt guilty, but what could she have done? She couldn't give Paul to them.

Sonya continued her work with Blessed Hope, but in spite of her busy schedule, the plight of Bryon's parents haunted her. And the day Daniel telephoned that her divorce had become a reality and that Bryon had given her full custody of Paul, she said, "I've been thinking about asking Bryon's parents if they would like to visit with Paul sometimes. I wouldn't make any legal commitment, simply let them have the opportunity. What do you think?"

"You're great to even consider it after what they tried."

"I'm thinking of Paul, too. I'm afraid that if I keep him to myself, I'll become too possessive. And is it fair for him to be cut off completely from his father's family? I intend to be honest with him about his lineage, but as he grows older and lives in the same city with his grandparents, it seems cruel for them to be strangers.''

"You realize that if Paul visits his grandparents, he's apt to see Bryon."

"I've thought of that, but now that I have full legal custody and the funds to care for the child, I feel more benevolent. He's mine, but I can't make a prisoner of him, and probably the best way for me to be sure he remains with me is to set him free.''

"You're a wise woman, Sonya, so I don't know why you ask me for advice. I would suggest that you follow your heart on this matter as well as others. You know in what direction I want your heart to lead you. I won't pressure you for a while, but whenever you're ready, I'm waiting.''

"Right now just be my friend, Daniel.''

After Sonya discussed with Adam Benson her thought of allowing Bryon's parents visiting rights and he agreed that she would feel better about sharing her son with his grandparents, she wrote them a short note. She had written to thank them for their generous gift, but had not spoken to them since the custody hearing. Still, she addressed them respectfully, as she always had:

Dear Mother and Father Dixon,
I want to apologize for my part in the unpleasantness between us that has marked the past year. It's unfortunate that the problems between Bryon and me also affected your happiness.

After that beginning, Sonya pondered long over her next sentence. The Dixons shouldn't think that her change of heart meant she wanted any financial help from them, but rather that she was being considerate of their feelings.

Perhaps you know that Edith York left most of her estate to me. It came as a surprise, but a pleasant one, as the extent of her holdings has guaranteed a secure financial future for Paul and me. For the present, I intend to continue with the crisis center, for it is a worthwhile project, but next fall I hope to enter the university for a degree in social work.

All is well with Paul and me; however, I can't be completely satisfied to keep you isolated from your grandson. Would you like to visit with Paul occasionally? If so, feel free to contact me when you want to pick him up for a few hours, or I can bring him to your house. I believe you'll enjoy him. He is an adorable, happy boy.

                                        Sonya

Two days later Bryon's father telephoned. "Bless you, Sonya. Anna's health has plummeted this past year. She's lost interest in everything, but your letter has done wonders for her. May I come and pick up Paul tomorrow afternoon, or do you want to come with him? Will he be afraid of us?"

"No, he's happy with everyone, and you'll enjoy playing with him. If you will come for him around one o'clock, it will give me time to do some Christmas shopping, and I can come by to get him after that."

"God bless you, Sonya."

The next day as Sonya prepared Paul for a visit with his grandparents, she thought how different her circumstances were from a year ago. Then she was almost penniless and with more worries than she could contemplate. A year later she had money, she had friends and the freedom to do what she wanted. But was she happy? This was a question that plagued her daily. She had everything but love, and could she expect happiness without love? She liked and appreciated her friends, but she felt no deep emotions for anyone except Paul, and that didn't seem to be enough. Why couldn't she be satisfied with her life as it was now?

The doorbell rang and she looked at the clock. Too early for Mr. Dixon, but she soon heard steps approaching down the hall, and she turned as Bryon entered the room. Anger stirred at his intrusion into her well-ordered life, and she sank down on the couch beside Paul. She stared at him, speechless.

"Please don't order me out, Sonya," Bryon said in a quiet voice. "I arrived home this morning for a few days, and I persuaded Father to let me come after Paul. Do you trust me to have him?"

"I've decided that it's selfish for me to keep the boy to myself."

"A lot of things have happened between us in the past several months, Sonya, perhaps things that can never be forgiven or forgotten, but I've come to ask you once more. Will you take me back? I want to be a part of your life, and of Paul's. Surely I deserve a second chance."

For a moment Sonya's thoughts turned to that May morning when she had stood beside Bryon and had taken the vow, "I, Sonya, take thee, Bryon, to be my wedded husband, to have and to hold, from this day forward, for better, for worse, for richer, for poorer, in sickness and in health, to love and to cherish, till death do us part, and thereto I pledge thee my faith."

Emotion tightened Sonya's throat, and she desperately wanted to relive the past, but it was no use. The spark was gone, and there was no way she could rekindle it. Instead of seeing the handsome Bryon she had loved, all she could remember was the long months of heartbreak, his rejection of her and his attitude toward his son. For herself, she might have taken a chance on Bryon's change of heart, but she couldn't risk having Paul's childhood marred by a possessive father. Yet the boy needed a father, and, unbidden, the words of Daniel entered her mind, "I'm more than willing to adopt him. I love the boy already." This thought annoyed her, for she had to make her decision independent of Daniel.

"No, Bryon, I will not give you another chance. I begged you for months to return to me, but now it's too late. My love for you is dead, and I can't revive it."

He turned on his heel, without even taking Paul with him. Sonya didn't shed a tear as she watched him leave the house.

Later, when Mr. Dixon came for Paul, he said, "Bryon telephoned from the airport. He's leaving this afternoon for San Francisco. I'll come back with the boy in a couple of hours."

After Mr. Dixon left, she realized she was too disturbed to go shopping. Had she really put the past behind her? Was she ready to admit she had made a mistake and start again? She reached for the telephone, but replaced the receiver. She walked around the room several times before determinedly she dialed a number, and when her mother answered, Sonya said, "Do you have room for two more people during the Christmas holidays? I've decided to come home for a few days. I want Paul to meet all of his Ohio kin."

Her mother's elation confirmed that the decision was wise. Last year she couldn't face her family, but now she was ready.

An hour later, after long deliberation, Sonya made another phone call.

"Daniel, I've decided to go to Ohio for the holidays. When I return, maybe we could start that long, old-fashioned courtship you mentioned?"

She laughed at his reply.

Epilogue

"Daniel, I've decided I'll go to Ohio for the holidays.
When I return, maybe we could start that long-overdue
national campaign you mentioned."

She laughed at his reply.

Epilogue

The field was alive with color as the T-ball players gathered, resplendent in their red, green and yellow jerseys. This was the first game for most of the youthful athletes, and from her seat on the bleachers, Sonya watched with mixed emotions as five-year-old Paul ran to join his teammates. Tom and Anna Dixon sat beside her, eager to see their grandson participate in his first athletic event.

Daniel managed Paul's team, and a smile played around Sonya's lips and her heart gave a little somersault when she watched her husband on his knees in the midst of the excited boys. The players spread out over the field, and Paul was first at home plate. The umpire checked to be sure the defense was ready before he shouted, "Play ball." Paul took a mighty swing and missed the ball. Looking toward the bleachers, Daniel caught Sonya's eye and laughed.

The Dixons looked fondly at the child.

"Not a very good start," Sonya said, smiling.

"No, but he'll improve," Tom said. "He's going to be a fine athlete."

Tom and Anna exhibited the same pride in Paul that they had once showered on Bryon, but they didn't over-indulge him as they had their son. Bryon's actions over the past few years had apparently taught them a lesson.

As the game progressed, and Paul's playing improved, in light of her own happiness, Sonya experienced a touch of remorse for Bryon that he had separated himself so irrevocably from his son. Since the divorce became final, Bryon had never seen Paul nor had he evinced any interest in him. When Sonya and Daniel had married three years ago, Bryon had readily signed the papers for Daniel to adopt Paul, and they changed his name to Massie. As soon as he was able to understand, they had told Paul about his true parentage, putting Bryon in as good a light as possible.

The game was almost finished, and the score tied, when Paul stumbled over one of the foul line cones and fell headlong. Sonya jumped from the bleachers and started toward her son, but Paul scrambled to his feet, yelled, "Daddy," and raced toward Daniel.

Sonya resumed her seat and smiled at the Dixons. "Obviously he isn't hurt if he can run that fast. Daniel will take care of him."

"We have never ceased to mourn Bryon's broken marriage," Anna Dixon said, "but we are happy that you've found Daniel. He's a good father, and we appreciate that. Both you and Paul are fortunate."

Sonya took Anna's hand and pressed it warmly. Bryon seldom visited his parents, but the one day each month they had Paul to themselves seemed to make up for it. Sonya had kept up an amicable relationship with her former in-laws, and Daniel was hospitable toward Paul's grandparents when they brought the child home after his day with them.

Tom and Anna had to leave before the game was finished, and while Sonya waited for Daniel and Paul, she reflected on the past four years. She had managed the Blessed Hope shelter until she was married, and then with Daniel's blessing, she had deeded the house and surroundings to a private corporation that owned and operated homeless shelters and abuse centers throughout the state. She had enrolled in the university on a part-time basis and two more semesters of work would complete her degree.

When Sonya and Daniel married, Mrs. Massie elected to move into a two-room apartment in an exclusive retirement complex and left the large house for them. Sonya stirred from her reverie and watched with amusement as Paul tried to match his stride to Daniel's as they walked along hand-in-hand. Her heart was so full of love for both of them that she felt lightheaded.

"Mom, did you see me hitting the ball?"

"I certainly did, and I was proud of you. Grandpa Dixon said that you're going to be a great athlete. Did you hurt yourself when you fell?"

"Oh, Daddy said it was just a little scratch," Paul said, but he invited Sonya to take a look at his bruised knee.

Daniel put his arm around Sonya's waist as Paul ran ahead of them to the parking lot.

"You had a mysterious look on your face when we approached," Daniel said. "What were you thinking?"

"Oh, just being thankful for my happy home. When I think about five years ago…"

Daniel bent over and stopped her words with his kiss.

"No more thinking about the past," he said softly. "Those days will never come again."

"I don't expect them to, but I have to remember the past to know how fortunate I am now. I'm not sure that I deserve you."

He pinched her playfully on the side. "You probably don't," he teased, "but I'm going to keep you anyway."

"We're going to stop for a hot dog and cola," Paul called over his shoulder. "Daddy said we could."

Looking up at Daniel, her eyes full of tender affection, Sonya said, "If Daddy says so, I suppose that settles it. But don't forget we have another child to pick up at your mother's. She may be tired of babysitting by now."

"I haven't heard her complaining."

Although Daniel had told her to forget the past, Sonya's mind turned backward once more. Two years ago, their daughter, Jessica, had been born, and how different that experience was from the night of Paul's birth. Daniel didn't leave her once during a difficult delivery, suffering with her through every contraction, pain and scream, and in the midst of her suffering, Sonya thanked God for Daniel's presence. During Paul's birth she had nothing to rely on except the Scripture verse she had first heard from We Care on the darkest night of her life. *Weeping may endure for a night, but joy cometh in the morning.* She had put God's promise to the test and found it to be true. She had endured two years of grief, but happiness had blossomed in her life through Daniel's love and the support of her church family.

On the morning she bore Daniel's daughter, her joy was dampened momentarily. The position of the child had kept the sex secret until it was born, but when the pain was over at last, Dr. Hammer said, "You have a pretty girl this time, Mrs. Massie," and tears crept into Sonya's weary eyes.

"I'm sorry I didn't give you a son, Daniel," she whispered.

He bent over the bed and squeezed her gently. "But I wanted a daughter; I already have a son."

She had never doubted Daniel's love for Paul, but his words made her joy complete. Her life had been so abundant that Sonya no longer puzzled over the meaning of Romans 8:28. During the ups and downs of her life, she had learned that in all things God *does* work for the good of those who love him, who have been called according to His purpose.

* * * * * *

Dear Reader,

Childhood on a hillside farm in West Virginia was not conducive to a literary career, yet the lessons I learned there in responsibility, self discipline and faith in God have influenced my writings. At the age of ten I was inspired to write my first novel. Not one to dally, when I felt the urge to write I took a pencil and spiral notebook, went up on the hillside, sat under a hickory tree and started my first book, although that inspiration was soon superseded by other childish intersts. The desire to publish a book persisted, but it was not until 1977 that I began to think of myself as a "writer." I completed my first novel, though it was not published until 1990. In the meantime, I had published other books, however success in writing didn't come easy for me. As an editor once told me, "You can write, but you have to work at it." How right he was!

Child of Her Heart is my fifteenth novel. I have no firsthand knowledge of the trauma that accompanies divorce, for I've been married to the same loving and supportive husband for forty-one years. However, the many friends I have whose marriages have ended in divorce prompted my interest in the subject, and I hope that my fictional treatment of broken wedding vows in this book will be a source of inspiration to my readers.

I have devoted most of my writing to inspirational subjects encouraging readers to overcome their problems and redirect their futures by accepting God as an integral part of their lives, and that they will desire, as I do, to find and accept God's will for daily living. No problem is too big, or small, for God to solve.

In His Service,

Irene B. Brand

Welcome to *Love Inspired*™

A brand-new series of contemporary inspirational love stories.

Join men and women as they learn valuable lessons about facing the challenges of today's world and about life, love and faith.

Look for the following April 1998 Love Inspired™ titles:

DECIDEDLY MARRIED
by Carole Gift Page

A HOPEFUL HEART
by Lois Richer

HOMECOMING
by Carolyne Aarsen

Available in retail outlets in March 1998.

LIFT YOUR SPIRITS AND GLADDEN YOUR HEART

with *Love Inspired!*™

Steeple
Hill™

LI498